More praise for *Any Other City*

"I wanted to luxuriate and soak in Hazel Jane Plante's trans demimonde, bubbling over with queer desire, scented with longing. A hall of mirrors refracting space and time, *Any Other City* interweaves heartbreak, art-making, guitars and drums, all with electric aplomb and vigour."

—BISHAKH SOM, AUTHOR OF *APSARA ENGINE*

"Hazel Jane Plante's *Any Other City* is absorbing, funny, hot, tender, and punk AF. Her characters are so vividly rendered that it feels like Plante has actually manifested her novel's conceit: a musician who is a DIY punk icon and a trans woman invites a fictionalized version of Plante to collaboratively write a hybridized, experimental memoir. Both Plantes deliver, and the writing is wise and raw, joyful and subversive, messy and real. Heartbreak and pain drive some of the plot, but Plante also ensures that pleasure and creativity and creation are given equal space. Gloriously visceral sex scenes abound, provocative art installations are genuinely immersive and thrilling, and there's tangible exhilaration and exhaustion in the fits and stops of songwriting (and finding ways back to ourselves through our art). *Any Other City* will get inside your head and your heart, and it will change you in the best possible ways."

—ANDREA WARNER, AUTHOR OF *BUFFY SAINTE-MARIE: THE AUTHORIZED BIOGRAPHY* AND *WE OUGHTA KNOW: HOW FOUR WOMEN RULED THE '90S AND CHANGED CANADIAN MUSIC*

ANY OTHER CITY

A Novel

HAZEL JANE PLANTE

ARSENAL PULP PRESS
VANCOUVER

ARSENAL PULP PRESS
Suite 202 – 211 East Georgia St.
Vancouver, BC V6A 1Z6
Canada
arsenalpulp.com

The publisher gratefully acknowledges the support of the Canada Council for the Arts and the British Columbia Arts Council for its publishing program, and the Government of Canada and the Government of British Columbia (through the Book Publishing Tax Credit Program) for its publishing activities.

Arsenal Pulp Press acknowledges the xʷməθkʷəy̓əm (Musqueam), Sḵwx̱wú7mesh (Squamish), and səl̓ilwətaʔɬ (Tsleil-Waututh) Nations, custodians of the traditional, ancestral, and unceded territories where our office is located. We pay respect to their histories, traditions, and continuous living cultures and commit to accountability, respectful relations, and friendship.

This is a work of fiction. Any resemblance of characters to persons either living or deceased is purely coincidental.

Parallels
Words and music by Adrianne Lenker
Copyright © 2016 Domino Publishing Company Limited
All rights reserved. Used by permission.

Motion Sickness
Words and music by Phoebe Bridgers and Marshall Vore
Copyright © 2017 Whatever Mom and Pizza Money Publishing
All rights administered worldwide by Kobalt Songs Music Publishing
All rights reserved. Used by permission.
Reprinted by permission of Hal Leonard LLC

Cover and text design by Jazmin Welch
Back cover photography by Daniel Olah via Unsplash
Edited by Catharine Chen
Proofread by Alison Strobel

Printed and bound in Canada

Library and Archives Canada Cataloguing in Publication:
Title: Any other city : a novel / Hazel Jane Plante.
Names: Plante, Hazel Jane, author.
Identifiers: Canadiana (print) 20220412499 | Canadiana (ebook) 20220412502 | ISBN 9781551529110 (softcover) | ISBN 9781551529127 (EPUB)
Classification: LCC PS8631.L345 A79 2023 | DDC C813/.6—dc23

for Onjana

ANY OTHER CITY

A Memoir

TRACY ST. CYR

with

HAZEL JANE PLANTE

ARSENAL PULP PRESS
VANCOUVER

Foreword to Side A,

or

A Dose of Vinyl Hiss
Before the First Song Starts

by Hazel Jane Plante

YOU'RE ABOUT TO READ ANY OTHER CITY, Tracy St. Cyr's avidly antic-ipated memoir. Perhaps you're reading this book because you adore her band, Static Saints. Perhaps you were transfixed by her infamous appearance on *The Late Show with Stephen Colbert*. Perhaps you were intrigued by this book's tantalizing cover. I'm listed as the person Tracy wrote her memoir "with," so perhaps I should share how it came into being before you shake off your sandals and wade into its waters.

I met Tracy shortly after my debut novel, *Little Blue Encyclopedia (for Vivian)*, was published. Thanks to my cunning and tireless publicist, I was invited to chat with a musician of my choice for an episode of the *Talkhouse* podcast, which pairs artists for conversations about their work. I chose to talk to Tracy St. Cyr. I've been a fan of Static Saints since their stellar third album, *Esperanto A-Go-Go*, and I'd watched Tracy publicly transition while I was in the crux of my own gender crisis. We had a wonderful freewheeling chat that centred on shared artistic obsessions, including genius musician Rowland S. Howard and iconoclastic artist Sadie Tang.

Tracy and I became fast friends, and I wrote liner notes for the Static Saints album *Dress Rehearsals*. At some point, Tracy confided that she'd signed a contract to write a memoir. It happened during her transition-related media whirlwind. One week, she was profiled in *The New Yorker*; the next week, she was on *Good Morning America*. During that dizzying wave of wooze and schmooze, Tracy signed a publishing contract. Out of the blue, I awoke to an avalanche of text messages from Tracy imploring me to collaborate on her memoir, her last text (at 2:15 a.m.) being, *Help me, Hazy-Wan Kenobi—you're my only hope.*

We met for coffee and talked about what she'd written so far, what she was trying to do with her memoir, and what it might look like if I got involved. She'd delayed the delivery date for the manuscript a couple of times and was on the hook to write the book because she'd already accepted and spent a substantial advance. She unzipped a black leather duffle bag on the empty chair beside her and gave me a quick spiel on the contents. They included most of the remnants of her past that she'd been consulting while working on the book. "My brain is fucked," she said. "Everything feels super foggy. And this book feels like a jigsaw puzzle with too many missing pieces. Maybe you can help me solve it."

I took some time off work and sifted through the contents of the duffle bag, which was crammed with notebooks, diaries, photographs, and demos. I sorted the items into piles on the hardwood floor of my apartment. I filled coloured index cards and sticky notes with dozens of discrete details, trying to divine patterns within the chaos. Sure, Tracy could write a linear memoir, but that would be like building a Vancouver Special home. She told me she wanted her memoir to be "architecturally interesting," which was why she wanted to work with me. (Tracy, you had me at "Hazy-Wan Kenobi.")

I'd been chatting and texting with Tracy while delving into her past, and our brains converged on the idea of a two-story structure. One story would be a snapshot of her life at twenty, when she flew overseas and unexpectedly fell in with a clutch of trans women. The second story would be from a year earlier, when she flew to the same city, this time to weather a traumatic event. I created a shared document, and we started to populate it with moments from her life at the ages of twenty and forty-six. Before long, we started noticing reverberations. Perhaps we could show how it feels to travel through time with a complicated gender, including the ways our past selves ripple into our present selves.

At some point, Tracy sent me the demos for the next Static Saints album. I was knocked out and soon became fixated on the song "Useful and Beautiful." It will likely be heard as an ode to sexual debasement, but I think it's also an invitation to root your life and your art in utility and beauty. I've found myself returning endlessly to this question: How can we make Tracy's memoir more useful and more beautiful? I love that her song enacts what it extols: it reminds us that we can revel in sexual pleasure and perversity ("I've got uses / I've got bruises") while also opening up to become more expansive, more useful, and more beautiful ("Oh, let me be a crashing wave / Oh, let me be a secret cave"). The aesthetic and architectural decisions animating this book stem from the desire to make it as useful and as beautiful as humanly possible.

Tracy and I spoke many times about the voices we let into our heads, particularly the people we have imaginary conversations with, who often are our lovers. As a result, Tracy decided in her memoir to write directly to two women who deeply affected her life. In Side A, she writes to her first girlfriend. In Side B, she speaks to a lover who shattered her world.

I've seen sources claim that I'm the "ghostwriter" of this memoir. I want to dispel this notion. Tracy is this book's architect; I'm just someone who chatted with her about the two-story building she wanted to construct and provided some feedback on her blueprints and architectural models. The Side A / Side B structure is a case in point—that comes from Tracy. I was just along for the ride as a pedantic passenger, a light-fingered creative conspirator.

For what it's worth, I suggest reading *Any Other City* in several smaller sips rather than one long gulp. It's a slow work to metabolize and has lingering notes of leather, smoke, and licorice. While reading, please don't forget to keep hydrated and caffeinated. I don't think I helped Tracy "solve" her personal jigsaw puzzle, but I'm so glad she trusted me to help her identify and rearrange the pieces into a useful and beautiful shape that feels something like a life.

July 8, 2021

And you will lose yourself in the city
(You will unravel your riddle)
And you will find yourself in the city
(You will secrete all your secrets)

COSTUMES BY EDITH HEAD, "SECRET GIRLS"

WHEN I WAS SMALL, I dreamt of becoming friends with a peregrine falcon. It wasn't my pet. We were close friends. Maybe best friends. The falcon wanted so badly to be human. And I dearly wanted to have wings. We would sit together in a soft nest high above the city, sharing secrets and nibbling on black-licorice mice. Have you ever tried licorice mice? They are tender, gooey, and delicious.

After I told you my dream of befriending a falcon, you talked about the colony of vampire bats you believed lived in a cave on the outskirts of town. Your brother had told you about them to scare you, but you started asking your parents to take you to the cave. You didn't tell them it was because you wanted to be bitten and become a bat. We both wanted wings and adventures when we were kids.

Last night, I dreamt that we were together at a lake, drinking soda and dipping our toes in the water off the edge of the wharf. The water was glassy and smooth. A dragonfly landed on your shoulder, and you offered it some of your black cherry soda. I laughed, but it flew from your shoulder to the lip of the bottle. Then, it stunned us by zooming up and hovering between us for a few seconds before whirring off across the lake. You leaned over and kissed me. I felt a burst of electricity as your tongue touched mine. I woke up and remembered where I was and where you are. I couldn't fall back to sleep.

Somehow, your hands know my body better than I do, Astrid. And now your hands are on the other side of the ocean.

—

The Old Quarter of this city is crammed with long, winding alleys. I live in a tiny third-floor apartment in the middle of one of them. Apparently, it's called Seahorse Alley, though one of my guidebooks calls it Underwater Horse Alley.

You said you always pictured the continent we were on as a bird with outstretched wings perched on an ice cream cone. Ever since then, whenever I look at a map, that's what I see too. You realigned my vision. Now, I'm living on a continent that you once said was shaped like a galloping buffalo. And you're still in that watery city located near the bird's breast.

I know you don't understand why I left. You asked why I couldn't create art in the sleepy, cloudy city you love, the city where you became yourself. I didn't have words to explain why I needed to leave. I'm here because something in me told me to come here.

But now that I'm here I miss you more than I can explain. My heart feels swollen and heavy. It's like a rusty, aching anchor. I'm weighed down with want. I'm a wanton thing. Somehow, I failed to recognize that I'm tethered to you. I miss your eyes and your hands and your lips and your voice. I want you to ease me open. I want your fingers to fill me.

—

I'm working part-time in a bakery. I get up at 3 a.m., which shapes my days in weird ways. I'm groggy until I've had two cups of coffee. (Yes, I've started drinking coffee!) And I curl into bed around 7 p.m.

When we lived together, I was always the night owl, and you tended to drift off while we cuddled on the couch. I tried to paint while you slept, but I found myself wanting to snuggle next to you more than I wanted to paint. For some reason, the phrase "nuzzle and doze" is coming to me. Maybe I read it in a poem once or in a translation of a poem. It sounds like a translated phrase. Nuzzle and doze. That's all I ever wanted to do when it was dark out: nuzzle and doze alongside you. But unlike you, I find sleep elusive. I often feel myself start to fall asleep, as though I'm tumbling over the edge of a cliff, and I jolt awake, my heart hammering. Sometimes when I'd awoken you, you would cradle me and kiss my shoulders and neck and tell me it was okay. Sometimes you would sigh and turn your back to me.

Sometimes your crabby cat, Buttons, would wake me by biting my toes. She never bit you. I was the one who fed her, so she'd come to me whenever she was hungry. She came to you when she wanted to cuddle. She'd sit in your lap and glower at me. Her expression was 85 percent "What the fuck are you doing here?" and 15 percent "She loves me more than she loves you."

—

You grew up in an old house that you once said was a fixer-upper nobody was ever going to fix up. Your parents mostly left you alone to do whatever you wanted. Your yard was sprawling and wild.

I was just remembering the first time I rode my bike to your place. We were both sixteen. You poured me a cup of sugary orange juice. Then, you took me into the backyard, and we kissed under a tree you used to climb. After a while, you led me past a collapsed barn. I wanted to go inside, but you said that its muddy floor would muck up my shoes. Behind the barn was a broken-down Volkswagen van surrounded by shoulder-high grass and weeds. The van was a faded military green except for one of the doors, which was painted safety orange. You opened the bright-orange door, and we went in.

You swivelled the little kitchen table against one of the walls in the van, and we sat on the couch. Your lips were sugary. Your tongue tasted like smoke. You turned on a small portable radio. It was broadcasting a song about heartache. You took off your top. Your bra was light blue with one white flower on it. I traced the edges of the flower with a finger.

You folded out the couch to make a small bed. Then, things happened so quickly that my memories are tangled together. I forget if you took off your bra before you slipped one of my fingers into your mouth. I forget if you were staring into my eyes while you sucked on my finger, or if you started staring into my eyes when you guided my finger inside you. And you must have taken off your skirt and panties at some point, but I don't remember when that happened. And a song must have been playing on the small radio while I fucked you with my finger, but I don't remember what song it was. And, really, I think you were fucking me, because I was probably trying to be gentle and not hurt you. You asked me to fuck you harder. Then, you asked me to use two fingers, telling me to put them in my mouth before I put them in you. When I slid my fingers into my mouth, I expected you to taste fishy, but you didn't. You tasted like a tangy, salty fruit that was just ripening. My body was flooded with desire. It was trickier to find your pussy on my own. I felt silly. You smiled and guided my two fingers inside of you. You were more slippery than I'd expected. Then, you pulled me down onto you, kissed me, taught me how to fuck you. When you came, you gasped and your eyes widened and you looked so tender and fragile and I saw tears at the edges of your eyes. Later, when we were lying together, you gently tugged my earlobe with your teeth and whispered, Wow, you fucked me good, like really good. My body is humming.

When you tried to unbuckle my jeans, I shook my head. Next time, I said. You looked disappointed, but I insisted, and finally you kissed me and said okay.

—

Ever since arriving here, I've been walking a lot. Mostly, I explore the alleys. Glass Alley. Alley of Branches. Blood Alley. Alley of Gems. Silver Alley. The alleys here are all crooked and crammed with shops and bicycles and spiral staircases that twist this way and that way.

I tried doing watercolours of your face, but they made me miss you too much. So I've started mapping one of the alleys instead: Alley of Branches. So far, I've discovered a print shop, a barber, a few families, a cul-de-sac where dozens of people park their motorcycles, a locksmith, and a small swimming pool. I've never seen a public pool as small as this one. It's affordable and never crowded. I've become one of a handful of regulars. My favourite patron is an older woman with a purple-and-yellow swimsuit who wears goggles and floats on her back, smiling. I've never seen her not floating. I'm jealous of how open and serene she seems to be. Her eyes always appear to be closed behind her goggles.

For a while, I thought I could stay with you in the watery city you love, but it's too crowded with memories. They're stuffed into every corner and every cranny. All the stuff from the past is stacked on top of what's there now, like a layer cake. And I have to remember stuff that I don't want to remember. And I have to feel stuff that I don't want to feel.

For me, it's a city forever stuffed with sadness. It's a city where I have to share space with obsolete versions of myself. It's a city of gunpowder and hand grenades.

I've never lived anywhere else. I needed to get away for a spell.

Why couldn't I tell you this before I left? I have no idea.

If I understood myself, I'd be a different person.

—

The older woman who floats in the small swimming pool came into the bakery today. She ordered an espresso and a croissant. After my co-worker Effie delivered the order to her table, the woman gently tore off one end of her croissant and slowly poured the espresso from its tiny cup into the soft, airy centre. It was like watching a magician pour a jug of milk into a newspaper funnel. The croissant absorbed the entire double shot of espresso. Then, she slowly nibbled on her espresso-infused croissant while reading a mystery novel. I've never understood why people are fascinated and comforted by reading about other people being murdered. Without her goggles on, I could see that the floating woman has the most brilliant blue-green eyes.

—

It took a long time for me to let you unbuckle my jeans. I'd only had sex once before, and it was not good. I couldn't come. Not even after nearly an hour of fucking. I'd thought maybe it was the condom or the lack of friction. But now I think my body just didn't want to. And I didn't know how to pretend, so I just stopped and told her my tummy was upset and awkwardly left her house and walked to the mall and bought a candy bar and grape soda and wolfed down the candy bar and took the bus home and gulped down the grape soda and jerked off and sobbed into my pillow and felt more ashamed and broken than I'd ever felt before.

When I finally let you take off my jeans in the abandoned van in your backyard, I was so nervous that I felt lightheaded. You told me to lie down on the small bed. Then, you asked me what I wanted. I covered my face with my hands and said, I don't know. You kissed my forehead and my cheeks and my throat and my shoulders. You put your ear to my chest and listened to my heart beating. You've got a good heart, you said. It makes a nice thump. You moved your fingernails across my inner thighs. You dotted my torso with kisses. You paused, looked up at me, your hair falling in your face. Is this okay? you asked. Yes, I said. Very okay. You smiled. Somehow you knew I needed slowness.

—

One day while walking through Glass Alley, I followed a faint hum that grew louder and more shimmery as I travelled to its source. Finally, I poked my head into a doorway and saw a dozen or so musicians creating a sound unlike anything I'd heard before. It was so soft and airy that it barely qualified as music. It was the prettiest drone. No melody. Pure atmosphere. Their instruments reminded me of a documentary on an avant-garde composer who created dozens of unique instruments to play his experimental songs on. But these instruments were less ornate, largely consisting of warped metal bowls and hubcaps played with felt mallets, wire-strung wooden planks played with violin bows, and a few distressed woodwinds.

Besides the musicians, there were a dozen or so people sitting on folding chairs, their heads lowered. It looked like they were listening intently or meditating, but they could have been unconscious. I listened at the doorway until I noticed a man watching me from the other side of the room. I blanched and hastened back into the alley.

Before long, I felt a hand at my elbow. I turned, alarmed and defensive. It was the man who had spotted me. I made a gesture of apology. He said something that I couldn't understand, something that might have included the word for "please" a couple of times. After a baffling back and forth, I understood that he seemed to be inviting me into the room. I shook my head, said no a few times. He kept insisting, almost pleading. Eventually, I nodded my head and followed him into the room. The musicians were still filling the space with their pretty, shimmery drone. It felt like entering a church.

The man poured me a cup of tea. Then, he poured one for himself. He raised his glass and smiled, and I did the same. The tea was sugary and warm. The music also felt sugary and warm. Somehow, it was comforting to be drinking tea with a stranger, listening to a soft, ethereal wash of music made by strange instruments.

—

The first time I fucked you and was inside of you, the first time I fucked you without my fingers or a toy, that first time, I kept thinking of waves, of a dolphin undulating in the ocean. Maybe that helped me to feel okay about being inside of you. And the way your eyes kept looking into mine also made it feel okay, made it feel good, so gushingly good. Your eyes, my eyes. An ocean, a dolphin. And, oh fuck. Fuck. My body crashing again and again against the waves of your body. Staring into your eyes as I came. Your arms wrapped around me, pulling me down while you ground against me, as I shuddered and collapsed into you, poured myself into you. And then. A calmness. An okayness. A smoothness, soothing and liquidy. Then, you cradled me and kissed my cheeks, my throat, my lips. You broke the stillness, saying, That was so fucking hot. Just. I don't even know. Fuck. That was the best thing ever. And you were right. It was.

The next time we fucked, I couldn't get to that place again. For some reason, I felt awful and started crying. Somehow, you got it, got that sometimes sex wouldn't work for me, and you folded me into your arms.

—

I haven't seen the older woman at the swimming pool lately. Watching her floating on her back, smiling and open to the world, was so soothing. I tried floating in the pool today. It's hard for me to calm down, lie back, and trust that my body will float. Sometimes I start to panic and worry I'll suddenly sink and my lungs will fill with water. To help me relax and make myself buoyant, I often think of you holding my hand, whispering, Everything is okay, over and over. When I picture you holding my hand, we're sitting on a train, scenery whipping by us. In the water, I let my arms and legs turn to driftwood. Everything is okay. We're still on the train, passing through a forest. Your hand is holding my hand. Now I'm a bright starfish floating in a bed of water. Everything is okay.

—

The first time I came in your mouth, you told me I tasted oceany.

—

I've finally finished mapping Alley of Branches. It's an incomplete map, but even the best maps are incomplete. I have a stack of sketches. In this one, I tried to capture the texture of the cobblestones. In that one, I tried to show the chockablockness of the print shop. In a few of them, I tried to put to paper the tangles of bicycles and motorcycles. And there are more sketches of the small swimming pool than seem necessary, but its gravitational pull kept bringing me back. When I moved on to making watercolours, I started with small studies of the older woman in her purple-and-yellow swimsuit and tinted goggles floating calmly in the blue-green pool.

I've been thinking about painting individual watercolours that can be assembled into a massive kaleidoscopic painting, a painting that will show the meandering contours of the alley, its spiral staircases, its dwellings, its businesses, its juxtaposed and jumbled glory. While you live in a watery city, I'm dipping my paintbrush to drag watery colours across cold-pressed paper.

I can't stop doing watercolours of you, even though they make me miss you terribly. Your face. Your breasts. The nest of your pubic hair.

A few years ago, I read an article about a legendary art school located in this city. I mentioned to you more than a few times that I wanted more than anything to go to that school. You said, You're already an artist. You're my artist. I didn't know what to say. I don't want to be a Sunday painter. I don't want to be a disgruntled dishwasher at a greasy spoon diner who also happens to be an artist. I want to be swimming in art, to be surrounded by other artists, to make things that are unwieldy and weird and learn from my mistakes, to devote myself to creativity. In my vision, you're there with me, sharing coffee and fresh pastries each morning in our small apartment, holding my hand in a gallery, reading aloud to me while I make dinner, knitting a pair of fingerless gloves while I sketch you, exploring the alleys alongside me, urgently kissing me against a brick wall.

After months of hesitation, procrastination, and self-doubt, I finally applied to the art school in this city. It's notoriously difficult to get in, and I didn't. I tried again. I got rejected again. You suggested that I study art somewhere nearby, but I'd been dreaming of this art school for too long to let it go. So, I told you that even though its art school didn't want me, I still wanted to move to this city and make art, and I asked you to come with me. But everything you wanted was already in the sleepy city where we lived. You wanted to be near your family and friends; you liked your job and loved living surrounded by water and mountains and weren't enamoured by the thought of leaving everything behind to live in a city of strangers and serpentine alleys.

One time we walked past an empty car with its motor running and the keys in the ignition. I told you I was tempted to jump inside, drive off, and start an entirely new life in a new town with a new name. You looked horrified, like I'd just broken up with you. Why, you asked, why would you want to do that? You had no idea why someone would want to shrug off their past and reinvent themselves.

—

After being away for two or three weeks, I returned to the small swimming pool. In that short span, it had somehow been transformed into a coffee shop. I walked down the pool's concrete steps with their gleaming silver handrail into a cozy sunken café. It felt odd being in the drained swimming pool. I was so used to feeling the resistance of water against me in that space. My combat boots clacked on the blue-green tiles. I hung the bag that contained my swimsuit and a towel on the back of a chair and sat down. All the tables and chairs were bright yellow. There were far more people in the coffee shop than I'd ever seen in the pool. I looked around for the older woman with the purple-and-yellow swimsuit, but I didn't see her. I wondered if she went somewhere else to float now or if she'd simply phased that out of her daily routine and moved on to something else, like tai chi. For the first time, I noticed that the concrete sides of the pool had faint illustrations of birds and fish. Some faint birds were swooping down with their faint talons extended toward faint fish under faint waves, while other faint birds were carrying faint fish into the air. I glanced at the menu and saw that the price for a coffee was similar to what I used to pay to swim in the quaint, uncrowded pool. According to my language dictionary, the coffee shop was named Mr. Swim. I had a watery cup of coffee and a disappointing Danish and left.

—

My first crush was on a girl named Tracy in kindergarten, and I've been crushing on girls ever since. I've always told you that my crush on you started when we were about fifteen, taking Earth Science together. But that's not true. I first had a crush on you when I was about ten. That was the year we had the teacher who used to sing opera over the PA system in the morning, the teacher who seemed clueless about why he was standing at the front of the room, the one who would digress during a lesson on grammar to bemoan the dinky dessert portions in TV dinners. I started hovering near you, eavesdropping on what movies and music and snacks you liked. One time, I took a few things from your desk during recess. I don't even recall what I took—probably small things you wouldn't miss. I might have taken one of your scrunchies. My crush on you lasted until you relocated your desk to the back of the room to sit beside Lisa. As soon as that happened, I knew Lisa would convince you that I was a loser. So, I drifted away from you and let my crush wither.

Several years later, you were friends with my friend Aaron, who I sat beside in Earth Science, so we started chatting. And then, just like that, my crush on you was revived, and I couldn't stop thinking about you. I've always told you that I knew I loved you from the first time we kissed. It was a fantastic kiss, but I think I fell for you deeply the first time you came over to Aaron's place to watch us jam.

For some reason, I trusted you right away and was willing to be silly in front of you. And then, while I was tuning my guitar and Aaron was saying his usual Fuck, one two, one two, fuck you, into the mic to adjust the levels, you suggested a weird and wonderful name for our band: Lubricated Sagan. You laughed. Aaron laughed. I laughed. I kept flashing on the countless videos we'd watched in Earth Science with Carl Sagan reeling off facts about the universe in a never-changing monotone and an ever-changing turtleneck. Our laughter would subside, then one of us would say, Lubricated Sagan, and we'd all burst into laughter again. I remember you laughing at your own joke until you had to wipe tears from your eyes with your jean jacket sleeve.

I wanted you to keep laughing, so I broke out my shaky Carl Sagan impression. At present, I intoned, an enormous wang appears to be thrusting forcefully into my lubricated rectum.

Through tears, you added in your best monotone, I must admit the sensation is not entirely unpleasant.

We collapsed into laughter, and Aaron's mom yelled down from upstairs to see if everything was okay. Aaron yelled back that everything was fine, and we tried to stifle ourselves. You probably don't remember, but our eyes connected right then. A shiver ran down my spine. I wanted to spend the rest of the night with you, the rest of the week with you, lying in bed, staring into each other's eyes until one of us got peckish or had to pee. That's when I first felt a pinch of love for you.

Until you suggested Lubricated Sagan, we'd been oscillating between a name Aaron liked (Osiris) and a name I liked (Cubistic Barbeque).

I remember when our Earth Science teacher, Mr. Roseblatt, introduced mnemonics to help us memorize the order of the planets. After giving us a few options, he said the mnemonic he found most memorable was **Many Very Eager Men Jumped Sally Under Neil's Porch.** He chuckled and segued into another topic.

Excuse me, Mr. Roseblatt, you said. Are you saying rape is okay?

Visibly uncomfortable, he adjusted his custard-stained sweater vest and stammered something along the lines of, Well, no, no, I didn't, um, that's not. He had a doe-eyed science-teacher-with-a-tobacco-stained-moustache-in-headlights expression.

But, Mr. Roseblatt, you said firmly, "many very eager men jumped Sally under Neil's porch" sounds like rape. It sounds like you're saying it's okay for these men to rape Sally.

Mr. Roseblatt tried to make what he'd said go away, but you wouldn't let it go. He got more and more flustered. I'd never seen a student make a teacher yield like that. Finally, he realized that he was stuck, like a mouse squirming on a glue trap, and the only way he could get unstuck was to apologize. And, to his credit, he did. Looking back now, I suspect he was probably worried you would report him to the principal. Once he'd apologized, you just let it go. A few girls came up to thank you after and you just brushed it off, like it was no big deal.

Your bedroom walls were covered with posters of metal bands and bats. I remember being transfixed by one massive poster filled with dozens of bat species. Some of them looked like they were smiling. You tried to unpack for me the wonder of bats. I kept cutting you off with kisses. I asked if you had a favourite bat on the poster, and you couldn't choose a single species, so you talked about a few of your favourites. I remember you pointed to a bat with a long, slender tongue and said, I bet he'd be fun to date.

I asked you to put on some music. You rooted around in a milk crate filled with cassettes, found the one you wanted, and popped it in your boom box. It was a local influential industrial band that had recently covered every song on Meat Loaf's *Bat Out of Hell* album. You asked if it was okay, and I said it wasn't my favourite. You slipped one of your hands into your jeans, took it out, and slid a finger into my mouth. I tasted your tanginess. A faucet twisted inside me. You asked again, Is this okay? Yeah, I said, it's perfect.

The first time you kissed me wasn't when I fell for you, but that first kiss was when I knew I was so deeply into you that I didn't know if I could ever dig my way out. You were the quintessential rocker babe with your feathered hair, tight jeans, doom metal shirt, and jean jacket, smoking in the smoke pit with all the other rocker babes. You kept offering me a drag, but I kept saying no, even though I was so tempted every time I glanced at the lipstick-stained cigarette between your fingers.

Follow me, you said. Then, you started walking somewhere. I followed. I remember being nervous that you were setting me up, because I wasn't like the cooler-than-thou rockers I'd seen you flirting with in the halls. I was one of the weird queer kids who got teased for wearing eyeliner and mostly hung out in an alcove with my weird queer friends.

I followed you to a dumpster at the back of the parking lot. Look, you said, I like you. Do you wanna kiss me? I felt woozy. I had that top-of-the-roller-coaster-oh-fuck-oh-fuck feeling in my tummy. Yeah, I said, I do. But I couldn't move. I was a statue. I watched you close your eyes, lean in, and open your mouth. You tasted like spearmint and smoke. It's hard to know how long our first kiss lasted. Was it just the tender moment of your soft lips against mine, your tongue sliding tentatively into my mouth before retreating? Or did it also include when you kissed me more deeply and pushed your jeans against my jeans, your denim softness against my denim hardness. I was overwhelmed, couldn't think, could barely breathe. A bulb in my brain burst.

After we kissed, you lit another smoke and inhaled. You offered me a drag, and this time I took it. I felt dizzy, coughed, and handed it back to you. We stood there behind the dumpster, pressed against each other, sharing a lipstick-stained cigarette.

—

Last night, I made a handful of drawings based on scenes from *Already Yesterday*, the time travel movie we saw on our second date. But in my drawings, you and I starred in the story instead of River Phoenix and Lisa Bonet. In my revised version, you travelled back in time to prevent a devastating pandemic and fell in love with me. First, I drew from my memory of the film. Then, I watched a VHS tape of it that I rented from a video store tucked in a corner of Alley of Gems. (The store is so small that my guidebook says to find a jewellery store with a neon sign of a glowing emerald and then to turn around. Even with those directions, it was hard to spot. But it was teeming with tapes, and the woman working there knew exactly where to pluck out *Already Yesterday* from the stacks of tapes around her.)

The first time I saw the film, I was distracted by sitting beside you in the theatre, feeling your leg against mine, your hand in mine, watching you sip from our shared straw and drop popcorn in your mouth. (Your lips seemed extra glossy that day.) I was so besotted that I simply remembered *Already Yesterday* as a sweet romantic film rather than a bittersweet tragedy. River Phoenix plays the son of an eccentric epidemiologist whose unexpected infatuation with a quirky postal worker, played by Lisa Bonet, distracts him from preventing the pandemic. He's busy charming her by juggling fruit at a grocery store on a side street when he should be preventing Forest Whitaker's character, who has just been infected with the deadly virus, from piloting the first in a series of international flights that will rapidly spread the virus to the most populated cities in the world. The final scene shows the doomed lovers cuddling in bed as their symptoms get worse, and the dreamy, haunting song "Already Yesterday" by the Church surges through the speakers. You wept through the credits. I kept trying to cheer you up with banter and felt a bit miffed when you shook your head and murmured, Please, don't. Eventually, you tidied yourself in the washroom. When you came out, you took me to a park nearby and we smoked a joint.

—

I'm at the laundromat. It rarely rains in this city, but it's bucketing down right now. When we do get rain here, it's as though some pipes in the sky have burst. I'm sitting on a faded chair with stuffing leaking out of it, reading the letter you sent me. I've never cried in a laundromat before, but there's a first for everything. I don't know how you can be unsure whether I love you. I desperately want to come home, but my body won't let me. Something in me needs to be here for a little while longer. I know you need me. I know you feel distant from me. I know cuddling with Buttons isn't enough for you. Last night, I held my own hand and imagined it was yours. But I also know that we'll always be in each other's lives. We belong together. Being apart for a while isn't ideal, but we're both where we need to be right now. And I'll come back to you soon. I promise. As soon as I wrote that, the rain stopped on a dime.

Now my laundry is tumbling in an oversized dryer, making a rhythmic *whoosh* and *tink* as the metal buttons and zippers on my pants and hoodies clink against the metallic insides of the dryer. You tried to teach me to meditate a few times, but I just can't do it. I try to focus on my breathing, but my brain won't stop whirring. The sound of the dryer reminds me of when I try (and fail) to pay attention to my breathing. Inhale. Pause. Exhale. Pause. *Whoosh tink.* Pause. *Whoosh tink.* Pause.

The end of your letter made me happier and sadder than I can say. I'm sitting in this ratty chair, letting good and bad emotions wash over me as I listen to the *whoosh tink, whoosh tink, whoosh tink* of the dryer. My heart feels like it's on a tumble cycle.

—

I spotted Sadie Tang while walking past a restaurant today. I resisted dashing inside and interrupting her meal to tell her she's the reason I want to go to art school here. She was with a couple of other people—I'm certain they were younger artists she's mentoring—and I longed to be sitting at that table, drinking cocktails and eating oysters with them.

The first time I saw Sadie Tang's work was a revelation. It was as though I'd been groggy, wiping the sleep from my eyes, and someone handed me a triple espresso. Suddenly, I was awake.

I went to an exhibit of her work with my friend Cory when we were thirteen or fourteen. (I think that I might have told you about a friend of mine who spat on me in gym class after he fell in with a crowd of more popular kids. That was Cory.) We arrived with our black-dyed tumble-weed hair and our goth getups. We looked like almost-identical shadows, except my sixteen-hole boots were cherry red and his were black. He'd suggested we go to the art gallery, which sounded achingly dull, until he told me we were going to see a show called *Platypus Pornography*. I was tickled and intrigued by that provocative, preposterous title.

The exhibit was by a transsexual artist named Sadie Tang. After reading the artist's statement, you entered a small darkroom. Red safe-lights illuminated the equipment around you. Some photos were being processed; others were hung up to dry with clothespins. All the black-and-white images I could see showed transsexual Asian women smirking and shoving their middle fingers toward the camera. Their defiance and exuberance was tangible. I felt a tinge of jealousy at how free they seemed to be. The piece was called *The Flipped Birds*.

When we stepped out of the darkroom into the bright gallery lights, Cory turned to me, smiled widely, and flipped up both his middle fingers. I gritted my teeth, snarled, and mimed chomping on his fingers, like a goth pitbull. He jumped back and giggled. A museum guard glared at us, waggling an index finger as a warning. I pursed my lips and nodded. He nodded back.

At that moment, I noticed the guard was standing in a room filled with smooth life-sized mannequins. There was a mannequin just a few feet from him with enormous breasts and a massive cock. I quickly looked away so the guard wouldn't see me biting my tongue to prevent myself from laughing. Cory leaned in to discover why I'd turned away, and I gestured toward the mannequin-filled room. He glanced over and said something like, Holy fucking shit, dude. He grabbed my arm and tried to pull me toward the room. Let's go slow, I said. We strolled over as casually as we were able.

The naked mannequins were in a range of poses. Some were standing around. Some were sitting down. Others were walking or gardening or playing sports. The way the mannequins' smooth lavender bodies reflected the bright overhead lights in the stark white gallery was weirdly soothing. No two were alike. Some had flat chests, and others had breasts. Some were thin, some were muscular, some were fat. Some had pussies, some had cocks, some had both. But they were all messing with our expectations of male and female bodies, which threw me for a loop.

There were signs around the room stating that the mannequins enjoyed being touched, but only with gloves. Several boxes filled with black latex gloves sat on a white table in the middle of the room. Cory was already fitting his fingers into two black gloves. If I'd been there on my own, I wouldn't have had the guts to put on latex gloves and touch the smooth, naked mannequins. But I wasn't alone, so I followed Cory's lead and fumbled my hands into a pair of gloves too.

Cory walked over to the mannequin we'd seen from the other room, the one with enormous tits and a gigantic cock. I felt a jolt of panic. Was he going to start groping the mannequin? Was the guard going to kick us out? But when Cory stood in front of that lavender mannequin, he hesitated. I'm not sure if he stopped because I was there, or because the guard was there, or because he was caught short by how exquisite the mannequins were up close. He hovered briefly before touching an index finger to one of its shoulders and slowly gliding his finger down the length of its arm to its wrist. Then, he ran his gloved fingers over its open palm, curling his fingers into its outstretched fingers. He was holding hands with the shiny, smooth lavender mannequin. Its protruding erection was only a few inches from his ass, but he didn't seem to notice.

We both floated around the room, stopping in front of mannequins and running our black latex fingers over their backs, their hands, their torsos, their arms, their cheeks. We moved silently from smooth body to smooth body. When a tour group arrived, we exchanged looks and walked over to drop our black latex gloves in a stainless steel bin.

—

That day you came over to Aaron's place, we played a few covers and our one original song, "Nuclear Reactor." We'd written it in science class the year before, during a lesson on nuclear power. Aaron wrote the opening couplet and the chorus, and I wrote the rest.

I once worked in a nuclear reactor
I knew the engineer and I fucked her
Cuz we did it I got her radiation
Now I am a mutation
I went through a process of ionization

Yeah, fuckin' yeah
Yeah, fuckin' yeah

I'm starving for some hot apple pie
All this radiation killed my cell nuclei
My girlfriend's name is Carol
Because of my job now I'm sterile

Yeah, fuckin' yeah
Yeah, fuckin' yeah

Do you remember how much you hated "Nuclear Reactor"? After we played it, you made little devil horns with your fingers and said, "Yeah, fuckin' yeah" rules, but the rest of that song blows.

We always ended our jam sessions by playing "I Wanna Be Your Dog" two or three times. After we'd played it once, Aaron handed you the mic. You mumbled your way through the opening verse, but you gave me goosebumps when you sang the chorus. You sounded husky and sultry. You sang the second verse directly to Aaron, who was rattling a tambourine in time. I briefly wondered if that meant you were into him. But then you rushed over to me for the chorus, your nose an inch from mine, screaming into my face about how you wanted to be my dog. Your eyes were wide, and you were spitting out the words. You looked like you meant it. I never sang in front of people back then, but for the last line of the chorus, I yelled in unison that I also wanted to be your dog. You smiled.

—

All the cool clothing shops here suddenly have camouflage in their window displays. Camouflage T-shirts, camouflage tunics, camouflage bras and panties, camouflage handbags, camouflage boots. It's just like how the cherry blossoms that line the street outside our apartment seem to agree on the perfect morning to pop open and flaunt their soft pink petals. I walked out the door one day, and all I saw in boutique windows was camo. I know it's just fashion, but it feels like a bad omen, like maybe I'm being told to prepare for battle.

—

While I was mapping Alley of Branches today, I kept asking myself why I was devoting my time to exploring alleys. I couldn't drop that question.

The longer I pondered what I was doing, the more it felt like a meaningless distraction. I'd been captivated by Sadie Tang's *Platypus Pornography* exhibit because it did something I'd never seen done, because it was saying something about gender, about bodies, about expectations, about pleasure.

I ducked into a tea shop tucked behind a candy store. I ordered a small pot of Lady Grey tea and settled into a corner table in the nearly empty shop. I took out my little sketchbook and made a list with two columns: *Why am I here?* and *What do I want to do here?* I jotted down a handful of things in each column. Then, I ranked them by importance. The top item in both columns referred to Sadie Tang. I'm here because she's here, and I dearly want to meet her. If I were to leave the city without meeting her, I know I'd regret it.

I've already been turned down twice by the art school where she teaches. Perhaps she saw my portfolio when I applied. Perhaps she had personally rejected my work both times. I imagined her expression turning sour as she eyed the work in my portfolio, muttering, Oh god, anything but this rubbish. If I did get to meet her, maybe I should pretend to be someone else. Someone who wasn't an artist and someone with a different name. And I'd need to invent a reason to meet her. Maybe I could interview her? Yes, I could interview her. But why? Maybe I was interviewing transsexual artists. That sounded good, but why transsexual artists? I didn't want to come across as a creep who saw her as a fetish. Maybe instead of saying I was interviewing transsexual artists, I should just say I was interviewing artists. That sounded less creepy, but the question of why lingered.

Maybe I had a college radio show. What was I studying at the college where I had a radio show? Carpentry? Nah. Psychology? Nope. Criminal justice? Fuck no. Even though I wanted to invent a non-artsy version of myself, I desperately needed Sadie Tang to know that I was an artist. Plus, it made sense that someone in art school would want to interview an established artist for a college radio show. Where was I studying? The first place that came to mind was the Rhode Island School of Design, because I'd pored over one of their brochures before deciding not to apply, and my friend Irene had gone there for a while and we'd chatted a bit about her classes, her teachers, the other students, life in Providence. If Sadie Tang asked me any questions about studying at RISD, I figured I could fake it.

But I still had to give myself a new name. What name would you pick if you could rename yourself? It's so hard to settle on one thing. You'll think you've got the perfect name. Then you'll notice that it seemed shiny for a while, but it's already become dull. Astrid is such a good name. I know you think it sounds like the title of a corny sci-fi cartoon. To me, it sounds like the name of a flower that grows on one of Jupiter's moons, its velvety silver-and-black bulbs only blooming on the coldest and darkest days.

I've always liked androgynous names. I suspected Sadie might like them too. I started jotting down a few possible names. Tracy. Ash. Robin. Charlie. Dusty. Casey. Pat. Frankie. Sandy. Leslie. Jo.

—

I'd been drawn to art ever since being dazzled by Sadie Tang's exhibit, but it felt like making art for a living was beyond me. All the adults I knew who were employed had blue-collar jobs, like sawmill workers or welders.

When people said their parents worked in offices, I had no idea what their parents did or how they'd gotten jobs working in offices. I assumed you probably needed to be a whiz at typing. Unfortunately, I had not done well in typing class, which involved typing without looking at the keys for an hour while tinny classical music from a boom box filled the little room. It didn't help that our teacher sat at the back of the class, wearing sunglasses and slurping coffee from a ceramic Snoopy mug. Did you ever have Mr. Fairchild? I forget.

At the start of every class, he'd point us to the appropriate pages in our typing textbooks and remind us that we should only disturb him in case of emergency. If we had a question, we should ask one of our friends, because they probably knew the answer. I didn't have any friends in that class, and I never had what I felt was a touch typing emergency. I was fine with the home row of keys, but as soon as we started adding other rows, I struggled. And when we added numbers and punctuation, I was sunk. While I floundered on my electric typewriter, Mr. Fairchild slumped behind his shades in the back corner, looking like an unkempt vampire.

On the last day of class, Mr. F (as he preferred to be called) wore a piano key necktie and popped a demo cassette of his bar band into the boom box. He wrote his band's name on the chalkboard: Big Bad Woof and the Tweeters. A few students snickered.

Dallas Mullins asked, Are you Big Bad Woof? We bit our collective tongues.

No, Mr. F said, I'm one of the Tweeters. He paused, daring us to laugh. We didn't. He continued, I think that's enough dilly-dallying for today. Time to roll up your sleeves and type to the beat.

He hit "Play" on the boom box and wandered around the room, strangely energized, peering over our shoulders as we fingered our type-writers. Occasionally, he tapped out piano riffs on the sides of our desks. I still remember nervously typing while he stood behind me, softly singing along to "Pour Some Sugar On Me."

When I received my report card, I discovered that Mr. F had given me an F in typing. It looked like I'd probably never work in an office.

You've known since elementary school that you wanted to study bats. It didn't matter to you that your parents ran a dry cleaning business, that no one in your family had ever gone to university. You knew what you wanted to do, and you never doubted you could do it. I remember telling you how much I loved choose-your-own-adventure books as a kid. It was thrilling to be given some degree of control rather than being told what to do. You told me they always bored you because the options were so limited. What if you didn't want to a) open the door, or b) go upstairs? What if you wanted to ride your bike to the mall? What if you wanted to climb a tree?

In some ways, being here is me finally opting out of my own choose-your-own-adventure scenario. Do I want to a) wash dishes at the diner and try making art part-time, or b) enroll in the art stream at the community college? Maybe crossing an ocean to dwell in a city of endless alleys and camouflage leather skirts is my version of climbing a tree.

—

Oh, my gorgeous time-travelling genius. Leave it to you to go to the largest public library in town and sit down with newspapers for both of our cities so you could scan the film times and find a way for us to watch the same movie at the same time on opposite sides of the ocean. It was 7:20 p.m. for me and 10:20 a.m. for you. I sat with my popcorn, red licorice, and cream soda, imagining you sitting beside me, sipping from our shared straw and dipping your fingers into the tub of popcorn in my lap while you nuzzled against me, still a little groggy because you only fully become yourself around 11 a.m.

And *Fang Fatale* was the perfect film to watch together. A steamy lesbian vampire flick. When they made out under the blinking neon sign. When Jennifer Jason Leigh sank her fangs into Ione Skye's neck. When that cute guy with glasses lit Jennifer Jason Leigh's cigarette and she French inhaled before leaning in to suck him dry, finally leaving him whimpering and twitching on the sidewalk. As I said during our brief long-distance call afterward, I loved it, even though it was pretty trashy.

What was the last thing you said before you hung up to run to class? It sounded like you said that hearing my voice through the phone wires was turning your cunt into pudding. Now I can't think about anything else.

Before *Fang Fatale*, the theatre I was in showed an old black-and-white short film. It was about seahorses, and it was in French. Seahorses look so peculiar and delicate, with their bony bodies and their spindly tails. For a while, I couldn't tell if they were real seahorses or marionettes, but I think they were real seahorses. They are goofy-looking creatures.

At least half of the short film was footage of a male seahorse giving birth. There were no English subtitles, but my French is pretty good. The female deposits eggs in the male's pouch and floats away. And when the male gives birth, he spurts so many teensy-weensy seahorse babies out of his swollen pouch. Even after all those teensy seahorse babies have squirted out of him, he keeps spasming from birth contractions for a few more hours. It's hard not to feel bad for that seahorse dad with his endless spasms.

Only when I wandered back home did I realize that I live in Seahorse Alley.

—

Lately, I'm finding it difficult to make myself come. The ways I used to jerk off don't feel that good anymore. There's a new technique I've discovered that I call "cup and rub." It's difficult to describe, but it seems to be working. I'll show you the next time I see you. I miss your hands and your mouth on my body.

—

I wrote a letter to Sadie Tang in care of her school, asking to interview her for my radio show. I told her my name is Tracy.

—

I was just remembering when your dad helped us paint our overpriced one-bedroom apartment. He was bemused that I had no idea how to paint. I helped clumsily lug the paint cans from his truck. It was kind of him to pay for the paint and to lend his expertise, but he treated me like his dim-witted sidekick the entire time.

I never told you, but I overheard the two of you talking while you painted the bathroom magenta and absinthe green. It sounded like your dad said I was growing on him; then, I think he asked if you were sure I wasn't gay. I didn't catch your answer, but whatever you said made him laugh so hard that he had to reach for his puffer.

—

I met Sadie Tang today. She wanted to go for coffee before agreeing to do the interview for my imaginary college radio show. When she asked me over the phone what my show was called, I blanked. Oh, my show, I blathered, I thought I already told you the name. No, she said, you didn't. Oh, okay, I said. It's called *Art Attack*. Well, it used to be called *Art Attack and Vine*. Then I shortened it. To *Art Attack*. (Sometimes, when I start making things up, I just can't turn my mouth off. I'm like a faucet with a broken handle.)

She met me near a well-known monument related to the war. A few tourists were standing around it, snapping shots and studying their guidebooks. Sadie had told me she would be easy to spot. She was unmissable in her black leather jacket and white T-shirt with three lines of bright red text:

trans

sexual

artist

I waved at her. She drifted through the tourists to where I was standing and smiled warmly. It's good to meet you, Tracy, she said. I know a great coffee shop that way. She pointed toward an alley. Follow me.

She led me down Blood Alley, up a dark, twisting staircase, past a couple of family dwellings, past a barber and a butcher and a florist, and then, just like that, we had arrived at the coffee shop. Actually, it was a coffee shop and a shoe shop housed in the same small space. Sadie introduced me to the Thai lesbian couple who ran it, El and Em. El was quiet and androgynous, dressed in a black T-shirt, black jeans, and black sneakers, with a shaved head and dark hazel eyes; she ran the coffee shop. Em was flamboyant and flirty, wearing a denim dress and shocking-pink motorcycle boots; she ran the shoe store and was a skilled cobbler. I felt embarrassed for Em, because she looked like an overweight man in a dress. She had wide shoulders and a five o'clock shadow.

Sadie said we were just there for coffee. She muttered something to Em that I didn't catch. All three of them laughed. Em smiled at me and said in English, She told me that maybe she will talk you into buying a pair of my boots. Em winked. Nice meeting you, she said. With that, she disappeared behind a paisley curtain on her side of the store.

Once we were seated at a table with our cups of coffee and a couple of pastries, I realized Sadie was probably the first transsexual person I'd ever met. Of course, I'd just met Em, but it was hard for me to think of her as a woman. She seemed more like a drag queen or something.

It was warm in the coffee shop, so Sadie shrugged off her leather jacket and folded it gently on the chair beside us. She reminded me of a Vietnamese Juliette Binoche. Her dark hair was in a pixie cut with a streak of silver along one side.

I sipped my coffee and scalded the roof of my mouth. Be careful, Sadie said, they make the coffee piping hot here. She'd ordered Vietnamese iced coffee. It was slowly dripping through a small metal filter, a tall glass full of ice waiting beside it. I nodded and made an "okay" sign with my fingers. I had no idea about transsexual etiquette, but I sensed it would be rude to ask her how and when she'd known she was a transsexual.

So, she said, resting her elbows on the table and leaning toward me, why do you want to interview me? You don't really have a radio show, do you?

Well, I stammered, I don't know, uh. Well, okay. I don't know how you know, but you're right. I don't have a radio show.

She nodded and cut a piece off her raspberry scone with a butter knife. And, she said, you aren't going to RISD, are you? She buttered the piece of scone and popped it in her mouth.

How did you know? I asked. I felt defeated and deflated. Within a few minutes of my sitting down with her, Sadie Tang had already clocked me as a fraud.

I have friends who teach there, honey, she said. Hell, one of my exes worked there the whole time we were dating. Bloody Providence. Now, that city really wasn't my city. If you want to concoct a cock-and-bull story for me, you need to make sure your cock-and-bull story is airtight. She

pointed her butter-smeared, crumb-encrusted butter knife at me. Got it?
Air. Tight.

I nodded. I felt like a hermit crab trapped in a shell two sizes too small.
I tried to sit up straight in my smooth plastic chair. I touched my tongue
to the scalded spot on the roof of my mouth. A piece of skin had been
burnt off by the piping-hot coffee. I gently nudged the flap forward and
backward with my tongue. It reminded me of when I was small and had a
loose tooth that was happy to wiggle back and forth but wasn't quite ready
to come out yet.

It's okay, Sadie said. I'm not upset. I'm intrigued. You've piqued my
curiosity. They say curiosity killed the cat. But they also say that satisfac-
tion will bring it back.

I'm really sorry I lied to you. I just didn't know what else to do.

That's fine, she said. Apology accepted. Water under the bridge. Now
you need to tell me why you lied to me. My curiosity is piqued. Ergo, I'm
dead. It appears I've had an art attack. She winked at me. But you can
revive my exquisite corpse by satisfying my curiosity.

Well, I said, I lied because I wanted to meet you.

Okaaaay, she said. She buttered another chunk of scone. Now why did
you want to meet me? She whispered loudly like a character in a play:
Here's where you spill the beans, Tracy. She bit into the buttered scone
and gestured with her palm for me to talk.

I touched my tongue to the tender, scalded skin on the roof of my
mouth again. *Okay*, I thought, *here we go.*

As soon as I started to talk, everything tumbled out of me. Visiting
Platypus Pornography with Cory. Getting rejected twice from the art school
where she teaches. Flying across the ocean to live in this city of myster-
ies and alleys. Missing you fiercely, but still feeling the pull to stay here.
Working at the bakery. Making watercolours of the meandering chaos of

the alleys. And, finally, deciding that I needed to meet her, that I wanted more than anything to make art that was as energetic and emotional as hers, but I didn't know how to do it yet.

When I'd finished, Sadie sat silently for a moment, pursing her lips and nodding. Okay, she said. Thank you for all that. I need to pee. But I'll be back, and I have a few things to say. She grabbed her purse from under her leather jacket.

El came over to refill my cup and check if we needed anything else. I shook my head. I nibbled on my raspberry Danish and snuck a glance at Em, who was adjusting a row of colourful cowboy boots in her store.

Sadie returned to the table a few minutes later. She poured her Vietnamese coffee over the ice cubes and took a sip. Oh, that's good, she said. She had another sip. She rested her elbows on the table and leaned forward. Look, she said, if you think you should be here, you probably should be here. I don't believe in fate or whatever, but I've seen some spooky shit, and sometimes your gut knows more than you'd think. I'll meet you here for coffee once a week for the rest of the term. So, that's like four or five weeks. Then, I have to fly to Tokyo for a thing. How does that sound?

It sounded unreal. Wow, I said, that's so nice of you. I don't know how to thank you.

You can thank me, she said, by thanking me. Which you just did. And by buying the coffee and snacks next time. This time it's on me. First time is always free. You'll need to bring some of your art next time. And, yes, this is a nice thing I'm doing for you, isn't it? Keep the unbearable niceness of my being in mind if I become a total fucking bitch to you later, okay?

Okay, I said.

She finished her iced coffee and put a few wrinkled bills on the table that must have been at least twice the price of our coffee and pastries. She hugged El and Em and exchanged goodbye kisses with them.

El waved goodbye to me, and Em blew me a theatrical kiss. Next time, she shouted, you will buy some boots from me, yes?

Uh, maybe, I said. I knew that wasn't true, so I quickly added, Probably not. Sorry. I found it hard to make eye contact with Em because I didn't want her to notice that I thought she looked like a linebacker playing dress-up in girly clothes. I wondered what her life was like.

Em and Sadie laughed.

You lie to me, Sadie said, and you tell her the truth. Interesting. Well, sometimes the truth sets you free, and sometimes it brings you a tsunami of bullshit.

Sadie whisked us through the alley back to the tourist-infested war monument. Until next week, she said. Then, she gave me a quick goodbye hug and disappeared down an alley.

—

I don't think I've ever told you about how my brain is often counting things or doing weird little calculations. Oh, actually, you might have noticed it, because I'll often check the door three times before we leave the apartment. Then, I'll occasionally walk back and check it another four times. (My brain likes the number seven. 3 + 4 = 7.) I do something similar with the stove, looking at all of the element dials and the oven dial to make sure nothing is turned on. With the stove, I need the numbers to add up to 21, which can get complicated because there are only five dials. Why do I need it to add up to 21? I don't know. That's just the way it is.

Now I wonder if I'm worrying you. You don't need to be worried. I went and saw a therapist a couple of years ago because I was worried there was

something wrong with me. She listened to me unspool the bendy calculations my brain does with the numbers and objects it encounters. When I
stopped talking, she asked if "all these little number rituals" kept me from
being able to do things. I said it was sometimes distracting or annoying,
but it didn't really affect my life too much. She said that if things "escalated"
and started to interfere with my life, I should visit her or another therapist
for "possible interventions." But she assured me that it sounded like there
was nothing wrong with me. It's just something my mind does "to find
order within chaos," she said, and plenty of people have similar quirks. I'm
fine. Really, everything is all right.

For some reason, there are certain numbers that make me feel comfy.
2. 3. 7. 12. 21. 34. 43. 47. 102.

I'm mentioning this because the address for El and Em's coffee shop /
shoe shop is number 47, which feels fairly auspicious.

—

After my shift at the bakery today, I sifted through pieces of art, considering which to show Sadie Tang. I hate all of them. I don't know how to
make art. Now I wish I'd never contacted her.

After spinning my wheels for an hour or two, I dropped the mixtape
you made for me before I left into my boom box as a quick pick-me-up
and started sorting things into three piles: awful, maybe, not bad. When
I finished sorting, there were only a few things in the not bad pile and a
handful in the maybe pile, so I decided to just bring those items with me.
(There were more things than I could count in the awful pile.)

Now I have to wait almost a week for Sadie to dismiss my flimsy pieces
and bury me under an avalanche of honesty. I can already imagine her
giving me a tight-lipped smile, wanting to be encouraging in the same way
a mom is encouraging when her toddler poops or when a cat lady thanks

her kitty for leaving a decapitated mouse on the doormat. Then, her tight-lipped smile fades as she morphs into the merciless bitch she warned me she might become. Oh dear, I see her saying, these are not good. And they're not good in a way that I rarely encounter. These are—what's the right phrase—oh yes, spectacular failures. Then, I picture her waving El and Em over to gawk at the crap art I've brought in.

Your mixtape ended, so I popped in the new album by the Dalloways, which opens with "Song for Edmond Edmont." Have you heard that song yet? It's catchy and weird and has an off-kilter, herky-jerky beat. In an instant, that song pricked a hole in my inflated emotions. And I was laugh-ing at my insecurities and flailing around in time to the pulsing beat in my cramped apartment.

According to the liner notes, "Song for Edmond Edmont" is about a language surveyor who rode around nineteenth-century France on a bicycle, recording different French dialects. My favourite part in the song (maybe it's what musicians call a "bridge"?) is where the singer, Ginger Astaire, ecstatically sings four words again and again and again:

Bicycler!
Topographer!
Stenographer!
Lexicographer!

Each time she sings it, another member of the band joins her, so it becomes like a spell or an incantation. Finally, all four members are sing-ing, and it's glorious. And then it goes into the catchy, off-kilter chorus.

After the music ends, Ginger Astaire yells, "Que sera, sera, baby!" and we can hear a couple of her bandmates laughing. For some reason, her tweak on the title of that Doris Day staple calmed me down about seeing Sadie Tang next week. Whatever will be, will be, baby.

I spent the week working at the bakery, obsessing over the flawed pieces I was going to show Sadie, slinking through alleys, and drinking beer under a tree at a popular park near the canal.

Wherever I went, the latest Dalloways album provided the soundtrack. At the bakery, I played it whenever my colleagues would let me. At home, it never left my boom box. In alleys and at the park, my whirring portable disc player broadcast it to my earphones.

It feels like it's been years since an album has pulled me in so completely. All I want to do is listen to those ten songs on repeat. All the tracks on *Forgotten Songs for Forgotten Souls* are about obscure historical figures. Besides Edmond Edmont, there are songs about overlooked oddballs like Capability Brown (an eighteenth-century English gardener), Anastasius Lagrantius Rosenstengel (a gender-bending eighteenth-century Prussian), Ching Shih (a nineteenth-century Chinese pirate and sex worker), and Huda Sha'arawi (a twentieth-century Egyptian feminist revolutionary).

Today, my favourite is "Song for the World's Greatest Actor." It's sung from the point of view of an actress playing Desdemona in a production of *Othello* in the Wild West. According to the album's liner notes, a sozzled cowboy in the audience became infuriated watching devious Iago convince his friend Othello to murder his own wife. Apparently, the drunk cowboy sprang up from his seat, shouted, You lying bastard! and shot the actor playing Iago dead.

The part of the song that always gets me is its devastating ending:

> You still walk in my memory's hallways
> I'll visit you in the cemetery always

I drink a drink at your gravestone, my dear
"Here lies," it says, "the world's greatest actor"
And here lies our baby girl in a basket
And here lies my whole world in a casket

Those last two lines are like a dagger to my heart. Please pick up this album so we can fill our ears with the same weird sound waves. These songs are also making me want to play the guitar again. Maybe I'll buy myself a ukulele. I bet "Nuclear Reactor" would sound amazing on a cute little uke. Yeah, fuckin' yeah. Just imagine me singing those lines in a Hawaiian shirt with a lei around my neck while strumming a ukulele. As I write this, I can already hear you saying, Oh, I'll give you a lei. Yeah, fuckin' yeah, indeed.

—

I think about going down on you all the time. The way you grab fistfuls of my hair and push my head down hard as you fuck my face. The way you tell me exactly how to suck your clit, sometimes tenderly, sometimes with more pressure, sometimes with a flickering tongue. All the ways you want me to fuck you with my fingers while I give you head. The way you breathe, sometimes shallowly, sometimes whispery, sometimes throaty. The way you cup your breasts and arch your back. The way you dribble down my chin. The way you gasp and quake as you come in my mouth. The way my body fits against yours as we cuddle afterward.

Now I'm remembering you and me in that pizza joint on Main Street. While I was sprinkling chili flakes on a slice, you leaned over and whispered, When we get home I'm going to need you to pussyburger me, and then you let out a short, tight laugh. And I knew exactly what you meant, because "pussyburger" had just become part of our sexual shorthand. Earlier that week, you'd trained me to get my right hand in a Vulcan salute and squeeze you between my fingers. While I was gripping you like that, you held me with your gaze and said, It's like your fingers are the bun and my pussy is the patty. Like a pussyburger. You laughed and propped yourself up with your elbows to kiss me. Then, you showed me so many ways to make you feel good with my fingers by moving them this way or that way or by using my thumb or my mouth against your clit. At times, you are greedy for pleasure, and it's incredibly hot.

I asked you, If my fingers are the bun and your pussy is the patty, what's your clit? You shook your head and said, Oh fuck, I don't know. Maybe it's the pickle on top. All I know is that right now more than anything in the world I want you to make me come with your mouth. Can you do that for me?

—

I arrived much too early for my meeting with Sadie, so I wandered around Blood Alley to kill some time. I lingered for quite a while in a pet store that used to be a public restroom. It was strangely charming, even though I was baffled that they hadn't removed or disguised the trough urinal behind the cash register. Most of the kittens were napping, but the puppies were barking and tussling and wagging their little tails. After wandering the aisles and watching the puppies for longer than any other customer, I felt like I should buy something, so I bought a couple of foam balls. The cashier asked a question that I didn't quite understand, but I assumed she was probably asking how I was doing or how my imaginary cat was doing. I said the word for "good" a couple of times. She smiled. Then, she said in English that she'd never seen me in the store before and asked if I lived nearby. I told her that I didn't, that I was meeting a friend at a coffee shop around the corner.

Oh, she said, I love that coffee place. El and Em are so special. You should ask Em to make you a pair of boots! She stepped from behind the till. I bought these boots from her. She angled one of her ankle boots so I could see the silver buckles on the side. They are expensive, she admitted, but they are for sure worth it. Do you want your balls in a bag?

What? I asked.

She laughed. Your balls. For your kitty cat. Do you want me to place them in a small bag?

I laughed. Oh right. No, I can just put them in my backpack. Thanks.

Okay, she said. See you next time.

I opened the door and a bell tinkled. Have a fun time with your balls, she called out.

Oh, I said, don't worry. I will. She laughed. The door closed behind me.

When I entered the coffee/shoe shop, El and Em both smiled and called me "Tracy," which startled me. People always forget my name. Maybe I look like a Tracy. I hoped Em would stay on her side of the store because I kept worrying that I might blurt out that she reminds me of Divine from those John Waters movies, and I was pretty sure that a transsexual woman wouldn't want to be compared to a man in a dress. I felt my face redden as I wondered what kind of sex El and Em have.

I settled in at the same table where Sadie and I sat last time. Remembering how I'd scalded the roof of my mouth last week, I planned to let my coffee sit for a while before taking the first sip. I dug out the pieces of art from my backpack and put them in a neat little stack on the table. I spotted the blue foam balls at the bottom of my bag and wondered if the cashier had been flirting with me back in the pet store. Had she really been talking about these cat toys the whole time? Or maybe it just seemed like she was flirting because English wasn't her first language. As you're well aware, I find it impossible to tell when someone is flirting with me. Obviously, I'm not interested in the cute pet store cashier, but it feels like it would be a useful life skill to be able to discern whether or not someone is flirting with me. You are blessed with the gift of flirtiness, which is hot, even if it makes me a titch jealous at times.

Sadie arrived exactly on time for our meeting. I tried not to notice how tight and shiny her leather pants were. She sat down across from me with her croissant and Vietnamese iced coffee.

It's good to see you, Tracy, she said. How was your week?

Oh, I said, yeah, it was okay, thanks. How about you?

I don't want to make you uncomfortable, she said, but you're going to need to give me more than "yeah, it was okay." It would be nice to get a sense of each other outside of our art.

I nodded. My coffee was probably somewhat less piping hot now. I touched the cup and it was still pretty hot, so I sipped it slowly. I made a slurping noise, and Sadie smiled. You're learning, she said. You should try iced coffee. It's really good. I nodded.

Actually, I said, it's been a pretty slow week. I worked a few shifts at the bakery, which always leaves me kind of zonked for the rest of the day, because I have to get up crazy early. I hung out in the park. I don't know anybody here aside from the people at the bakery, and we don't really hang out. So, really, I just kind of walk around. I love the alleys here. They're my favourite thing right now. I sent a letter to my girlfriend. That's about it, I think.

See, she said, that was relatively painless. Yes, the alleys here are incredible. They're one of the reasons I love this city. There are very few cities that I truly love, but this is one of them. It still carries a lot of pain and sadness from the war, and it's got its fair share of shit, but it's also kind of magical. I think some famous dead philosopher said something near the end of his life like "from time to time there is magic." And that dead white dude was right: from time to time, there is magic. There's a lot of crumminess in the world, but there's also some magic. And this city has more magic than most. Can you walk me through a little of your art?

While she nibbled on her flaky croissant, I showed her the works I'd brought and spoke very briefly about each of them. She nodded and listened. When I'd finished, she thanked me for sharing my art. I blushed, wishing I were a better artist, wishing I had a point of view, wishing I'd brought her something substantive.

Rather than critiquing my art, Sadie asked me a series of questions. Why did I want to make art? Who had been the most influential person in my life so far? What did I think I would learn in art school? What was I reading and listening to lately? What did I think about when I was wandering through the alleys and hanging out in the park? Why hadn't I met anyone in the city yet?

I squirmed in my seat and muddled my way through her questions. Every answer I gave sounded dumber than the previous one. Eventually, I stopped myself midsentence and said, I'm sorry, but I don't even know what I'm talking about right now. I think I'm wasting your time. I'm sorry.

Tracy, you're not wasting my time, she said. I'm just trying to get a feel for who you are. Hold on a sec. She took out a tiny gold pen from her purse and jotted something in a little red notebook. Then, she put the notebook and the pen on the table. You probably thought you'd show me your art and I'd give you some feedback and some homework for next time, and that would be that. She took off her silver jacket and draped it across the back of her chair. She was wearing a black SILENCE=DEATH T-shirt.

Look, she said, I think you need to think deeply about the art you want to make and why you want to make it. A lot of my early work didn't really need to exist. It didn't have a purpose. If you devote your time and energy to making something, it should matter. Galleries are already crammed with shit. You don't want to make meaningless shit, do you?

No, of course not, I said.

Think about what you want to do, then, she said. Making meaningful art is really bloody hard. It's like learning to ride a wild horse, but it's a different horse every time. It can run away or trample you if you don't respect it. Art is mysterious and powerful, Tracy. Every time I set out to make Great Art—capital G, capital A, Great Art—I failed miserably because my little ego got in the way. Do you get what I'm saying? Did I get too esoteric there?

Uh, no, I said. I think I get it. I thought of things I could say to show her that I understood, sort of. But all my ideas sounded silly, so I took a slow sip of coffee.

Sadie pulled out a thick book from a black tote bag. It might seem weird, but I'm going to lend you this. It's a book we made for a recent show I did in LA. She slid it across to my side of the table. It had a lavender cover with SADIE TANG in big white letters. So, she said, why am I lending you this book of my own work? Well, I'm going to try something that I think might be helpful for you. You said you saw *Platypus Pornography*. The pieces from it are in here, along with a bunch of work from before and after. She tapped the cover of the book with one of her silver fingernails. Take this week to spend time with the pieces in here, and I'll answer any questions you might have next week. What was my process for a specific piece, and why did I make it? Why am I doing so much video work lately? Why do I focus on Asian transsexuals? You know, whatever. She finished the last sip of her iced coffee. When she set the glass back on the table, the ice cubes tinkled. I get the sense you haven't thought deeply enough about your own work, so this might also prompt you to climb into a little bathysphere and sink to the bottom of your brain. Pay attention to the goo in there. You probably need to sit and think. A lot. Or maybe you need to walk and think. I don't know. Oh, you should always have a pen and a notebook with you. She pointed to hers on the table.

El came by and refilled my coffee cup.

I thanked Sadie for the book and for her time. She hugged me good-bye, whispering in my ear, Tracy, you better tip El well. I told Sadie not to worry.

As soon as she was gone, I started flipping through the art book she'd left me. A couple of minutes later, I felt a tap on my shoulder. It was Sadie. I forgot this, she said, placing a postcard for an art opening on the table. I meant to invite you, but it slipped my mind until now. If you come, I can introduce you to a few people. I looked at the postcard and realized it was happening on a day when I had an early morning shift at the bakery. I could make the opening in the evening, but I'd be turning into a pumpkin by the time it began.

I'd love to go, I said. Thank you.

Yes, of course, she said. Ta-ta, Tracy. Then, she was really gone.

—

I'd been to the art bookstore in our city—the one that's always overflowing with calendars at the start and end of every year—but I'd never seen a book of Sadie Tang's work there. Then again, most of those books are pricey, and the photographed art in them seems puny if you've seen the real thing with your own eyes. I don't want to cloud my memory of the actual art by swapping it for an image in a book where the work is shrunk down to the size of a candy bar.

I remember I took you to an exhibit of Yvonne Cone's work. You went in skeptical, but when you left, your eyes were as round as saucers. For the next week or two, you kept mentioning how overwhelmed you'd been by the massive yellow and blue canvases. And they were definitely overwhelming. I've still never seen anything like her interlocking canvases jigsaw puzzled together to cover every inch of wall space. But when Yvonne Cone's paintings are reproduced in books, you don't get a sense of how, in person, they make you feel like a sugar ant bedazzled by gushing tidal waves of blue and yellow paint.

While paging through Sadie's book, I remembered one of the rooms at her exhibit that I'd visited with Cory. As soon as you walked in, you were surrounded by four images of transsexual Asian women. The photos glowed in large, square light boxes, one on each wall of the room. All four of the photos featured a lamp, a fridge, and a vacuum in front of a pink wall. Of course, I immediately recognized this as a nod to the cover of the Cure's first album, *Three Imaginary Boys*. Hence the title of Sadie's piece, *Three Imaginary Girls*. Three of the light boxes were portraits, each of a different transsexual woman standing in front of the recreated album cover, and the fourth light box showed all three women standing together. According to Sadie's book, the women in the photos were named Naomi, Sabine, and Algy. In the photos, the women were glaring at the camera with their hands on their hips. If I'd had to guess the title of these photos without any context, I'd probably have guessed it was *The Defiant Ones* or *What the Fuck Are You Looking At?*

In the middle of the room, there were several recliner chairs, each with its own side table, lamp, and set of earphones. The side tables also had small yellow booklets with the title of the work, *When We Were a Girl*, in pink cursive letters on them. Inside the booklets, you discovered photos of girls playing with dolls, riding bikes, visiting a petting zoo, posing in their Sunday best for portraits, etc. In other words, you saw the sort of snapshots you'd see in any family photo book. When you put on the earphones, you heard three women talking about their girlhoods.

As the art book for Sadie's show in LA says,

> It generally takes gallery visitors at least a few minutes to realize that the three women reminiscing about their childhoods are the three transsexual Asian women staring at them accusingly from the gallery walls. They are literally surrounded by these three women. Only then does it dawn on the gallery visitor that the three women they are listening to weren't raised as girls, that they're imagining what their childhoods might have been like if they'd been raised as girls. They are witches casting spells to conjure their missing girlhoods.

I wasn't sure how I felt about that last sentence, but I did remember most of the other feelings described. It was strangely magical. And there was an additional disconnect because the childhood photos in the booklets were of white girls, not Asian girls.

But that magic was instantly dispelled when we left the small, snug room, because Cory started snickering and saying one snide thing after another. I remember joining in, saying it should have been called *Three Gaylords* instead of *Three Imaginary Girls*, which made him double over and nod his head vigorously. As soon as I said that, I felt ashamed, because I'd been spellbound in that room, but I couldn't help wanting to convince Cory that I also thought it was the gayest thing I'd ever seen.

Sitting with my legs crossed on the floor of my apartment, with Sadie's heavy art book on the carpet in front of me, a stream of questions about that installation bubbled up. Why the weird grammar of *When We Were a Girl* rather than *When We Were Girls*? Had she referenced that Cure album because the name seemed clever? What was the seed that inspired that work? Which had come first, the idea of the defiant portraits, or the idea of the imagined girlhoods? Why the light boxes? Why those three women? Had they come up with their own girlhood visions, or were they reading from a script?

—

In elementary school, I read a book about a child who ran away from home to live in a hollowed-out tree. He stayed there for months, living on fruit and berries and whatever small animals he could catch and eat. And no one came to get him. One day, he nabbed a baby peregrine falcon from a nest, which he nursed and trained to hunt.

After reading that book, I dreamt of running away from home, befriending a peregrine falcon, and living in the woods. I wouldn't snatch the bird from its nest. Instead, it would notice me and start to tag along on my walks, flying from branch to branch. I'd talk to it calmly, letting it know that I was its friend. Eventually, it would swoop down and rest on my shoulder, showing that it had decided to trust me. We'd share a soft nest of moss and twigs and feathers, and I'd build us a tree house for the rainy days and the wintry months.

I told my best friend Julia about my plan, and she was perplexed.

It would be nice, she said, to live outside for a few days. But why would you want to stay for so long? Wouldn't you miss TV? Wouldn't you miss your parents? And your bed?

I couldn't explain it to her, but I knew that I wouldn't miss those things. I knew that I'd feel safer with my sleek, protective peregrine falcon.

What would you call your falcon? she asked.

Oh, what a question. I hadn't thought of a name for my falcon yet. Well, I said, I think a good name for it would be Julia.

You can't call it that! she said. You can't give it my name. It needs a new name.

What would you call it? I asked.

She clapped her hands together. Ooh, she said, I love naming things! I'm much better at it than my grubby little brother. He named our cat Walkies! What a dumb name. Walkies!? She rubbed her hands together. It has to be a good name. It's a falcon.

It's a peregrine falcon, I clarified. There are different kinds of falcons.

Yes, I know! she said. She walked over to a nearby tree and gazed up at its branches. I imagined her picturing a peregrine falcon perched above her, its alert eyes darting from her to the sky and back to her. A falcon, she said. A peregrine falcon. The first name I have for you is a good one. She looked at me.

What is it? I asked. What's the name?

Be patient, she said. The name is … Ginny!

Jenny?

No, Ginny. G-I-N-N-Y. Ginny! It's a good name. Trust me.

Ginny, I repeated. I picked up a small rock and threw it at the base of the tree with the imaginary peregrine falcon perched in it. The small rock hit the tree trunk and made a gentle *thunk* sound. I turned to Julia. What's the second name?

The second name I have for you … is … Perry!

What? Like Perry Mason?

No, not like Perry Mason! Jeez. Like Perry the Peregrine Falcon.

No offence, I said, but you suck at naming things. Maybe I'll call it Walkies.

Fuck you, she said. Maybe you should name it after yourself. Fuckface the Falcon. Now that's a good name!

Within a few months, Julia had a different best friend. It wasn't because of the peregrine falcon naming debacle. That bomb was defused after a couple of heated days. It was because boys and girls began drifting into different groups, and things like crushes and boobs started to come between us. During this wave of crushes, my friend Jeremy briefly tried to woo Julia. Every day at recess for about a week, he handed her a small paper bag full of her favourite sour candies from the grocery store near our school. The bags of candy stopped coming when she said in front of everyone that she didn't want to be his girlfriend. After lunch that day, he handed her a torn piece of yellow lined paper with an itemized list of all the money he'd spent on sour candies for her. You need to pay me back, he said. She laughed and tore it up in front of everyone. Fuck you, she said. You gave me those candies because you're in love with me. Now, please go away, Jeremy. Can't you see I'm busy talking to my friends? Why don't you go talk to your grubby friend over there? She pointed at me and smirked.

—

Sadly, the awful mnemonic for the order of the planets in our solar system that Mr. Roseblatt taught us is still burned into my brain: **Many Very Eager Men Jumped Sally Under Neil's Porch.** I've tried to write over it with other mnemonics, like **My Very Excellent Mother Just Served Us Nine Pizzas,** but I haven't had any luck. Instead, I just think of Sally's mother serving pizzas to the men under the porch, which is even more fucked up.

There are so many shitty things that I want to write over, the same way the pet store has written over the public toilet or the coffee shop has written over the swimming pool.

—

I arrived for the reception at the art gallery and thought I'd gotten the day wrong, because nobody was there. Then, I heard something clang and spotted a couple of people in a far corner. Right, they were still setting up for it, because nobody arrives on time for these events. Except me. I dashed back out the front door before they saw me and went to a coffee shop a couple of blocks away. The shop specialized in something called "egg coffee," so I ordered one. It was delivered in a small glass with a layer of frothy cream on top. It came with a spoon on the side, which made me wonder if I should stir it like an ordinary cup of coffee or scoop it like a dessert. I sampled a spoonful of the froth. It was rich, airy, and sugary. Then, I sipped it. The bitterness and punch of the coffee was softened by the sugary, yolky froth. I wiped away the froth moustache that I could feel on my upper lip. On the upside, perhaps this drink would give me the jolt I needed to keep my eyes open at the gallery; on the downside, it might also make me a tad jittery.

I returned to the gallery after nursing my egg coffee and killing some time meandering through a nearby alley. Dozens of people were there now, and most of them seemed to know each other. They were talking easily and drinking from champagne coupes. I remembered hearing that the very first champagne coupes were modelled on Marie Antoinette's breasts and wondered if that was true. Then, of course, I started thinking about your breasts and how perfectly they fit in my mouth. The perfect pebbles of your nipples. The magnificent champagne glasses we could make based on—

I heard my name. Tracy. Earth to Tracy. Come in, Tracy. It was Sadie. She was standing in front of me, offering me one of the two champagne coupes she was holding.

We said hi and clinked glasses, and I followed her on a quick circuit around the gallery. She briefly introduced me to people in every corner of the room. Then, she steered me to a couple of specific works that had caught her eye. It was a group show on cinema and feminism. The pieces Sadie showed me were fine, but I wasn't knocked out by either of them. Then, she fell into chatting with a clutch of artists.

After a spell, a stylish older woman leaned over and asked in English if I was here with Sadie. I nodded. She said, Oh, I adore Sadie's piece! It's so clever. I gave her a puzzled look. You haven't seen it yet? she asked. It's over there. She pointed somewhere. I'll take you, she said.

I noticed she was drinking tea from a floral teacup. Everyone around her was drinking champagne or wine. She had shoulder-length silver hair and was wearing a red-and-black camouflage dress. She started walking with purpose to the other end of the room, and I followed her. She stopped in front of a black booth with one white teardrop painted on the side of it. It was about the size of three phone booths and had a porthole at eye level. Above the porthole, a sign with glowing red letters read,

RECORDING
DO NOT ENTER

The woman pointed at a line of three or four people waiting to enter the booth and gestured for me to stand behind them. She tried to talk to me while we were waiting, but it was getting later in the evening, and someone had turned up the volume on the sound system. One of the speakers was in the corner near us. After a minute, I yelled in the woman's ear, Sorry, I can't hear you! It's really loud! She nodded. After that, we just stood in line, sipping our drinks and surveying the crowd and the art around the room. I kept trying to spot Sadie, wishing I'd told her I was about to be whisked across the gallery by a strange silver-haired woman.

Before long, I was at the front of the line. I could hear faint music leaking out of the black booth. I realized that the glass in the porthole showed a wonky view of the inside of the booth. All I could see was a brownish, frizzy shape, which I thought might be the hair of the woman who had been in front of me in line. I hadn't been anxious earlier, but I now realized that I had no idea what would be expected of me once the door to the booth opened. I tried to ask the silver-haired woman what would happen inside. She smiled and shouted in my ear that it was too loud to talk here, but this was the best thing in the room. She added, It's so clever!

At that moment, the door to the booth opened, and the woman with frizzy auburn hair stepped out. She looked a little dazed. I took a final sip of champagne, set my empty glass on a small table, and gingerly stepped into the booth. It was dim inside. A voice said, Please close the door. I closed the door behind me. It was even darker now. The voice said, Please put on the black gloves on your right. I turned to my right and saw a container of black gloves illuminated by an overhead light. I picked up a pair and put my fingers into them. They were quite tight.

The lights in the room grew brighter. A large screen on the wall in front of me clicked on, and a life-sized video of Sadie Tang materialized on the screen. She was standing in a living room, dressed in a studded black leather jacket, a bright top, dangly earrings, cut-off denim shorts, and black knee-high riding boots. She was wearing sunglasses, but she took them off almost immediately.

Darling, she said, I want you to come a little closer. Please put your feet on the feet. She gestured in front of her. On the floor of the booth, I saw white foot outlines. I did what I was told and stood on the glowing feet. That's better, Sadie said. I noticed she was speaking with an English accent. Her faux English accent was soft, more BBC than cockney. Now, she continued, I want you to sing a little song with me. Can you do that, darling? I think you can. Don't worry. I can see you're a little scared. I'll make this as painless as possible. I'll tell you exactly what to do, sweetie. Just follow my lead. You don't need to do anything at first. Just relax. Are you ready?

A stuttering synth loop and a drum machine started up, followed by a familiar-sounding twangy guitar part. It was one of those songs that had seemed to be everywhere for a while. The guitar was twanging the song's vocal melody. It was Boy George's version of "The Crying Game." As soon as I recognized it, Sadie started singing into a microphone, looking directly at me. Watching her sing on the screen six feet in front of me was disorienting and thrilling. She danced while she sang to me about the steps in the crying game: its kisses, its sighs, and its goodbyes. After a minute or so, there was an instrumental break. While the guitar twanged and Sadie shimmied, a light from above clicked on to illuminate an object rising up through a hole in the floorboards. When it was fully raised and in place, I saw that it was a microphone on a mic stand. An instrumental section of the song looped in the background as Sadie started talking to me. Now, she said, I want you to sing with me, baby. I'm getting lonely singing by myself. Please don't be shy. She gestured to the microphone standing between us. You can touch my mic if you want to, baby. It won't bite. She winked. Now, we're going to sing together. Are you ready? Okay, here we go.

The words for the next line appeared at the bottom of the screen in white letters. They turned yellow as the words were sung. I tried singing into the mic and heard my voice in the room, which I now realized resembled a sound booth. My voice was louder than I would have liked. I sang more gently and tried to blend with Sadie's voice. I'd been closing my eyes. When I opened them, I noticed that the microphone in front of me was, in fact, a large black dildo. When I looked more closely at Sadie, I saw that she was also singing into a dildo. Now I understood why viewers had to put on gloves. I was reminded of the time Cory and I put on gloves years ago to interact with Sadie's smooth lavender mannequins in the gallery. The light shining on the black dildo microphone made its swollen head and the raised veins along its shaft hard to miss. I remembered the silver-haired lady calling this piece "clever" and wasn't sure that was the first word that came to my mind.

Suddenly, Sadie said, Keep your eyes on the prize, darling. The prize isn't down here, she said, pointing to her crotch. It's up here. She pointed to her face. My sparkling eyes are the crackerjack prize. When she pointed to her crotch, I saw that she was no longer wearing her cut-off jean shorts. She was wearing a leather harness with a strap-on dildo. The dildo was large and lavender.

Oh, don't look so shocked, Sadie said to me. You knew what you were in for, sweetie. After all, my name is Dil. She smiled and raised one of her eyebrows. Let's sing the last part together. Then, I'll send you on your merry way.

I murmured my way through the last lines of the song. Then, the music stopped. Sadie said to me, We had our kisses. We had our sighs. Now is when we say goodbye. With that, the screen went black. The voice from before, which I now recognized as Sadie's, said, Please deposit your gloves in the bin to your left. I did as I was told. And now, Sadie said, please leave, or I'll really give you something to cry about. I have other lovers to see. The door to the booth opened, and I walked through it, back into the glaring light of the gallery.

I went to find Sadie to tell her how powerful her piece was. I looked and looked, but I couldn't find her. While doing my second or third round of the gallery, the silver-haired woman approached me, wanting to talk about Sadie's piece. I told her I was trying to find Sadie. She wandered over to speak to a few women gathered in one of the corners. When she returned, she told me Sadie had been called away unexpectedly. Apparently, it couldn't be helped. A woman in pearls walked over and offered me a champagne coupe. To Sadie! she said, flashing me a toothy grin. We clinked and sipped. I decided to chat with Sadie's friends until I'd drained my champagne. Then, I would head home. Maybe I'd even take a taxi, because it was quite late.

The music was even louder than before, so I could only catch some of what was being said. As I was taking my last sip of champagne, a line from the song that was playing cut though the conversation and stunned me. I must have misheard the lyrics. I excused myself and walked over to one of the speakers. I listened intently. The song had a throbbing bass line and a piercing guitar part. Then, the singer sang that he could drug me and fuck me out here on the cold tundra. Why would someone play this song at a feminist art show? And then the song ended, and a different song was playing. But I just kept hearing that menacing line about drugging and fucking the listener on the frozen ground in the middle of nowhere. The singer sounded bored, which made it even more chilling. He sang in a detached way that declared, I could do this to you and I could get away with it. You could be defiled and discarded. You are nothing.

On the taxi ride home, the driver kept wanting to talk to me in English. He kept asking if I was having a fun night or if I wanted to have a fun night, something like that. I asked him to drop me off at a busy corner that was a five-minute walk from my apartment. I went into a convenience store and bought a candy bar and a bottle of orange juice. When I came out, I was glad to see the taxi was gone.

That's when I realized that I was hearing a lyric looping in my head. I could drug you and fuck you out here on the cold tundra. No wonder I'd been wary of the taxi driver. While walking back to my apartment, I tried to conjure different catchy songs to blot this one out. None of my usual songs worked. "Push It." "Burning Up." "Tainted Love." "Pull Up to the Bumper."

I don't think I've ever really told you about how awful my earworms can get sometimes. It can take hours to shake a sticky song out of my head. It hasn't been too bad lately, but it used to be horrible. It could really mess me up until I replaced it with another loop, or it eventually evaporated on its own.

When I got home, I tried to blot out the menacing tundra loop with other songs. Finally, around 1 a.m., I obliterated it with the Corduroy Tomboy song "My Eiffel Rifle" that you'd put on the going-away mixtape you made for me. Those silly singsong lyrics made me swoon as I remembered you singing them the first time you wore a strap-on for me: "Please feel my Eiffel rifle / Please kiss my Eiffel rifle / Please taste my Eiffel rifle / Please love my Eiffel rifle."

We were in that hotel room on a long-weekend road trip, and you were a little tipsy and really getting into it, swaying your hips and singing with a faux French accent, just like that girl who sings the song. It was so funny, so sweet and so hot. You said a friend of yours had a boyfriend who liked being fucked in the ass by her, and you thought I might be into it too. Oh wow, you were so right.

Remembering you wearing that strap-on got me really worked up, so I tried to jerk off with my cup and rub technique. It did the trick. Afterward, I drifted off to sleep.

When I awoke, even the loop from "My Eiffel Rifle" was gone. I decided to leave my disc player at home for a while to avoid possibly getting stuck with another sound loop.

—

I arrived early (as usual) for my next meeting with Sadie. As soon as I settled in at the coffee shop, Em sat down in the seat across from me. She smiled. Her lips were candy-apple red. I could see she'd missed a spot near her Adam's apple when shaving. I felt awful for her.

Hi, Tracy, she said. Maddie asked me if I could please ask you about your balls.

My what? I asked. My balls? Who said that? My voice wavered.

Maddie, she said. She met you in the animal store where she works.

Oh right. I remember her. She sold me some cat toys. Her name is Maddie? My scalp felt tingly.

Yes, Maddie, Em said. She pressed her palms together and leaned forward. Maddie said also she thinks you are pretty. Em's long bright-pink fingernails were nearly touching as she kept her hands in a prayer position. One of her arms was covered with tattoos of pin-up models, while the other arm teemed with marine life, including a jellyfish, an octopus, an eel, and a manta ray. Em continued: She said you should go and see her at the animal store if you also think she is pretty.

That's so sweet of her, I said. I do think she's very pretty, but I already have a girlfriend. And, oh, it looks like Sadie is here now.

Okay, Em said. But I think you should go to see Maddie in the animal store. She is very special. With that, Em went over to give Sadie a hug hello. As Em walked away, I noticed she seemed surprisingly comfy in her body, even though she didn't look particularly feminine. She was living the life she wanted to live, regardless of what society told her. I still had no idea who the fuck I was or what I wanted. I wanted to make art, but maybe I just wanted to make art to feel talented and validated. Em didn't seem to be grasping for the approval of the wider world. I wondered what it would be like to get to a place where I didn't care, and I felt a kernel of jealousy.

When Sadie sat down, I was better prepared this time to make small talk. I also told her how much I'd loved her piece at the art gallery.

That one, she said, was pretty fun to do. I mean, Dil is such a great character! Yes, that shitty IRA dude pukes when he sees her naked, and Dil says and does things that you know she would never do. Well, maybe you don't know, but I do. No offence. But she's really the heart of that movie. And that IRA guy is totally smitten with her. So was her soldier boyfriend. And so is that skeezy douchebag who follows her around.

I nodded. I haven't seen *The Crying Game*. But I know the film's "secret" is about Dil's genitals.

Anyway, Sadie said, I see you have returned my book in pristine condition. Thank you. She tore off a piece of her chocolate croissant. I can give you one hour of my time. I hope that's sufficient. She removed her red-and-white polka-dot watch and put it on the table. Now, she said, what questions do you have for me?

For most of the hour, I asked her questions that had been percolating while I'd studied her book. Most of my questions were about *Three Imaginary Girls* and *When We Were a Girl*, because I'd become fairly obsessed with them that week. One tidbit she shared was that she'd heard through a mutual friend that Robert Smith of the Cure had seen Sadie's *Three Imaginary Girls* photos somewhere and said they "almost made him like that album cover. Almost."

At the end of the hour, she slipped back into her leather jacket and gave me some homework. You seemed particularly enamoured, she said, with my girlhood room. I have to admit that surprises me. For next week, I want you to come up with something to transform a room. I'm mostly looking for ideas. You don't need to execute anything. Maybe just a sketch of the layout and a rough drawing or two of what would be in the space. And here's the hard part: I want it to be something that nobody but you would ever create. It should be so specific that if you saw it in a gallery, you would think it was created by your identical twin. Does that make sense?

I think so, I said.

I'm sure everything will go swimmingly, she said. It would be good for you to think on a grander scale, to take your mind for a walk and do something you've never done before. Sadie paused. I'm having some friends over this weekend. It's not a party. Just a handful of friends, some cocktails, some hors d'oeuvres, some chit-chat. You can say no, but it would be lovely if you wanted to join us. What do you think?

I think that sounds amazing, I said. Yes, please.

She jotted the time and location on a napkin. You will be wondering, she said, what you can bring. I'm not one of those people who says just bring yourself. You should bring something. I'd recommend a nice bottle of wine.

—

Yes, I'm okay with you taking other lovers. I'm not worried that you seeing other people will gum up what we have. I know that sex is important to you, and I want you to be happy. Will I be jealous? Yes. I will. I'm not going to lie. But I'm not worried that you'll fall for someone else. There are very few things that I know in this world. But I know that we belong together. And, truthfully, if you'd rather be with someone other than me, you should be with them. I'd be gutted, but I want you to do what you want to do. I can't go back to being the trembling kid I was when you met me. I love you. And I trust you.

I was just thinking about the first time we had sex in a public place. Do you remember? We were in that Second Cup downtown. The one near the library. I was so nervous, but you just took my hand and led me into an out of order bathroom and locked the door. You sat on the edge of the sink and hiked up your skirt. You kissed me hard. Then, you cupped my chin with your hand and told me to pull off your panties. I fumbled them off of you. The room smelled like urine and cleaning products, but by the time I took off your panties, it had already started to smell a little like sex. I need you, you said, to put your fingers in me right now. I slid a finger into you, and it went in so easily. It's like your pussy was pulling me in. You smooshed yourself against me. (That might have been the afternoon when I suggested the band name Tractor Beam Snatch. You made a clicking noise with your tongue and rolled your eyes. Anything with the word "tractor," you said, is gonna sound like country music.)

You got into a better position on the sink and told me to fuck you hard with two or three fingers. I slid two fingers into you, and you felt so good inside. I wanted more than anything to taste you, but you'd started rubbing your clit, and I could tell you were already on the verge. Then, with your eyes shut tight under the fluorescent lights, you came, holding on to the sink with your free hand so you wouldn't fall as your body shook against mine. I started to slow down and fuck you more gently. No, you said. More. I need you to fuck me more. I went back to fucking you hard and imagined my fingers dripping with warm honey, imagined the honey oozing over the lip of the sink and pooling on the concrete floor. After coming a while, you told me to stop. You'd had your fill. Your face was glowing. You stood and tidied yourself. You pulled a fresh pair of panties from your purse. I used to be a Brownie, you said.

Always be prepared, I said. Isn't that your motto? I kissed you. You tasted like coffee and smoke. I washed my hands with the gunky pink soap from the dispenser. Then, I dried them on my jeans because they were out of paper towels. Maybe that's why the bathroom was out of order.

Actually, you said, our motto in the Brownies was "lend a hand." You pulled my right hand to your lips and kissed my damp fingers. Then, you kissed my left-hand fingers. Those ones get all the love, you said, eyeing my right hand, but these ones are also very useful and comely. Did you know "comely" means attractive?

Oh, I know, I said. I used to play D&D.

Oh really, you said. I bet you were a Dungeon Master. I nodded sheepishly. You smirked. Let's get out of here, you said. This room reeks of piss and pussy.

—

Sadie's apartment is located in Alley of Branches, the same alley I spent days mapping after moving here. Before going to Sadie's place, I popped into Mr. Swim, the swimming-pool-turned-coffee-shop, for a pot of green tea. I wondered again about the older woman in the purple-and-yellow swimsuit and goggles.

I arrived at Sadie's precisely five minutes after the time she'd scrawled on the napkin. When she opened the door, I hugged her and handed her a bottle of good red wine. (I'd found it in a display with a sign that translated to "Yummy and Cheap." I've always tended to select bottles based on their labels, and this one had an illustration of a black cat licking one of its paws. I asked the androgynous salesperson, Is it good? They nodded and punched up my order.)

Sadie toured me around her charming apartment and introduced me to her friends Rosetta and Naomi. I recognized Naomi as one of the women Sadie had photographed and interviewed for *Three Imaginary Girls* and *When We Were a Girl*. I told myself I wouldn't ask Naomi any questions about that unless Sadie brought it up. While nibbling on the spread of charcuterie, I was also introduced to Sadie's cat, Tufty. Her paws looked like furry little pompoms.

Sadie, Rosetta, and Naomi all talked very quickly and kept toggling between languages. Whenever they mentioned someone I didn't know, Sadie would turn to me and distill that person's essence into a phrase. One person was "a vile, vile man"; another was "a dashing but pervy gallerist." After a while, another friend of Sadie's arrived. Her name was Algy. I recognized her as another of the women Sadie had featured in *Three Imaginary Girls* and *When We Were a Girl*. Seeing her up close, I saw that Algy had the faintest wisp of a moustache. I was reminded of the peach fuzz moustaches grown by the boys who used to punch me in junior high hallways. Those boys often wore Led Zeppelin T-shirts and had ugly stick-and-poke tattoos. The peach fuzz had looked awful on them, but it was positively adorable on Algy.

Hey, Algy said, half waving at us. Eloise has a date with a bricklayer she could not break.

I'm jealous, Naomi said. I'd like to be broken by a bricklayer. Everyone laughed.

Sadie poured Algy a glass of sparkling wine and topped up all of our glasses. Then, she raised her champagne flute, saying, May we all follow in Eloise's footsteps and have our bodies broken by beautiful lovers. We said cheers to that. I might have blushed.

After Algy arrived, I found myself stealing glances at her. I tried to be discrete. Everyone else in the room intimidated me, but Algy seemed open and welcoming. She reminded me of a gregarious, graceful bird. Maybe I saw her as a bird because she was wearing a blue T-shirt with the silhouettes of two crows perched on a telephone wire.

Later in the evening, when Algy was sitting on the couch beside me, I leaned over and said to her, I like your shirt. Isn't that the logo for American Crow?

She beamed. Yes! I love the American Crow! My band mailed them a demo, but we never got a letter back. She sipped her wine. She seemed pretty tipsy.

Wait, I said. You have a band?

Yes. We're not that good. Pause. We are okay. Pause. We have some moments.

What do you play?

I play guitar. Eloise also plays guitar. We both sing. Our drummer, Lottie, left us to join a band called Kelp Goblet.

Kelp Goblet, I repeated.

Yes, Kelp Goblet. Like dark metal. Lottie has always been a metal girl. Now it's just me and Eloise.

What's your band called?

So okay, we used to be called Ink Moon. Not Pink Moon. Ink Moon. Now we're Blood Moon.

What kind of music is Blood Moon?

Kind of like soft and hard. Like pretty and angry. Like quiet and loud. You look confused, and that is perfect. It's kind of like music for confused people. We will be quiet and pretty, like background music. Then, we will be loud and angry, like with a punk attitude. We play with volume.

You're talking about music? Sadie asked. Algy is so good! Suddenly, Sadie was standing before us, topping up our wineglasses. Algy and Eloise, she said, are two of my favourite people in the city. And the music they make is raw and simple and smart.

Yes, Algy said, we are certainly simple! She sipped her wine.

Now, Algy, you know I meant that as a compliment.

I know, Algy said. Yes, I know. She smiled.

A few minutes later, Algy surprised me by asking if I ever wore makeup. I told her that I used to wear some makeup when I was a mopey teen.

Mopey? she asked.

Like sad, I said. I was so goth.

Goth is good, she said. But the goth makeup is like a ghost style. You'd make a pretty ghost. You should let me do your makeup one time.

Maybe, I said. I need to go soon, but I want a little more wine.

Algy snatched my glass off the table. She disappeared for a moment. When she came back, both of our glasses were full. She held my glass just out of reach. I have a glass for you, she said. But you must promise that you will let me do your makeup. It will be fun. And you can meet Eloise. Do you agree?

I agreed. She handed me my glass, and we softly clinked glasses to seal the deal.

—

All week, I kept puzzling over what imaginary art to put in my imaginary room before my next meeting with Sadie. I had vague ideas, but they all seemed like watered-down versions of her room. I found myself looping back to the questions she'd asked at our first meeting. Why did I want to make art? Who had been the most influential person in my life so far? What was I reading and listening to lately? And then there was her other condition that the art filling the room needed to be something nobody but me would ever create. So, I had a week to invent something that mattered, something that would resonate, and something that was incredibly specific to my life. What could I come up with that would meet the overlapping needs of that weird artsy Venn diagram?

I started with the simplest question: Who has been the most influential person in my life so far? My dad. He was undoubtedly the answer to that question. I haven't really told you much about growing up with my dad, but you've heard flashes here and there. My mom left when I was six. Much later, I learned that she'd fled to a women's shelter with me when I was four after enduring several years of verbal and physical abuse from my dad. But he had tracked her down, threatening to kill her if she ever took me again. She knew he meant it. Within a couple of years, things became unbearable again. When she left this time, she left me behind, knowing it was the only way to keep us both alive. Later, she filed for divorce, granting my father sole custody with the stipulation that she have visitation rights. She strove to make our visits cheerful, but I was a sullen and distant kid.

I remember once offhandedly telling a friend that my dad was someone you might read about in a newspaper article that ended with the phrase "before turning the gun on himself." I'd shrugged and smiled, but my friend appeared shaken. He pursed his lips, scrunched his face slightly, and asked if I was okay, if I needed to talk to someone. I rarely talk about my dad because I don't know how to be honest without eliciting pity. And I've never wanted you to pity me.

I tried to be invisible when I was a kid. I wanted to shrink to the size of a thimble and sleep in a matchbox in a small hole in the wall. I wanted to walk into the wilderness and find a peregrine falcon to share a soft nest with me in a sturdy tree. I wanted to be a different person. I wanted to stop feeling worthless and clumsy and stupid. When you fell for me, I was astonished, because I saw myself as a black hole, physically, emotionally, and socially. And, truthfully, I was trying to be a black hole, because being visible made me feel so vulnerable, like I was walking around without skin.

Eventually, I managed to stitch together some imaginary art to fill the imaginary room. I decided to recreate my teenage bedroom and scatter little memories of my dad around the room on recipe cards, like the kind my grandma still keeps in a metal box beside the cutting board. The memories related to my dad would be a mixture of mundane things and intense things. I jotted down a few memories, which unearthed more sadness than I'd like to admit.

I also decided to put a boom box on a dresser to blast some of the music I'd listened to when I was at my most angsty. I'd make a mixtape that was heavy on the Cure, Public Image Ltd, Joy Division, and Siouxsie and the Banshees. I was less sure about what to call the imaginary work, but I figured something would come to me.

As usual, I arrived early for my meeting with Sadie and ordered my standard coffee and pastry. While waiting, I wondered if Em would ask me about the girl in the pet store, Maddie. But as soon as I sat down, a customer appeared in her shoe store, and soon she was busy being her naturally gregarious self.

Sadie breezed in wearing a long dress with diagonal white and grey stripes. Everything else was grey: her bag, her tassel earrings, her kitten heels. Her lipstick and her chunky bracelet were both blood red. I've never understood how certain women seem to effortlessly coordinate their outfits. I remember when you introduced me to one of your favourite movies, *Heathers*. There's a line about how Winona Ryder's character "can't accessorize for shit." To me, it seemed like throwaway dialogue, but you said something about how perfect that line was. You paused the VHS tape and broke it down for me. You explained how women put outfits together and how they accessorize. It was dizzyingly complicated. Sadie is the opposite of "can't accessorize for shit," whatever that is. Her outfits have a harmony, and there are always one or two pieces that really sing. I was wearing my usual uniform of jeans, T-shirt (today, forest green), leather jacket, and black combat boots.

We caught up on what we'd each been up to since Sadie's cocktail party. I tried to be expansive in my description, but my life was pretty small. She, on the other hand, had just been invited to sit on a jury at the Venice Film Festival.

After sharing that news, she said, Tell me about your room, Tracy.

I was an apprentice baker with a crummy sketchbook and she was a famous artist, but okay, no problem. I gave her a quick overview of my idea to recreate my bedroom—the memories of my dad on recipe cards, the music on the boom box. And I told her my tentative title, *In My Room*.

When I stopped talking, Sadie nodded and said it was "interesting" and "clever." Then, she peppered me with questions. First, she asked about the title, saying she thought it was the name of a Beach Boys song. I agreed that the title needed work.

I like the idea of the memories, she said. But I'm not sure about this scavenger hunt situation. I'm imagining visitors prowling around the room, bumping into each other, like they are participating in an Easter egg hunt. It seems too playful. Too much like a game. Maybe there's a way to make it more intimate. You mentioned that your grandmother keeps her recipe cards in a metal box. Maybe it would be possible to have little stations around the room, each one with a metal box filled with a set of cards. People might take the cards. Hmm. We might need to think more about that idea. The music rattling the walls in the room is nice, but I think I'd be worried while I was in your recreated bedroom in the gallery that your dad might burst in. If you want visitors to get a sense of the room as a sanctuary, maybe you should use headphones. The memories that you've drawn up for the cards are a nice mix of unremarkable and harrowing. You've included how these memories make you feel, looking back on them. You might want to remove your feelings from the cards and let people simply sit with your memories. To have them feel what you might have felt. She paused. Does all of that make sense? I know it's a lot. I'm trying to be helpful and give a sense of how this might actually work in a gallery, which I know is difficult. But I think your ideas are great. I'm impressed. And we're both fans of post-punk.

We talked about bands for a while, and then she talked about how making this kind of art can stir up "weird and hard emotional gumbo." I was surprised to hear her use the word "gumbo."

Sometimes when you create art about painful things, she said, it can be cathartic. But sometimes it can just bring you back to the pain you're trying to turn into art. It's a weird alchemy with no guaranteed formula. Sadly, there are no safety goggles that can protect us. Are you okay? Do you have people you can talk to?

I'm okay, thanks, I said. I didn't really have anybody nearby to talk to, but I felt fine, and I didn't want to saddle her with sadness.

Okay, she said. But if that changes, let me know. I can put you in touch with someone. I nodded. Algy said she's going to meet up with you this week.

Yeah, I said. Algy seems cool. I decided not to mention that I'd promised to let her put makeup on me.

Algy is very pretty, Sadie said. She's quite the heartbreaker.

Oh, I said, it's not like that. I have a girlfriend.

I know. But distance can complicate things. From my experience, at least. She smeared some butter on a corner of her scone. Unfortunately, she said, next week is the last week I can meet with you. After that I fly to Tokyo. Then, I fly back to Vietnam to spend time with friends and family and maybe a couple of old lovers. That should be interesting. Anyway. What do you want to do next week? She bit into her scone.

Oh right. Tokyo. I forgot. I don't know. I sipped my coffee.

If you're still thinking about art school, she said, maybe we could talk about that? I could answer any questions you have and give you a sense of what to expect. Do you like oysters?

Uh, I've only tried them once. They feel weird in your mouth. But I liked the juice in the shell.

Well, Sadie said, they don't feel weird in my mouth, but I know what you mean. They're an acquired taste. Like avocados or cock and ball torture. Sorry. That was strange of me to say. I should be more professional. How would you like to meet for cocktails and oysters next week instead of coffee? It would be my treat.

I'd love that. Thank you. Just tell me where and I'll be there.

—

The address Algy gave me for her apartment was in the middle of Silver Alley. True to its name, the cobblestones in the alley were brushed with silver paint, though they had lost most of their shine. (The next time I visited Algy, they were dazzlingly silver. According to my guidebook, they are spruced up regularly with fresh silver paint.) It took me a long time to find the furniture store she lives above, because it's also a restaurant, which she neglected to mention. There was no street address, and after circling the same part of the alley several times, I spotted a simple hand-painted wooden sign hanging above a doorway. It depicted a bowl of noodle soup with a couch, a dining table, and a bed floating in the steamy broth. At the edge of the sign, a soup spoon with a tiny chair in a puddle of broth was being raised to someone's lips. According to my language dictionary, the shop's name translates to "Tasty Furniture." I went in.

All around me people were slurping from steamy, fragrant bowls of noodle soup. All the tables, chairs, and lamps in the restaurant appeared to have price tags on them. I glimpsed an adjacent room down a hallway with couches, coffee tables, beds, and desks, and yet more customers lowering their heads to soup bowls. There were a few people wandering around, discreetly checking the furniture prices. A woman dressed in black with her hair in a high ponytail approached me with a menu. No, thank you, I said. I finally found the staircase tucked between the toilet and the kitchen.

At the top of the stairs, I was surprised to see that none of the doors had numbers. I spotted the door Algy had described to me. It was bright pink, with a black cartoon heart drawn on it. I was ten minutes late, and I'm never late. I inhaled deeply, exhaled slowly, and knocked.

The door swung open. Algy waved me in. You found me, she said. She was wearing a black tank top and shiny pink leopard print spandex pants. We hugged. She smelled like an intoxicating blend of vanilla, lavender, sweat, and sex.

What is the poison you like? she asked. Coffee? Tea? Beer? Whiskey?

Oh, coffee sounds amazing, I said, if it wouldn't be too much trouble.

Eloise! she yelled. Tracy needs a coffee! Me too! Thank you, sweetheart!

A voice yelled back, Okay!

Algy showed me around the small apartment. All the walls were bubble-gum pink with black cartoon hearts of varying sizes painted here and there. She paused at the doorway to the bedroom, saying, We needed the really big bed. I looked past her and saw that the bed nearly filled the room. There was no space for any other furniture. The living room seemed surprisingly large compared to how tiny the other rooms were. Algy invited me to sit in an elegant-looking rocking chair. I wondered if she'd bought it downstairs in Tasty Furniture. Perhaps the tenants in this building got a discount.

Eloise came in and set down two cups of coffee on the coffee table. She introduced herself and shook my hand. She looked more androgynous than I'd expected. She was wearing a baseball cap, a flannel shirt, and jeans. Her fingers were covered in silver rings.

What do you take? Milk? Cream? Sugar? she asked.

If you have it, I said, I'd love cream and sugar. Thanks.

I've got you covered. She smiled. Her pupils were dark brown with flecks of gold. She brought over cream and sugar from the kitchen and asked me if I needed anything else. I shook my head and thanked her again.

Eloise returned to the kitchen before coming back with a bottle of beer and sitting beside Algy on the couch. We settled into some small talk. After a few minutes, an orange and white cat emerged from under the couch.

Hi Lola, said Eloise. This is Tracy.

Lola scanned the room, her eyes settling on me for a moment, then made a beeline for the bedroom.

Lola has less energy since we got her fixed, said Eloise. But she's also less angry. She was always in the window, because there was a cat howling outside. And Lola really wanted to fuck her, so she kept trying to escape. She was so sneaky because she was so horny.

Wait, I said. Do female cats try to have sex with other female cats that are in heat?

Lola is a girl, said Eloise, but she also had a cock before she had an operation.

Lola is a transsexual cat, Algy explained.

Oh, I said. Okay. I gestured to the amplifiers, guitars, and coils of black instrument cords in the corner. Do you practise here, or do you have a jam space?

We practise here now, said Eloise. When we played with Lottie, we rented a rehearsal space in the industrial area. But now that it's just us, we play here.

I'm so curious about your music, I said. Do you have any recordings? Sorry to put you on the spot.

What do you say, Algy? Do you want to play? Eloise asked.

Yes! said Algy. I'm always wanting to play!

Eloise drained her bottle of beer, went over to the corner, and turned on two amplifiers. Algy sat on a stool beside the bookshelf, bringing her cup of coffee. They started to check the tuning of their guitars.

I saw two cats in two windows on the other side of the alley. They looked like they were only about ten feet away. They were close enough that I could have tossed a couple of foam balls into their apartment if all the windows were open. One of the cats was dark grey, and the other was a tuxedo cat. They were both in a bread loaf position in side-by-side windowsills. I wondered if they were siblings.

I also couldn't help noticing the glass display case beside the stereo. It was similar to my great-grandma's display cabinet, where she kept her Delft Blue pottery and her bone china. Algy and Eloise's display case had two glass shelves: the top shelf held an array of guitar pedals, and the bottom shelf held an assortment of sex toys in various shapes, colours, and sizes. I'd never seen sex toys on display in someone's house before. As I was pondering whether to casually say something or not, Lola came back in, flopped in front of the stereo, and started cleaning her stomach. *Lola,* I thought, *I have a feeling we're not in Kansas anymore.* In the end, I didn't know what to say, so I kept my lips sealed. In the bedroom with the massive bed, I'd also glimpsed a range of sex-dungeon-type things dangling from the walls, including whips, paddles, riding crops, canes, chains, handcuffs, leather straps, and a gas mask. I imagined myself saying to Algy, *That's a cool gas mask.* I pictured her pouncing on the bed, taking it off the wall, and telling me I had to try it on.

Did Algy tell you about what kind of music we play? asked Eloise.

A little bit, I said. I think she said it was music for confused people.

Yes, that's true, said Eloise. It's music for misfits and tomboys. Girls who wore overalls with a slingshot in the pocket. We play slingshot rock. We play transsexual rock. Blood Moon sounds so dark, but it's also funny because we don't get our periods. We get the moon, but not the blood. Transsexual women are like teenage grandmas.

Yes, said Algy. We are the sexy grandmas with the nice boobs! Blood Moon sounds like an angry witch name. We are witch women, Tracy. It's okay if you don't understand. Men don't understand us.

Eloise leaned over to whisper something to Algy. Algy nodded.

This song is called "Deep Wound," said Eloise.

Eloise played some complicated jazz chords that sounded open and bright. I only know enough chords to play the Stooges, the Ramones, and maybe a few songs by the Cure. She was playing lush arpeggios. I know what an arpeggio is, but I tend to flub notes bouncing between guitar strings.

While Eloise played chiming arpeggios, Algy started singing.

I wrote your name
I wrote your name on my hand
I wrote your name
I wrote your name on my hand

At first, she sang so softly that it took a moment for the words to register. Her voice sounded vulnerable and delicate. Then, her singing became more forceful, and she started to strum her guitar when she sang the phrase "on my hand." Her guitar was drenched in grit and distortion.

After a while, the dynamics and the chords shifted, and Algy's distorted guitar started to overpower Eloise's clean guitar.

Then, Eloise started singing. Her voice was more urgent and raspy than Algy's. She sang the same refrain several times:

> I wish I could open a wound
> So deep it would never heal

I sat upright in the rocking chair, feeling my jaw and shoulders grow tense.

Suddenly, Eloise stopped singing and Algy stopped playing her distorted guitar. Eloise strummed an open chord and let it ring. Algy quietly sang a line that made me ache inside: "You make me feel." She sang the line again and again as Eloise played a string of chiming guitar chords:

> You make me feel
> You make me feel

After singing that line several times, she sang "You make me feel so fucking real" once, and the song was over.

Algy looked at me with puppy dog eyes. How do you like our "Deep Wound"? she asked.

That was incredible, I said. I don't have words for it. I tried to say the phrase "holy shit" in their language, and they both burst out laughing.

You should not say this in public, said Eloise, trying to stifle her laughter. It's like. It's almost like spitting in someone's face. Or even worse. Like pissing in someone's face.

Yes! said Algy. Saying that is like a pissing thing! It's okay. You can piss at me, Tracy. But you need to keep the piss in your pants in a public place.

Yes, said Eloise. Please keep your piss in your pants. Can I get you more coffee? Or a beer or something?

A beer would be nice, if that's okay.

Me too! Algy chimed in. Beer me, baby!

Eloise came back with three bottles of beer and two glasses. This princess, said Eloise, jerking a thumb in Algy's direction, only drinks beer out of a glass. I'm a bottle girl. I brought a glass for you so you can do what you want to do.

A bottle is fine, thanks, I said. I figured it would be one less glass for them to wash.

Eloise leaned over and clinked the neck of her bottle against mine. To the bottle babes, she said, sticking out her tongue at Algy.

Algy shrugged. Only one can wear the crown, she said. I will be your princess. She sipped from her glass.

How long have you been playing music together? I asked.

About a year, Eloise said. We met through Lottie. We both used to date her. Lottie and I started playing music together. Then, she introduced me to this one. She playfully poked Algy in the side. Algy tittered. She had never played guitar before, Eloise continued, but she had a fantastic voice. Just look at her lungs. All three of us looked at Algy's breasts, which were perky (I'm tempted to use the word "nipply") under her black tank top. I taught her to play guitar, and she is such a natural. We're playing a show next week. You should come.

Yes, Algy said, come to our concert! I can do your makeup. Not the ghost makeup. Good makeup!

Oh okay, I said. I'd love to come.

As I was putting on my shoes to leave, Eloise handed me a cassette tape. It had a pink cover with a black cartoon heart and the words "Ink Moon" in the middle of the heart.

This is a demo from when we were called Ink Moon, she said. So it has Lottie playing drums. It's just three songs.

While walking back through Silver Alley, I popped into a tea shop and got a small pot of Earl Grey and a thin slice of cheesecake. I took out the demo tape and pored over it.

Typewritten on its spine: The Legendary Ink Moon EP.

On either side of the spine label were two hand-drawn black hearts, like cartoon bookends.

INK MOON EP was scratched into both sides of the cassette (with a razor blade, I suspected).

The typewritten liner notes on the bubble-gum pink insert read:

3 hit songs:
1. Deep Wound
2. Punk Rock Shebam Shebam
3. Apples & Oranges

Ink Moon is:
Algy – femme vox, butch gtr
Eloise – butch vox, femme gtr
Lottie – skins

We are transsexual women. We are your worst nightmare. We are your wettest dream.

These songs were recorded at Greta's Place with help from Naomi. Love always to Lola.

xoxo

© *Transsexual Riot Grrrl Music*

I smiled at the over-the-top-ness of calling their lo-fi handmade demo cassette "legendary" and proclaiming that it included "3 hit songs" and that the band members were the listener's "worst nightmare" and "wettest dream."

I tried to use my fork to gather all the graham cracker crumbs on my small plate. In the end, I had to resort to using my finger to collect all the last bits of crumbly goodness. I popped the cassette into my backpack and headed home.

—

I'm glad to hear you've gone on a couple of dates. Yes, I'm still okay with you seeing other people. I'm glad you had an amazing orgasm with that guy who works in a fancy restaurant. I don't own you. You get to have sex with whoever you want. You are your own person. And I love the person you are so much. I can't wait to give you a bouquet of orgasms when I get home. I know we belong together. Nothing can change that.

My love for you reaches to the edge of the stratosphere and down to the deepest depths of the ocean. I started to describe my heart as an anchor and a kite and a million other things with weight and wings, but then I remembered those lines from your favourite Scurvy Babies song:

> My heart is not a time bomb
> My heart is not a mobile home
> My heart is not a rhizome
> Oh no, oh no
> My heart is a metronome
> A bloody, bloody metronome

So, my heart is not an elegant crane soaring in the Himalayas. My heart is not a vampire squid swishing in the dark-blue sea. Yes, my heart is a bloody metronome, and it keeps time for you, always.

—

I've been listening endlessly to the Ink Moon demo. I try listening to other things, but I keep being pulled back to those three songs. They have a strange gravity. I spun the Scurvy Babies' "Bloody Metronome," but it felt too polished. The Ink Moon demo glistens in lo-fi ways that I don't even understand. There is tape hiss and the cymbals are too loud and Eloise's vocals are muffled on "Deep Wound," but I've listened to it so many times now that those flaws are part of what makes it so charming.

All three songs are profoundly simple. Each one has only two or three parts. And they are so repetitive. But that repetition lodges them in my brain, and they whiz around like toy cars on a tiny track, looping and looping. I'll be walking along and suddenly realize a line from "Apples & Oranges" has been spinning in my head for several minutes. That song is the perfect example of what they do that I don't understand.

Algy sings the opening lines a few times:

Feed me
Feed me apples and oranges

It has the singsong feel of a nursery rhyme.
Then, she sings,

Make me someone healthy and new
Please make me someone healthy and new

The entire song sticks with honey-coated femme vocals (Algy) and shimmering femme guitar (Eloise), except the line "Please make me someone healthy and new," which includes slashing distorted chords from Algy's gritty butch guitar. The entire song is so pretty, but that one line where she pleads with the listener is tinged with desperation.

There's an underlying sense of darkness on all the songs, especially "Punk Rock Shebam Shebam," which includes the disturbing couplet, "I put the gun in my mouth, put the gun in my mouth / Just to clean, clean, clean the cobwebs out." Where does a line like that come from? I hate when that line loops in my head.

I bought a cheap acoustic guitar at a pawnshop in Blood Alley. I'm trying to learn to play the three songs on the demo cassette. So far, I've mastered "Apples & Oranges," except for the chord during the "healthy and new" part, which is some kind of an A chord, maybe an A7 or an Asus2. (I also bought a guitar chord book because I've gotten so rusty.) It's tricky to tell because it sounds like Algy is playing a distorted power chord, while Eloise plays a chord that rings and shifts between the words "healthy" and "new." Maybe I'll ask Eloise when I see her next week.

I painted a portrait of myself with a guitar in my hands. I've given myself long black fingernails in the painting. It's a pretty sexy look. My hands would look so good cupping your breasts. I might ask Algy to paint my nails black. Or should I go with a more colourful colour?

—

I killed time in a bookstore near the oyster joint before meeting Sadie. Spaces brimming with creative work calm me down. Bookstores. Libraries. Art galleries. Record stores. Video stores. The idea of being surrounded by art is deeply comforting. You once told me that I should work in an artsy bookstore, but I don't know if I'd feel like creating art if I was constantly reminded of how much of it already exists. It would be like being a librarian who's trying to write a novel. How could you feel like you had something to say if you were always aware of how many books have already been published? I mean, what kind of narcissist would be able to sit down and write a novel thinking, Oh yes, millions of other novels have been published, but wait until you read the humdinger I'm going to write?! I feel sorry for any person who thinks that way.

I started flipping through a book about an artist who refuses to let her art be photographed. The idea seemed so preposterous and misguided. I thought, *Who the fuck does she think she is?* But the more I waded into the book, the more she started to convince me. If I'd initially encountered Sadie Tang's work through photographs, would her art have knocked me sideways when I stumbled on it in a gallery? If I'd known what to expect in her girlhood room, would I still have been spellbound? One problem is that without photographs, works of art would become even more elitist, because you'd only be able to see them by travelling to where they're housed. For example, the entire oeuvre of the anti-photography artist is in a gallery in Milwaukee. Besides visiting her art, what else would I do in Milwaukee? Seriously, do you want to travel to Milwaukee with me to spend an afternoon admiring paintings by a semi-obscure, semi-legendary artist who creates works about oppression and pleasure? Afterward we could nibble on Wisconsin cheese and guzzle Wisconsin beer. I didn't think so.

I bought the book and walked over to the oyster joint.

Sadie was already sitting inside with a swanky cocktail in her hand. Her early arrival threw me for a small loop, because I was used to being able to sit for a while and compose myself before seeing her. After greeting me, she strongly suggested that I get the same drink as her. Trust me, she said, it goes unbelievably well with oysters. I said to the waiter (for the first time in my life), I'll have what she's having. Sadie also ordered us a dozen oysters.

We each talked about our week, and she told me a bit about the show she's putting together in Tokyo next week. I'm a bit nervous, she said, about a new video piece I'm showing there. It's called *Detachable Penis*. I nodded. The name sounded familiar. Oh, she said abruptly, what's in that bag, Tracy?

I realized that I'd put the bright-yellow bag from the bookstore on the table when I'd arrived. This was our last time together, so she probably thought it was a gift. I'd forgotten to get her a gift! Oh crap, oh crap, oh crap. A wave of how-the-fuck-did-I-forget-I'm-the-worst-person-ever panic washed over me. Sadie had been so generous with her time and her ideas and had taken me under her wing, and all I had done was pay for coffee and snacks. And now she was treating me to cocktails and oysters.

Oh, I said, I bought you a small gift. I can never repay you, but I hope you like it. I handed her the yellow bag.

Aw, thank you, Tracy. I really appreciate it. That's so thoughtful of you. And you really outdid yourself with the wrapping. It's so ... She ran her hand over the plastic bag from the bookstore. It's so shiny and yellow. Psssst, Tracy, she stage-whispered, you should get wrapping paper next time. It's a small thing, but it's also a big thing.

She took out the book. Oh, Félicette! I love her work! This book is so good! I lent my copy to a student a while ago and he never returned it. Thank you! She came around to my side of the table and hugged me.

My cocktail arrived, and we clinked glasses. The drink was lemony, bubbly, boozy, and surprisingly salty. What appeared to be leaves were spilling over the edge of the glass.

This is so salty, but it's delicious, I said. What's with the leaves?

Oh, those are twists of seaweed. The gin they use is infused with seaweed. And yes, I agree, that saltiness is something special.

I took another sip and tried to taste the seaweed. I'd never tasted seaweed before, but I vaguely recalled that it smelled fairly fishy. Thankfully, the cocktail didn't taste fishy.

I'm thinking about making the title *Albatross* or *Metal Box*, I said.

What or what what? Sadie asked.

Oh sorry. I was thinking about a new title for the installation, the one in my bedroom. Maybe *Albatross* or *Metal Box* would be a better title?

Sadie smiled. Yes, you're right, Tracy. Either title would be better. I'm so pleased that you're still thinking about it. A title can make or break a piece. I watched the wheels turning behind her eyes. She leaned forward and fastened her eyes on mine. I think I like *Metal Box* better, she said. It feels like an opening, an invitation. I think *Albatross* might limit your work too much. Bonus points for making your title a clever reference to Public Image Ltd. She winked and made an "okay" symbol with her index finger and thumb.

I took a sip of my seaweed cocktail and hoped I didn't look as flustered as I felt. I could hear the whoosh of my heart beating in my ears. *Ba thump, ba thump.* The artist in there, I said, gesturing at the book I'd accidentally given Sadie, doesn't let anyone photograph her paintings, right? What do they look like?

They're incredible! Sadie said. Félicette makes these intricate paintings that are just explosions of colour. I don't know how she does what she does. I think she calls it neo-pointillism, which makes sense because she's leaping off from all those pointillist paintings by Seurat and Signac. She does a new thing with dots! She's literally a genius. And her idea to not let her paintings be photographed is also a kind of twisted genius move. She definitely has balls.

Her name sounds French, I said. But I think her work is in Milwaukee. What's up with that?

Sadie laughed. Oh, Félicette is an American girl. Sadie picked up the book from the table. Hold on, she said. I'll find the spot where she explains why she decided to call herself Félicette. Ah, here we go, she said.

> I didn't like my birth name. It was so simple and boring, like dry toast or oatmeal. I was reading a book on animals in space and learned that France had a space program for cats. All of the cats were female because they were calmer than the male cats. They chose one of the cats to shoot into space. She went up and came down, and she was fine. The space cat survived! The cats hadn't been given names because the scientists didn't want people at the space lab getting attached to them. The media dubbed the space cat "Félix" because of the cartoon and, of course, because any creature that does anything amazing must be male. The French space program

made that name female and, voila, the space cat had a name: Félicette! So, I took on her name.

Isn't that wild? said Sadie. I nodded and wondered about all the animals shot into space who hadn't been as lucky as Félicette.

Our waiter materialized with a plate of oysters on a bed of crushed ice. She described the three different types of oysters on the plate and asked if we had any questions. We shook our heads no.

Sadie gestured for me to go first. I confessed that I wasn't very skilled in the art of oystering. Is that a word? I said. "Oystering"?

It is now, Sadie said. Oh, I think I forgot to tell you, this is a lesbian oyster bar. There are a lot of puns on the menu. It's hard to go wrong with "oyster shucking" and "pearl diving" and all those other expressions that are pretty clearly about ladies doing sexy things for their lady companions. Ladies helping ladies. I'm telling you now in case you get weird looks. Sorry. But you're pretty androgynous, and they know me here, so I think we'll be okay. Do you want me to show you how to eat an oyster?

Yes please, I said. Oyster me.

I don't know what that means, she said, but here we go. She gave me a slow tour of the components on the oyster plate. Lemon wedges. Horseradish. Tabasco. Mignonette. Cocktail sauce. She invited me to dip my tiny fork into the mignonette and sample it. I did. It had a tart, vinegary bite. Then, she showed me how to check that the oyster had been shucked properly by gently wiggling it back and forth with my tiny fork to make sure it would slide smoothly out of the shell. She warned me not to spill any of the briny liquor while wiggling the fork.

This might be a dumb question, I said. But do I swallow the oyster whole, or do I chew it?

You need to chew, she said. That's how you taste it.

She walked me through the whole process of choosing toppings (she went with a little lemon and a little mignonette for her first one), sliding it out of the shell and into your mouth, briefly chewing, and swallowing. She smiled and put her drained shell back on the bed of crushed ice, face down. And that, she said, is how it's done. She mimed a stage bow.

I followed her lead and everything was peachy, except I accidentally took a few bits of shell into my mouth, which made everything a little less elegant because I had to fish shards of shell out with my fingers. But the oyster itself had a sharp, briny taste and was less slimy than I remembered. Maybe the first time I had them I'd mistakenly thought I was supposed to let the oyster slide down my throat whole, rather than chewing it? Looking at the smooth oysters resting in their watery shells, I couldn't imagine trying to gulp them down whole. It reminded me of the time when I was a teenager that I'd briefly taken up jogging to impress a girl. I'd thought it would be a good idea to swallow a raw egg for protein. After an early morning run, I stood in the kitchen, wheezing and depleted. I cracked an egg into a glass. It looked like a blob of fluorescent yellow mucus. I grabbed the glass, closed my eyes, and tried to gulp it down in one go. The yolk broke. Some went in my mouth, some glooped onto my chin, and some sticky goo burbled down onto my T-shirt. My days of gulping raw eggs were over in a messy flash.

Oh, I love eating oysters, Sadie said. Any animal in a shell, really. Under their shells, creatures tend to be tender and tasty. She set another empty shell on the crushed ice. Do you have any questions about art school?

I asked her a few questions, and she gave me blunt, bright answers. The swanky cocktails kept arriving. Then, there was shrimp cocktail and crab and lobster. Sadie cracked the crab and lobster for us, piling bits of juicy white meat in the middle of the table. Our fingers got buttery. More cocktails arrived. We talked about other topics, but I forget what we said.

The last thing I remember clearly was having shots of something strong, lemony, medicinal, and sweet. I think the shots were sent over by one of Sadie's admirers.

Somehow, I got home. I think Sadie might have delivered me there in a cab. I think some other woman was in the cab with us. She might have been wearing a dress with a banana print. I might have said a few embarrassing things in the cab that I hoped Sadie wouldn't remember. Strangely, she didn't seem that drunk. I'm so embarrassed. Why did I let myself get so drunk? I am an asshole.

I slept through my alarm the next morning and arrived two hours late for my shift at the bakery. I'd never been late for work in my life before. I apologized profusely, and Mavis told me to shut up and get to work. Effie threw me daggers with her eyes all morning. When I asked her if she could turn down the music, she walked over to the stereo and glared at me as she ratcheted the dial up to the hand-drawn red line that showed the maximum volume our neighbours would tolerate.

Is that good for you? she yelled in English.

Defeated, I turned back to the dough on the counter and channelled my emotions into rolling it like I was in a dough-rolling competition. The speaker was right above my head, and the electronica song was danceable and deafening. Effie came over to the opposite side of the counter where I was rolling dough.

Do you like this song? she yelled in English. It's a good one! The vocals came back on, and she sang along with the shouty singer: "I'll be a demon for you! I'll be a demon for you!" She yelled, Do you like it? "I'll be a demon for you!" Is this your favourite song?

Suddenly, I flashed to a moment from last night. Sadie had astonished me by singing along with "Jesus Built My Hotrod," which was blaring out of huge speakers. Her face was in my face, grinning, and she had a drink in her hand, shouting along with all the fucked-up, frenzied scat-singing parts that sound kind of like "wang dang ding dinga donga dang." The music was too loud and aggressive for a lesbian oyster bar, so at some point we must have gone to a club. A fresh wave of shame broke over me, and I knew for certain that I'd said things I shouldn't have, but I couldn't remember what they were.

Yes, I yelled back at Effie, This is an amazing song! Too bad we can't make it louder! The clanging percussion, the looping, distorted keyboard riff, and the shouted lyrics were all driving me apeshit.

She laughed and walked over the stereo. She put her hand on the volume knob. Just for you, she yelled, I will make it louder! She slowly spun the volume past the red line. The singer kept shouting the same punishing line over and over. "I'll be a demon for you! I'll be a demon for you!" It felt like my skull was being gonged by an invisible mallet. Then, there was silence. The song was over. Effie spun the dial back below the red line and walked out to the front counter.

When my shift finally ended, I fortified myself with as much caffeine as I could handle and called Sadie from my apartment. I'd been dreading calling her, but I needed to apologize before she left for Tokyo. I got her answering machine. I lurched into an apologetic message that was rambling and vague because I still had no sense of what I'd said. Or done? Had I done anything? Oh fuck. I hadn't even considered that. Eventually, her machine bleeped to let me know it had cut me off. I lay back and felt the bed spinning slowly, like a merry-go-round.

—

The phone was ringing. My body ached. I was in bed.

I reached over and picked it up. Hello? I asked.

Hi, Tracy. It's Sadie.

Oh hi, Sadie.

I'm calling you back. You left me a long message. Are you still drunk?

What? No, I said. I worked this morning. I was just taking a nap. Um. I'm sorry about last night. I don't know why I drank so much. I never get drunk like that. I'm so sorry.

Okay, she said. You said some weird shit. Do you remember any of that?

Not really, I said. I don't even. I'm sorry. Um. What did I say? I closed my eyes and braced myself like someone was going to punch me in the face.

Oh Jesus, she said. You talked a lot. Some of it was funny. Mostly, you were a charming drunk. But you—well, after a while, you started saying dumb shit. Like you asked a couple times how I knew I was a transsexual. And you prattled on about how I didn't really look like a transsexual. You kept saying, "You're the prettiest transsexual." It was shitty.

I'm sorry, I said. I'm so sorry.

Never do that again, okay?

Okay. Yes. Never. I'm sorry.

That's one strike, she said. One more strike and you're out. This isn't baseball.

Okay, I said.

One more thing. I was going to tell you this last night, but things went off the rails. Anyhow, I'm going to write you a letter of recommendation for art school before I go to Tokyo. I think you have some talent, and you'd grow a lot and learn a lot.

Oh wow, I said. Thank you so much. I don't know what to say.

You thanked me, that's fine. Just don't say dumb shit like that to me ever again. Deal?

Deal, I said. Never. Thank you, thank you.

What's the last thing you remember from last night?

Maybe drinking shots? I said. Or, well, I kind of remember you bouncing around and singing along to "Jesus Built My Hotrod." Did that happen? Did we go to a club after?

Sadie laughed. Oh fuck! Right, she said. "Jesus Built My Hotrod"! I forgot about that. I love that stupid fucking song. Yes, we went to a club after the oyster bar. It's kind of a secret club. It's behind an unmarked door at the back of a pharmacy, and you need a password to get in. It's very hush-hush. It's a good thing you don't remember any of that, because if you did, I might have to come over and smother you to death with your pillow. She laughed.

Okay, I said. I'm so sorry.

Yes, I know, she said. You can stop apologizing. Just don't do it again. I'll write the letter and have it delivered to you before I fly to Tokyo. Take good care of yourself, Tracy.

Thank you so much, Sadie. I appreciate everything you did for me. Have fun in Tokyo.

Don't worry, she said. I'll have a blast. I love that city. Bye for now.

Bye, I said.

I hung up and stared at the ceiling.

—

I couldn't renew my visa, so I've booked a plane ticket for three weeks from now. I left you a message on our machine. I can't wait to see you. I can't wait to hold you. My eyes miss your eyes. My ears miss your voice. My skin misses your skin. I always sleep better nestled beside you. I even miss the soft sounds you make in your sleep. You don't snore. You sigh and warble. You sound more like a bird than a bulldozer. It soothes me. I love you. I miss you.

—

When Algy opened the door to let me in, I awkwardly handed her a copy of the latest Dalloways album. I still felt bad about arriving late last time, so I didn't want to arrive empty-handed this time.

So sweet! Thank you! Algy said, hugging me. Today, she smelled like vanilla, sandalwood, and sex.

As soon as I took off my combat boots, Eloise appeared with two glasses of red wine. It's so good to see you, she said, handing me one.

Aw, thank you, I said. We clinked glasses and took small sips.

This one, Eloise said, pointing to Algy, never drinks before we play a show. She is so professional. She winked at Algy.

Yes, said Algy. I am the professional for now. After we play, I will drink all the drinks. I will be a sexy drunk girl for you.

I noticed a black-and-white photo beside me in the hallway. At first, I thought it was a classic shot of James Dean brooding in an open leather jacket with a white tee underneath, a cigarette dangling between his lips and his thumbs hitched in the belt loops of his jeans. It looked like James Dean, but it wasn't James Dean. The face was so familiar. Then, it hit me.

Holy shit! I said. Is that you, Eloise?!

She smirked, making her look bashful and proud at the same time. Pretty cool, right? she said. I was in a short film Sadie made about James Dean after that Luke Perry made-for-TV movie-of-the-week crapola came out. I kept saying no. I'm not an actor. I can't play James Dean. But she convinced me. You know her. She can convince people to do things. So, for one week, I was James Dean.

She was even more James Dean than James Dean, Algy said. It was really sexy!

Eloise blushed. That little film turned out pretty well, she said. And the James Dean I played is gay as hell.

Yes, Algy said. There are so many blow jobs in that James Dean movie.

After refilling our wineglasses, Eloise popped the Dalloways album into their disc player. The start-stop, off-kilter intro to "Song for Edmond Edmont" pumped out of their speakers. It really took off when Ginger Astaire came in with her giddy vocals: "I've got a song for you! It's about a French man with a notebook and a bicycle! Are you ready for it?!"

This song, said Algy, makes me want to bounce. She started to pogo in place.

You're right! Eloise said. She put down her glass of wine and joined in, jumping up and down beside Algy.

I nodded and sipped my wine. I didn't really want to start bouncing.

C'mon, Tracy, Eloise said. You should try it. It feels great. I smiled and shook my head no.

The next thing I knew, Eloise had placed a small trampoline in front of me.

Bounce time! Algy said.

I saw that the only way out of the situation was to bounce for a while. I put down my glass of wine and gingerly climbed onto the small trampoline. I jumped softly. I'd forgotten how springy trampolines are. When I came down, it boinged me back into the air. I started bouncing in time to the song. They were right, it was a good tune for bouncing. The off-kilter rhythm made it especially fun and challenging. It felt like when I was a kid and I'd spin around in circles with my arms out, pretending I was drunk, whirling and getting dizzy, imagining that was how adults must feel when they drank alcohol. While I was spinning around like a top, I'd often say the made-up word "lither" again and again. For some reason, this always felt right when I was spinning in circles, faster and faster, until I was wobbly and had to sit down.

The song stopped and Ginger Astaire declared, "Que sera, sera, baby!" Then, we were into the steady beat and synth drone that open "Song for Baroness Elsa von Freytag-Loringhoven." We all stopped bouncing.

Makeup time! Algy said. Are you ready?

Uh, sure, I said.

We went into the bathroom and Algy asked me to sit on the toilet. She cupped my chin in her hand and examined my face, gently turning it this way and that way, tilting it up and down.

Yes, she said. This will be good. Your face is good. You will be very pretty.

I'd really only ever worn makeup during my goth phase. I was coming out of that around the time when you noticed me, opting for a daily uniform of jeans, a T-shirt, and a pair of Chucks. I'd shrugged off the dark bells and whistles of goth and tilted toward anonymity. I know you liked how I looked with my long lashes coated in mascara and my dark eyes framed by eyeliner, but I was tired of being androgynous and mysterious, tired of being gawked at by strangers.

I think I told you that a handful of girls had crushes on me when I was thirteen. That's when I was at my cutest and most beguiling. There was one girl who was especially enamoured of me. Her name was Tina. She went to school at Acemink Junior High, so you probably didn't know her. She was a year older than me, and she lived across the street. Her family was building a house at the back of her grandparents' property. She invited me over once, and we walked through the wood frame of their new home. It was just us, and there were no walls inside yet, so you could see everything. It was like walking around inside the idea of a house. She showed me the sunken living room. I watched her walk down to a lowered part of the floor and say, This is where the couch will be. We're going to get a really huge couch. You can come over and watch TV if you want. I kept hearing the word "sunken" and imagining the couch underwater. I thought maybe it meant they were going to have a shallow swimming pool in the living room, which seemed cool, but it also seemed confusing and impractical. Wouldn't you be worried, I wondered, that the TV might fall in the water and you'd be electrocuted?

She wanted to show me her room, but it was going to be upstairs, and they hadn't built the stairs or the upstairs floor yet. Then, for some reason, she said that I should let her put makeup on me, that I'd look really pretty as a girl. I laughed and said, No thanks. A few minutes later, I told her that I had to go home. I added that maybe I didn't want to come over anymore, that I didn't really like her. Her smile crumpled. Yes, you should run home, she said. I invited you over here because I felt sorry for you. Because you're such a loser. I walked quickly down her long driveway, past her grandparents' house, down to the road, across the street, and up my long, crumbling driveway. The most fucked-up thing was that I had a crush on her.

Do you want to try on this dress? Algy asked. She was standing in the bathroom doorway holding a bright-red dress with a pattern of white bees. It's cute, I said. But I don't know if it will fit. And I might feel silly in a dress.

I think it will fit, Algy said. And this is a very good city for transsexuals and cross-dressers. I bristled. Will you try it on? she asked.

Um, okay. I'll try it on.

After worming my way into the dress and struggling with the zipper in the back, I looked at myself in the mirror. The dress was terribly cute, but I didn't like seeing my stubbly face in the mirror.

I slowly opened the door. Eloise was standing beside Algy.

Oh shit, said Eloise. Red is really your colour.

It looks amazing, Algy said. You should wear it with red lips. I have the perfect lipstick for you.

Do you have a razor I can use? I asked. I want to shave my face. I hate this stubble.

I think it's kinda hot, said Eloise, but my razor and shaving cream are behind the mirror. On the bottom shelf. Knock yourself out.

After I shaved my face, I let Algy fit me into a bra stuffed with rubber inserts. The bra was a little too tight, and the straps kept sliding down my shoulders, but she made a few adjustments and pinned things into place. She helped me wriggle back into the red dress with white bees and zipped me up. She left and returned with a necklace that had a small silver bee pendant.

Algy briskly walked me through a skincare routine. I washed my face. I ran a cotton pad with some astringent solution over my cheeks, nose, chin, forehead, and neck. I moisturized. Then, she sat me back on the toilet and tilted my face in various directions while she applied some of this and some of that. I did what she told me to do. I closed my eyes. I opened my eyes. I widened my eyes and resisted the urge to blink. I softened my jaw muscles. I made an O shape with my lips. I realized I'd forgotten to ask her about painting my fingernails. We probably didn't have time, so I didn't say anything. I kept asking her when I could look in the mirror. She kept saying, Very soon. She ran different brushes with different powders on different parts of my face. It reminded me of watching a painter work on a canvas. Eventually, she looked satisfied.

You are too pretty, she said.

Eloise appeared. Oh wow. You look fucking great! she said. You are going to break some hearts tonight.

I got up from the toilet and stood in front of myself in the mirror. I hated my reflection. I looked like an ugly drag queen.

I nodded, bit my tongue, and looked away. Thank you, I said.

You are so pretty! Algy said. I will take a photo, okay?

No, please don't, I said. Algy took a step back, surprised. No tabloid photos today, I ad libbed. I held my hand in front of my face dramatically. I didn't want them to notice I was on the verge of bursting into tears. The supermodel, I said, must pee now. Everybody out, please! Thank you, ladies. I closed the door and locked it.

I wanted more than anything to scrub off the makeup. I kept telling myself not to cry, that it would be terrible to smudge the makeup with my tears. But I didn't want to go to the club. I didn't want to be seen in public looking like that.

Last year, I decided to dress up as a woman for Halloween. I didn't want to look like a dude in a dress. I didn't want men to chuckle and give me drunk high-fives when they saw me. I wanted to stun people with how pretty I could be. I wanted your jaw to drop when you saw me.

The night before Halloween, you were out for dinner and drinks with a couple of classmates. I had a few hours to myself, so I decided to try out the look I'd put together in my head over the past week or two. I put on your sexy red bra stuffed with rolled-up socks, that red-and-yellow floral dress of yours (it was too short, but I could get into it), black wool tights (it was chilly out, so I was being practical), and a few pieces of your jewellery (including your necklace with the heart-shaped opal pendant). Then, I worked on my makeup. After an hour or so of fussing with my look, I put your brushes and makeup down on the bathroom counter and studied myself in the mirror.

Everything looked okay, except my face. There was something wrong with my face. Specifically, my jaw, my forehead, and my nose. I thought I'd be able to pull it off. I thought I'd be one of those jolie laide women. I'd assumed there would be a few flaws, that I wouldn't look perfect. But who wants to look perfect? We're drawn to flawed beauty, not perfection. But, looking in the mirror, all I saw were flaws. I'd imagined you seeing me looking gorgeous in your floral dress. I'd pictured you stunned, in a kind of reverie, saying, Wow, is that really you? I'd seen you hungry with want, kissing me hard, your tongue finding mine, your hand against my throat, your body pushing mine against the wall. But, no, none of that would ever happen. I looked like a man who was trying—and failing miserably—to look pretty. I wanted to punch my reflection in the mirror. Instead, I spat at it. I'd never spat on a mirror before. It felt like something I'd seen done in films, a cinematic self-hating gesture. I used to punch myself in the face, but I'd tried hard to stop that and had mostly succeeded. You caught me doing it once when I was overwhelmed with a fuzzy, inexplicable anger, and I could tell that it terrified you. I watched my gob of spit slide down the mirror and drip onto the faucet.

I hurriedly scrubbed the makeup from my face. I felt my body shake and realized I was sobbing. I buried my face in the towel hanging from my hook on the back of the door. When I finally stopped crying, I realized that I hadn't gotten all of the makeup off, and now some of it was smudged on the thick towel's flamingo design. I tried to scrub out the evidence of my shame and failure with soap before throwing it in the hamper.

The next night, I dressed up as a pirate radio DJ. All I had to buy was an eye patch from the drugstore. I already had a bandana, your black skull-and-crossbones metal T-shirt, a pair of headphones, and a small box of 7″ singles. You loved my costume and kept nudging me to stretch my mouth with my fingers and say, I was born on a pirate ship, like we used to do when we were little kids. It would have been funnier if I hadn't actually felt like a pile of shit.

What size are your feet? Eloise yelled through the closed bathroom door. I can't remember, I yelled back.

Can you open the door? she asked. I have some boots.

I looked at myself in the mirror. I'd been dabbing at the sides of my eyes with tissues and they looked slightly bloodshot, but the makeup hadn't been smudged too badly. I opened the door and forced a small smile.

Eloise was holding a pair of black leather knee-high boots. These are a 42, she said. Let's see how they fit.

At that moment, I decided to give up control and let myself drift downstream and just do whatever they said, so I stepped into the boots. Eloise pulled up the side zippers. Perfect! she said. Oh, those boots look great on you.

Algy put on a short black-velvet baby-doll dress with lace trim. From the living room, I could hear Eloise singing along to "Song for Edmond Edmont," so she must have found the lyrics sheet in the CD. I was glad she was as enamoured with the new Dalloways album as I was. I could already picture her reaction when she listened to the last track, "Song for Anastasius Lagrantius Rosenstengel's Device," which is an ode to a gender-bending eighteenth-century Prussian's leather dildo (a.k.a. "the device").

One aspect of Algy's makeup routine that surprised me was how she subtly darkened her faint peach fuzz moustache with a mascara brush. At first I thought, *Ah, right, flawed beauty!* Then, I thought, *No, it's just an aspect of how she looks that she likes and wants to accentuate.*

We took a taxi to the club where Algy and Eloise were playing. It was in the industrial district, just outside the Old Quarter. Before becoming a club, it had been a boxing gym. When we walked in, I was surprised to see a handful of scruffy maroon punching bags dangling from steel chains in the dance floor area. There was a boxing ring against the wall filled with amplifiers and musical instruments. Eloise and Algy rushed over to hug the bartender, a wiry woman with a striking rust-tinted pompadour. Her name was Westy. Her hands and arms were covered with tattoos of tiny stars. Eloise and Algy handed their guitar cases over the bar to Westy, and she stood them in a corner off to the side.

Welcome, she said to me. I love these two rock stars so much. If they like you, I like you. Gimme a second. I'll whip something up for all three of you. Let's see what your eyes are telling me to make you. She stared for a few seconds at each of our faces. When it was my turn, I felt so exposed and unattractive with my puffy face slathered in makeup. I imagined a magician decked out in a top hat and tails touching a magic wand to one of my broad shoulders and making me disappear. Abracadabra. Okay, Westy said. Got it. Your eyes have spoken.

She whirled around behind the bar and started filling three chilled cocktail shakers with different ingredients. After a couple of minutes, she vigorously shook each of the shakers and strained them into three differently shaped glasses. Each glass got a different garnish. Then, she nodded her head and slid our respective glasses in front of us.

Algy started to speak, but Westy cut her off. I know, she said. I know. No alcohol before you play. This is a straight-edge drink. Just for you, sugar. What are you waiting for? Bottom's up, girls.

The phrase "dude in a dress" kept running through my head. At least Westy hadn't laughed when she saw me. I tried to let it go and focus on the drink in front of me. My cocktail was pink and frothy with a cherry garnish. I picked up the thin stem of the martini glass and took a sip. It wasn't as sweet as it looked and had a tart aftertaste.

What's this called? I asked.

Do you like it? Westy asked. I nodded and sipped again. That's a Pink Shimmy, she said.

Eloise cozied up beside me and looked at my Pink Shimmy. Now that's a girl drink! she said. I reddened. Abracadabra. Abracadabra. Abra—oh please, oh pretty fucking please—cadabra. Eloise's cocktail glowed a greenish yellow under the bar lights with crushed ice and a lemon garnish. I gestured for her to try my cocktail. She took a small sip and smiled. That delicious pink drink, she said, has got a kick. Nice cocktail, Westy! We do what we can, Westy said, winking.

By the time Blood Moon started to play, I was teetering between tipsy and drunk. I kept reminding myself that I was with Algy and Eloise and that everything would be fine and I was in a safe place and would be back home before long. I also kept trying to remind myself not to drink too much. Then, I'd order another drink to calm my nerves. The last thing I wanted was to misspeak in the same ways I'd misspoken with Sadie. At some point, I recognized that I'd probably passed tipsy territory and entered the state of drunkenness, but I vowed to keep the word "transsexual" out of my mouth.

We're Blood Moon, Eloise said into the mic. We're transsexuals.

A handful of people at a table beside the boxing ring stage clapped and hooted.

Eloise started playing the bright, chiming chords to "Deep Wound," and Algy whispered the opening lines. Her voice was so soft that I could hear her breathing into the mic. I half expected someone to yell, We can't hear you! But no one did. Instead, we all pricked up our ears and leaned toward her.

> I wrote your name
> I wrote your name on my hand

Each time she said the lines, they were clearer and more defiant. After a while, Algy's distorted guitar chords started slicing through Eloise's shimmering arpeggios.

And then Eloise was singing her raspy refrain.

> I wish I could open a wound
> So deep it would never heal

Someone nearby was swaying with their arms around a tattered punching bag. It looked like they were slow dancing.

> I wish I could open a wound
> So deep it would never heal

A few people were turning to look at me, and I realized that I was weeping. I lurched to the washroom and stumbled into a stall. I stood there blubbering, wiping my face with a bunched-up mass of toilet paper, which soon became soaked with tears and snot and streaked with red and black muck. The makeup. I unwound another big bunch of toilet paper and tried rubbing as much makeup off as I could in the bathroom stall before eventually venturing to the sink and looking in the mirror.

I looked like a drunk gay brokenhearted clown. Suddenly, I started to laugh. I'd finally tipped past the point of giving a fuck. Partly, it was the alcohol. Partly, it was that I'd been shouldering a ton of tension and anxiety and fear all night and couldn't carry it any longer. I washed my face for a few minutes and managed to get most of the makeup off. There were smudges of it here and there, but I'd done what I could. My boxy body looked odd in the gorgeous red dress, but I liked how I looked better now than before. I looked like a cute art fag. It took me back to my goth days, and I sort of missed how I used to fuck with gender back then. Maybe it was okay to be seen, okay to stand out, okay to be mysterious and androgynous.

—

I awoke to ringing. It was still dark out. The phone. I fumbled blindly and finally felt it. I lifted it off the cradle, stopping the ringing.

Hello? I asked. Dead air. Hello?!

Hi, you said. I hope I didn't wake you. Your voice was soft and gentle and staticky in my ear.

Then, you proceeded to break up with me. You did it ever so softly, ever so gently. But, still, you tore my heart asunder. I was sad. I was shattered. I was still somewhat drunk, and I said things I shouldn't have. After a while, you said, I'm sorry, I'm so sorry. Then, you hung up on me.

I tried calling you back, but I kept getting your machine. I left a string of miserable messages. I pleaded with you to call me back. I pleaded with you to not break up with me. I pleaded with you to explain what the fuck had happened, what I'd done wrong, why you didn't want me. I might have yelled. I might have cried. Eventually, I stopped dialling your number.

I called in sick to work a few days in a row. I couldn't just show up and make pastries like everything was okay. Everything wasn't okay. I kept trying to leave my apartment, but I couldn't do it. I'd put on my shoes, open the door, hover in the doorway. Then, I'd close the door, take off my shoes, take off my clothes, and crawl back under the covers.

I called you constantly, but I couldn't get through. Eventually, your machine informed me that it was full.

When I finally checked my mailbox, there were two letters waiting for me. One was from Sadie, and the other was from you.

I opened the letter from Sadie first. It was her letter of recommendation for art school. It was generous, thoughtful, and perfect. This letter would open doors for me. Except I wasn't sure if I still wanted to go to art school. The only thing I wanted was you. And you didn't want me. Plus, the name in Sadie's letter was Tracy, which would be a problem.

I made myself a cup of coffee. I sat at my kitchen table and slit open your letter. In three pages, you tried to distill why we could no longer be together. After reading it, I sat with my head in my hands, my coffee getting cold, my heart on the linoleum floor.

You'd unexpectedly fallen in love with the guy from the fancy restaurant, the guy you told me had given you an amazing orgasm. You said you hadn't been looking to fall in love; it had just happened. You said he made you swoon. You said you still loved me, but your heart didn't twirl for me like it twirled for him. You said that we could still be friends, that we'd always be friends. You said he was moving in with you. You said your friend Max was looking for a roommate, that you thought we'd hit it off. You said you hoped I was doing well. You said you might go visit a colony of bats the same week I was flying home and your new boyfriend, Timothy, might join you. You said Timothy was a sommelier. I don't know what the fuck that is.

—

I worked my last couple of shifts at the bakery. Mavis baked me a goodbye cake. It was beautiful, moist, and delicious, but I only had half a slice. I wasn't feeling very festive. On the way home, I handed the fancy box with the rest of my goodbye cake in it to a homeless woman sitting on a blanket with her dog, who was wearing a red bandana. Cake for you, I said, trying to get the pronunciation close to what my guidebook said. Thank you, she said in English. Bobo loves cake, she said, nuzzling her German shepherd. I waved goodbye to her and Bobo. Have a good night, she said.

—

In your letter, you said Buttons purred like mad for Timothy.

—

I'm flying home tomorrow. And I'm not sure what's waiting for me. I don't have a job. I don't have a place to live. I don't have you. I bought you twenty small gifts. (One for each year of your life. I'm a hopeless romantic. With the emphasis on hopeless.) I was going to give them to you over a slow, cozy dinner. Maybe I'd have made ginger, carrot, and squash soup. Now I don't know what to do with them. Maybe I'll still give them to you.

Now I'm sitting in the airport, waiting to board the plane. I've been listening to the going-away mixtape you made for me. I just skipped over "My Eiffel Rifle." It hurts too much to hear that one. And now your favourite Scurvy Babies song is playing, "Bloody Metronome." As I listen to Alec

Scurvy sneer at all the flowery ways we describe our hearts, I imagine my heart, freshly torn from my body, bloody like a piece of raw meat, flopping on the airport carpet like a fish out of water, gulping for air. But, no, the song reminds me, it's just a metronome that pumps blood through my body. It feels like it's been damaged, but it's fine. Under my rib cage, it's still thumping, still keeping time, keeping me alive.

I just flashed on when you pressed your head to my chest and told me I had a good heart, that it made a nice thump.

Now I'm waiting in line to get on the plane, my passport and ticket in hand.

I once told you that the bloody metronome of my heart would keep time for you always.

And I still feel that way. I don't know how to not be with you.

Apparently, we don't get a meal on this flight. So far, I've eaten four bags of peanuts and two crumbly cookies. They're showing a movie about a bumbling bellboy who discovers he's a superhero. And now a stunning chambermaid has fallen for him. Of course she has.

—

I hope you don't visit that colony of bats with Timothy. I hope you're waiting for me at the airport. I'm sorry. I fucked up. I never doubted we'd always be together. I took you for granted. You once whispered that you'd love me forever. Then, you whispered, no, longer than that. I'll love you forever and a day. Do you remember? I want to scoop you in my arms and bury my face in the nest of your hair. I miss the way your eyes sparkle when you look at me. Why doesn't your heart twirl for me anymore? I love you, Astrid. My heart aches, my stomach aches, everything aches. I want to climb under the covers and nuzzle and doze with you. I feel sucky.

Preface to Side B,

or

Sex, Trauma, and Rock 'n' Roll

THE EDITOR IS HOUNDING ME. She says I'm too slow. I tell her I'm a late bloomer. I tell her my petals unfurl slower than most. I tell her they'll be gorgeous when they finally burst open.

When I signed a publishing contract, I thought I could stitch together a memoir that wasn't cut from the same sad cloth as every other musician and trans girl. I'd sit in coffee shops, jotting in my notebook. Brainwaves came and went. I'd crack the code and spool out the thread for my masterpiece. Then, I'd hit a snag. This went on for a few years. I got a couple of extensions. I finally admitted to myself and my editor that I needed a co-pilot. In despair, I reached out to Hazel Jane Plante to collaborate with me. Eventually, we found the memoir's two-story structure and wrote the book that you've been reading.

I've always loved architectural models. When I go to a museum that has models of buildings, I feel a shiver. I felt a similar shiver when Hazel and I hit on the two-story structure. I imagine my memoir as a skyscraper with an elevator that only stops at the twentieth and forty-sixth floors. You can get a sense of the other floors, but you don't have access to them. You've already visited the twentieth floor, and now you're zooming up to the forty-sixth floor.

I like gaps. I like things that wobble. I wanted my memoir to have gaps, to have a little wobble. I didn't want to dust my life with powdered sugar. Aging has changed me. Relationships have changed me. Hormones have changed me. Trauma has changed me. A body is a mobile home. A body is a slow time machine.

While working on this book, I was reminded of all the ways trans women's past and present lives converge and diverge. Hazel thinks there's a trans collective unconscious, but that idea sounds batty to me. (Fun fact: I folded a few details from Hazel's own life into my memoir. When I suggested it, she quickly agreed, saying it reminded her of a tailor sewing handwritten poems into the lining of a dress.)

When I sent a rough draft of this book to my sweetheart, she asked if I was sure about sharing this version of myself with the wider world. I've been asking myself the same question for a few months now. Am I sure? I'm not sure. My recent life has been steeped in sex, trauma, and rock 'n' roll, and it feels important to delve into those topics. I want to show how I write songs, how I process trauma, and how I fuck. These things feel deeply important. I'm fed up with fear. I'm tired of shouldering shame.

I often think of Algy informing me that trans women are witchy. She's right. We have power. We can transform things, including ourselves. We can muster magic. The truth is that we are too good for this world. It isn't safe enough for us. It's killing us. It's especially awful for Black, brown, and Indigenous trans women. They deserve safety. They deserve love and pleasure. They deserve to live with ease.

Sometimes I think, *There are countless ways to coexist on this beautiful pale blue dot, and yet humans are choosing to create this cockeyed world. How strange. How disheartening.*

I'm typing this on my laptop at a wobbly table outside a tiny coffee shop. Nat King Cole is on the speakers right now, singing "Quizás, Quizás, Quizás," which in English translates to "Perhaps, Perhaps, Perhaps."

Perhaps you will feel things in your body as you read this memoir. I hope you do.

Perhaps you will be reminded that trans femmes are smart, hilarious, messy, and hot as fuck.

Perhaps you'll think about how your own body has travelled through time, how you became the person you are, and how trauma, love, art, and sex shape your life.

Perhaps you will text a friend, *I'm reading Any Other City by Tracy St. Cyr. It's pretty fucking good. You should read it.* Perhaps after hitting "Send," you'll ponder whether or not this world deserves trans women. Perhaps you'll decide it doesn't and wonder how to change that.

t.

xx

July 17, 2021

Caterpillar on the floor,
Can you teach me to transform?
And I'll step right in and cocoon 'til I'm born
And I can't say that I'll miss my human form much

One hand to keep you warm
One hand to hold my chin
To be inside your arms, it's all I'm asking

I see all the parallels
I see all the parallels

BIG THIEF, "PARALLELS"

I FIRST FLEW TO THIS LABYRINTHINE CITY over twenty years ago. I found a cheap apartment in one of the less-desirable parts of the Old Quarter. That trip realigned my life in ways that were heart-mending and heart-rending.

This time I'm renting a small apartment in Silver Alley. Its cobblestones are brushed regularly with fresh coats of silver paint.

—

I couldn't stay in the same city as you, Johnny. After that awful night, I kept thinking I saw you everywhere. I needed distance to feel safe. You broke my brain for a spell. You scrambled my circuitry. I couldn't fathom what you'd done.

Now my brain is working again, but all the bits that were once coated with warmth when I thought of you are gone. You rewired me. I've deleted all the images of you from my phone, because whenever I scrolled past them, my pulse would push into overdrive, and I'd be blindsided by panic.

I still have plenty of photos you took of me. I'm often looking directly at the camera, my eyes brimming with adoration. I'm staring at one of those photos now. I'm in your *Unknown Pleasures* T-shirt, grinning and holding an ice cream cone.

Do you remember that day? We split a waffle cone with a scoop of pistachio and a scoop of rosewater and saffron. It was my birthday. That night, you took me to a fancy restaurant, and we got the server to take a few snaps of us. But I had to delete them. I need to let you go.

—

Last night, I dreamt the strangest dream. I'd just stepped out of the shower and heard a chittering sound, like a baby bird might make. I scanned the room. When I looked down, I saw the small head and spindly arms of a delicate creature growing out of my abdomen. It was blinking up at me. It resembled a freshly hatched chick, except it had no feathers and no beak. It opened its small mouth. It looked thirsty, so I filled my palm with tap water and tried to carefully drip it into the creature's mouth. It swallowed some water and licked the droplets that had splashed around its mouth. I'm doing my best, I said. I'm sorry I didn't notice you before. It blinked up at me and made that chittering sound again.

I shivered and reached for my T-shirt. I paused before putting it on and wondered if I should cut a hole in the side so the creature could look out. Maybe it would have trouble breathing under my shirt. Or maybe it would want to be hidden rather than have strangers gawk and poke at it. As I was debating what to do, the creature coughed, and I heard something spatter on the floor. I looked down, and its mouth was covered in blood and there was a splotch of blood on the bathroom tiles. It looked up at me, bewildered and frightened. I tried to calm it by cradling its tiny body with my hand. It trembled and blinked wildly. It coughed up more blood. It looked up at me with wide, urgent eyes.

Then, I woke up. I opened my eyes, but the room was dark. I touched my hand to my abdomen. Nothing. I felt bereft. I couldn't fall back to sleep.

—

The idea of you still occupies the space beside me in bed. And I still talk to you in my head. You hold a phantom power. Knowing this happens the world over doesn't make things easier. It's like when Hamlet is grieving for his father and his mom says, Buck up, kiddo, everyone dies. Fuck you, he retorts. I know everyone dies, but someone I love has just died, so please let me feel my feelings. I'm paraphrasing here.

I'm sure I'll miss you for a long time.

—

This morning, I remembered the demo cassette my friends Algy and Eloise gave me the first time I was in this city. They had a band called Ink Moon. After some searching, I found a video online with the three songs on their demo, and everything from that time flooded back. Meeting them. Meeting Sadie Tang. Working part-time in a bakery. Weird gender stuff that was starting to bubble up for me. Wandering the alleys with a soundtrack of post-punk on my headphones. My girlfriend breaking up with me over the phone.

I've been messing around with the Ink Moon songs from the demo. I had doubts about flying over here with my guitar and some gear. But now I'm so glad that I did. Music is something I need right now.

—

I don't have words for how I feel. I'm a muddle of emotions. In elementary school, we once had to make a poster that illustrated our lives. I wanted the background of my poster to include every colour imaginable. I squeezed bright tubes of paint over the thick paper and swirled the colours together. Eventually, the mixture turned poop brown. I added more colours, but that only made it a lighter shade of poop. I added even more colours, which made it a darker shade of poop.

Sometimes my sadness subsides and my frustration softens, but I never stop feeling bruised. Everything seems sepia-tinted and coated in sludge.

—

I got so lost in music this afternoon that I forgot to have lunch. I finally ducked out to get some street food at a stall nearby. After devouring some fried chicken and sticky rice, I washed the chicken grease from my fingers and started putting some basic tracks into Ableton. (We'll never share an order of fried chicken, salty fries, vinegary coleslaw, and lemonade again. We will never cuddle on the couch again. It's hard to get you out of my head.)

I've already recorded a ragged version of "Apples & Oranges." Singing that song feels healing, especially the lines "Make me someone healthy and new / Please make me someone healthy and new." I want to be made new. I want to stop feeling like an emotional geyser.

I recorded a sloppy, emotional version of "Deep Wound" today. I've been listening to the lo-fi video of Ink Moon's demo cassette on repeat. It's all I want to hear.

I'd hoped the Ink Moon video might allow me to track down Algy and Eloise, but it was posted by demoDemon99, who has uploaded thousands of lo-fi demos by obscure nineties bands. A potential path became a cul-de-sac. I'm allergic to social media, so I messaged my bassist, Marta, to see if she could find them. She said she'd see what she could do.

—

A friend recently reminded me that bodies don't understand time. So, if you think about a painful moment from the past, your body doesn't know it happened in the past; it thinks it's happening right now. My body remembers so much stuff that I don't want it to remember. I'm trying not to think about how you lashed out, because when I do, my body goes into a state of emergency. And I'm tired of being walloped by panic and sorrow. It's exhausting. But that's like trying not to think about a white bear or a pink dolphin. If you purposely try not to picture them, you're already sunk. I feel stupid because it's over and we're both kind of okay. But I don't feel okay.

—

In the apartment I'm renting, the previous tenant left a portable radio on an upper shelf in the bedroom closet. I took it down and plugged it in. A local radio station came in. It was broadcasting a song about heartache. Oh, now it's playing a song about falling in love. Same as it ever was.

I opened my laptop and started writing an email to Jax Perry at Sir Gaylord Records. I'd gotten in touch a few months ago to say how much I adored their 7″ covers series, particularly their split 7″ of Jackie Shane songs done by Slippery Elm and Thao & the Get Down Stay Down.

Jax had said to reach out if I ever wanted to record something and told me how much they loved my music, especially *Butterfly Valve*. Of course, they didn't mention my two newer albums, but even I knew they aren't my best. Everyone loves my "brave" coming-out album. Yeah, trans girls are brave, like that doomed blue-faced dude Mel Gibson played. Aye, you may take our lives, but you'll never take our freeeeeeedoooooom! Actually, I wanna stay alive, thanks.

I found my earlier email exchange with Jax, hit the "Reply" button, and started typing. I wrote some ecstatic sentences about Algy and Eloise's band, how much their music meant to me, and how I wanted to release a 7″ covering two of their songs. I paused. Inhaled. Hit "Delete." Exhaled.

As I'd been writing my message to Jax, I kept wondering whether they'd like my Ink Moon covers. I didn't want to have a tiny Jax hovering on my shoulder like a gay devil. The deal with my label had ended with my last album, and neither of us wanted to renew, so I was in the clear to do whatever the fuck I wanted. Why not just record the songs in a cheap studio and release them on my own? DIY. Just like Algy and Eloise. I felt myself relax. Decision made.

—

Remembering when I was here for the first time, I keep seeing myself as a twenty-year-old girl, but I know that wasn't the case. Or at least, that wasn't how the rest of the world saw me. I think my first girlfriend might have seen me that way, which made it particularly devastating when she broke up with me. She saw who I was and didn't want to be with me; she wanted to be with a cis guy. And when I returned to the city where I grew up, I tried to be a cis guy for a long time. And that's especially fucked up, because I'd seen life on the other side of that wall. I'd met Sadie, Algy, and Eloise. Looking back, maybe Sadie had seen the trans femme in me. Maybe Algy and Eloise had too. But I knew that if I fessed up as trans, I'd be seen as a freak. I kept thinking of Sadie's friend Em, the trans Thai shoemaker, about how I saw her as a dude in a dress. I figured that was how my friends would see me. And I couldn't handle that. So I tried to tamp things down. And that worked for a time. But it's like tamping down gunpowder. It gets even more combustible. Behind my denial beard, I was a femme powder keg.

Walking through the crooked alleys here, I recognize that I needed my life to twist this way and that way to get where I needed to go. A straight path probably would have led me to a land mine. I needed to take a circuitous route to keep myself alive long enough. But, of course, when I transitioned, shit was bonkers, because my band was just going from underground famous to almost above-ground famous. (You told me you loved *The New Yorker* piece on me that came out a few months after I transitioned. I still haven't read it. I was trying so hard to say the right things and to wear the right things. I felt like I had to be perfect.)

—

Before arriving here, I was deep into camo. Everything in the clothing shops here has a leopard print. So, my current look is a mixture of camo and leopard print. It makes me seem feral and militant.

Today my friend Clarice sent me an image of a T-shirt with a silk-screened submachine gun and the phrase "JOIN THE TRANS FEMME MILITIA." She added, *i'm a lover grrl not a fighter grrl but i'd go to war w/ yr dirtbag ex to protect you! i'm here if you ever need anything. (yes, ANYTHING!) sending luv across the ocean to you!!* She sent three kiss face emojis.

Thanks, I replied. *I'm still alive. I miss you, friend. XO.* I sent emojis of a leopard, a hug, and a bandaged heart.

—

I recorded one song on tour here a few years ago at a sweet little studio. It's gone now, but the person who ran it has a new studio. I dropped by to take a look today. It's a little unpolished, but it's affordable, and the set-up is perfect. It has one main recording room, good sound isolation, tons of classic mics, and a Neve 5316 console.

Sam, the owner/producer/engineer, recognized me from my session years ago. She was the first trans woman I'd ever met who ran her own studio. Oh hey! she said. Tracy! It's so good to see you. What was that song again? Oh, I know. "Suicide Pact"!

Great memory, I said. I'd kinda like to forget that song.

Oh really? I thought it was dynamite. She recited the chorus back to me: "We made a suicide pact / Then, I backed, yes, I backed out." So dark, she said. But brilliant. I cringed. I wasn't in a good place when I wrote that song. My label loathed it, but they eventually agreed to release it as a bonus track on the Japanese version of *A Year Without Moons*, along with a cover of Redd Kross's "Mess Around." (You always hated my playing "Mess Around" because of its lines about how hard it is to be monogamous. You accused me of playing it at live shows to antagonize you. I always denied it. You were right. I was kind of a cunt sometimes. I'm sorry.)

I want to book some time, I told Sam. This is a great studio. She smiled and shrugged and looked at the ceiling, manoeuvring away from my praise. But I'll need a drummer.

I've got you covered in the drums department, she said. What are you gonna record?

Sam had some time before the band recording that afternoon arrived, so I streamed some of the Ink Moon demo with the studio's Wi-Fi.

She said she knew the perfect person and started to open a folder on her computer.

It's fine, I said. I trust you. Let's book some time.

—

I awoke absurdly hotted up this morning, thinking about that time you whisked me away to a cabin in the middle of nowhere. We'd only been dating a few weeks. You said you had a long weekend planned for us, that all I had to do was pack a bag and hop in your truck. I assumed you were going to introduce me to rock climbing, because you were so devoted to it. But, no, when you picked me up at my apartment, you put me in my place right away.

Buckle up, fucktoy, you said.

I slid into my seat. You'd never called me a fucktoy before. I felt giddy.

We'll be at the sex cabin in no time, you said. I bought you an iced latte. You should drink it while it's still cold.

I sipped from the straw. Yummy, I said. Thanks.

Good girl, you said, grinning. You follow orders well. I like that about you.

You had a fuckmix blasting from your speakers. I think the digital display said it was called "Tracy is MY Fucktoy." You started nodding your head and singing along with the ascending "uh-huh" part on the Yeah Yeah Yeahs song "Black Tongue." You grinned, glanced down at my lap, and turned back to the road.

As soon as we were on the highway, you turned the music up. I wondered what would come on next. I'd have put my money on Grace Jones's "Pull Up to the Bumper." I was wrong. It was the Cramps' "The Hot Pearl Snatch." I was going to tell you about how wild they were the one time I saw them play live, how Lux Interior was like a scuzzy, unhinged Elvis. I wanted to tell you that Poison Ivy sometimes referred to Lux as a "tall girl." But, no, I bit my tongue. Now wasn't the time. You were revving up your over-the-top rockabilly drawl, particularly when you sang "snatch," savouring the word like it was a dram of well-aged bourbon.

Show me your tits! you yelled.

What?! I asked. We were barrelling down the highway with the windows rolled down and the wind whipping our hair. I felt shy suddenly. I wasn't sure I wanted to take off my top right then.

I said show me your fucking tits! I need to see them! Right now!

I turned to you. Reached back and unclasped my bra. Looked around. Pulled up my top so you could see my tits.

You're gorgeous! you yelled. I love your tits! You can put them away now, slut! You laughed.

We fucked in that cabin for three days. You'd brought along a leather duffle bag overflowing with toys, gloves, and lube. We didn't talk much. We ate when we got hungry. We went for one brief walk in the woods. We tried to watch a movie but started making out instead. Mostly, we fucked. Our bodies felt flammable.

—

I just tried jerking off, but I couldn't make myself come. Over time, I've learned to stick to the low thuddy settings on my wand, but sometimes I'm on the cusp for so long that I can't resist dialling up to the more intense buzzy vibrations. I was so close, so frustratingly close. My clit slowly became a raw, numb nub, and I felt the orgasmic horizon receding—then, the horizon vanished.

But I still want to get myself off and stop remembering that whirlwind weekend when I was your fucktoy. I'm so angry, because you've smeared shit on everything related to the years we were together. Even our flutter-ing honeymoon phase seems slathered in shit now.

—

I arrived at the studio about fifteen minutes early. Sam gave me a quick queer hug and introduced me to the drummer she booked for the session. This is Jay, she said. He's the brilliant drummer I told you about. He was wearing a Kill Rock Stars T-shirt. And, Jay, this is Tracy. She's the amazing force of nature I told you about. We half waved at each other. Jay was about a foot shorter than me, but he had presence.

Before we settled into recording, I streamed the two Ink Moon songs we were going to record. Jay nodded and listened intently. When they ended, he said, Cool. This is gonna be fun. He smiled.

I pulled my beat-up silver Fender Jaguar out of its case and checked the tuning. I ran it through my fuzz and delay pedals and plugged into a Twin Reverb in the corner. I fiddled with the knobs until it sounded pretty good. I'm not much of a gearhead. Cookie was always my resident guitar genius, so I'd typically let her fuss over the technical aspects of guitar sounds.

Jay and I noodled around while Sam placed mics and set levels and did all the other things she needed to do. I've always turned down gigs producing other bands, mostly because I'm not good under pressure when technical troubles arise—and they almost always arise. Plus, I'm too pigheaded. If I think something or someone is wrong, I'll speak up. That's not the best tack when you're making someone else's album. You should be making it sound how they want it to sound, not how you want it to sound. And if you're semi-famous, fledgling musicians often give too much weight to your words, even when you're talking off the cuff, with no expertise about what they're trying to do.

Once Sam gave us the ready-to-record thumbs-up, we did a run-through of "Apples & Oranges." Playing music for the first time with another musician is a little like making out with a new lover. You need to be attuned to the person you're playing with. And you need to be mindful of how the energy is flowing. In this case, I was clearly the top, but Jay was doing smart, subtle, and playful things (especially with his hi-hat and ride cymbal) that were elevating everything I was doing and snapping energy back in my direction. I'd play a guitar line, and he'd drop a beat to let the last note breathe. It was exhilarating, almost the musical equivalent of new romantic energy.

When we were done, we listened back to the run-through take—and it sounded kinda great.

Damn, Sam said. That first take was golden. I told you he can play! She put her arm around Jay.

Can we do another take? Jay asked me. I've got a couple of ideas, if that's okay.

We did another take, and Jay's playing was even more fine tuned and playful this time. Then, we launched straight into "Deep Wound." I hadn't sung it in front of anyone before and felt myself on the verge of tears during the middle section when I sang, "I wish I could open a wound / So deep it would never heal." It was like a switchblade in my spleen. (And while singing it, I kept thinking, *Oh fuck, that's exactly what Johnny has done: she's opened a wound that will never heal. And I feel like I've been bleeding out for weeks now. I want to be cauterized, stitched, and bandaged. I want to sit on the couch and heal with a pint of peanut butter brittle ice cream and some Buffy.*)

Jay's drumming throughout "Deep Wound" switched effortlessly between the quieter and louder parts of the song (or, in the words of Ink Moon, its "femme" and "butch" parts).

We listened back, and it sounded so good to me that I didn't think we even needed a second take.

Don't you want another one, just in case? asked Sam.

Nah, I think we got it. And, honestly, my last couple albums were probably too polished. We should have left some rough edges. When we were listening to the songs earlier, I was remembering how much I love the flaws on that demo tape. They give it life. There's a kind of flawed beauty.

Okay, flawed beauty it is, Sam said.

After that, we did a handful of overdubs and listened back. The songs sounded alive, with an urgent, unfussy feel. Sam would do rough mixes later and transfer the sound files to me.

We were all peckish, so we went up the street for a quick bite.

When we got back, I started playing a riff that had come to me a couple nights ago in my apartment. It was a sturdy, bare-bones guitar part with three barre chords and a lot of breathing room: G Bm A. I tweaked my fuzz pedal a titch and started banging out the chords. After a couple of bars, Jay joined in to supply a steady beat, sweetening the space between the final A chord and the opening G chord with some subtle snare and hi-hat.

I'd been looking at Sam's charm bracelet while we waited for our bowls of noodle soup to arrive. There were a few different charms dangling from it. Little skulls. Little crosses. Little stars. Little hearts. I'd been thinking about the word "charm." You can be charmed by someone's personality, and you can be charmed by a magic spell. The phrase "your charms" started swirling in my skull. And "charm" is one letter away from "harm." While jamming on that simple riff, I started muttering into the microphone, trying to divine what words wanted to bubble up from the sonic stew of my chords and Jay's beat. I flashed on how the three witches at the start of *Macbeth* throw different ingredients into the cauldron as they recite a magic spell.

I started singing into the mic, "Even your charms now nah now."

Jay and I had been hammering away on the same riff for a while, and I felt the need to move into a bridge. I thought the G Bm A chord progression was durable enough for the verse and the chorus. I'd never really done that before, but it felt like something Eloise would do. Find a great chord progression and stick with it. Maybe the chorus would just be one line repeated three or four times, Eloise-style. Simple felt perfect.

I locked eyes with Jay to let him know that I was going to do something different. I didn't know if it would work, but I had an idea for a straight-forward chord sequence for the bridge. He held my gaze and watched me and my fingers on the fretboard. I raised the head of my guitar and my eyebrows as I moved to a C7 chord. I shifted back and forth between C7 and C major, creating some tension. Then, I did the same thing with D7 and D major. I repeated that a couple of times. Jay added a sheen of shimmer with his cymbals and revved up the backbeat. His playing underscored the tension that was building as I toggled between those seventh and major chords. I gave him a signal that I was going back to the main riff, and he met me with his earlier beat. It felt good to release that built-up tension from the bridge. It was like whizzing through a dimly lit tunnel on a train and suddenly emerging into sunlight, with a forest on one side of the train and an expanse of glassy water on the other. I felt weirdly buoyant.

I sang into the mic, "Even your charms can't hold me now." Something inside me started to open, slowly and tentatively. I sang the line with more abandon and more freedom.

Even your charms can't hold me now
Even your charms can't hold me now
Even your charms can't hold me now

I imagined Eloise in the studio beside me, nodding and saying, There's a power in repetition. It's like casting a spell. I knew she was right.

I looked over at Sam. She threw me an "it sounds great in here" smile. I grinned and looked away. When I looked back, she was headbanging and making devil horns with her fingers. I started laughing, fumbled the riff, then just stopped playing altogether. Jay stopped at the same time, so it almost sounded like we'd planned to end it like that.

Sorry, Sam said. I just wanted you to know how good it sounded.

No problem, I said. I love the enthusiasm. How are we doing for time?

We're going to have to shut things down pretty soon, she said. Sorry.

Okay, I said. Let's cut this song right now, whatever it's called. I can listen to it later and come up with words. Jay, your drums sound killer. He shrugged.

That session felt so fucking good, I said, packing up my guitar and pedals. You have no idea how much I needed that. Thank you, thank you, thank you.

That was fun! Sam said.

Jay had come out from behind the drum kit. Sam tugged at the hem of his T-shirt and leaned against him. (I was willing to wager they were lovers, currently or formerly. Or maybe they would become lovers in the near future.) When is your band playing again? she asked Jay. Is that tonight?

Yeah, tonight, Jay said.

You should come! Sam said to me. Jay's band is incredible.

I wanted to be supportive, but I was wiped. I can't tonight, I said. Sorry. Rain check?

Okay, Sam said, rain check. It doesn't rain here often, but when it does— she whistled—look out.

—

A friend told me you've already swooped in to woo a young trans femme. You didn't waste any time, did you? When she told me, I wanted to cry and throw up. Another friend said she overheard you saying some shitty, untrue things about me. Please keep my name out of your mouth. I haven't disclosed what you did to anyone and I haven't maligned you, even though my heart is tattered.

I took my guitar out of its case to work out words for the song I'd started writing, but I couldn't get into the same headspace I'd been in earlier today. Instead, I was hit by memories of what happened that night. (Your bloodshot eyes. Your muddy motorcycle boots. Your chipped tooth. Your body, a taut tangle of sorrow and rage, swaying in the doorway. Your voice, trembling: You don't get to forget me.) I tucked my guitar back in its case and crawled into bed. I closed my eyes and let panic and sadness engulf me. I sobbed so hard that my body quaked. I gasped for air. It felt like something had died inside me that night and been decomposing under my rib cage ever since.

Suddenly, I was struck by a tsunami of anger. You gutted me because you couldn't stand to see me moving on. And now you're trying to fuck a young trans girl who you'll probably also damage. For weeks now, I've been flooded with sadness, thinking about how much you must have been hurting that night. I thought maybe when you came to your senses, sobered up, and realized what you'd done, you might be reflective, you might feel remorse. But no. It sounds like you simply dusted yourself off, shrugged, and ordered another drink. Fuck you.

—

When I finally got out of bed, I decided to fashion the song I'd started playing earlier today into a protection spell against exes. I started jotting down stray thoughts, just letting them puddle onto the page. I messaged Marta about my idea for the song. She texted back, *r u writing an ex hex???* I started laughing.

I replied, *Omg, yessssss!!! Ex hex = perfect!*

She texted back, *ex hex ftw bb!!! ur gonna hex that fucken ex right outta yr shit!!!* She sent a string of emojis: a crystal ball, a guitar, a magic wand, a microphone, a throbbing heart.

I wrote back, *You're the best, M! You made me laugh so hard I spat out some of my tea. Haha. And you know me, I'm a classy lady.* I added emojis of a laugh-cry cat and a teapot.

She sent me a dinosaur and a puff of smoke. It was her favourite one-two emoji combo because it looked like the dinosaur was farting. Sometimes she used other animals, but the dino was truly her jam, mostly because years ago she'd played bass in a scrappy dyke metal band called Clitoris-saurus. She joined my band for a tour a few years ago, and now I couldn't imagine playing without her.

I texted back, *Thanks, but I don't need your stinky dino today. I need an ex hex, stat!* I sent a broomstick, a black cat, gold dust, and a stethoscope. I added, *I love you, M!*

luv u too, bish!!! she replied. *don't let the exes grind you down!*

I picked up my guitar and started knocking out the main three-chord riff. I sang the line "Even your charms can't hold me now" a few times. Then, I started singing other lines and fragments I'd scrawled in my notebook to see how they fit with the chords and how they felt in my mouth. Most of them felt flimsy, but a few of them stuck. I got up, put on the kettle, and made some more tea. I sat back down and sifted through the lines that had stuck to see how they might cohere. I found a few good lines for the verses and decided to repeat the ones that resonated in my body when I sang them.

But I was still at a loss for the bridge. Maybe I'd sing "This is an ex hex" four times, turning it into an incantation. I grabbed my guitar and played the seventh and major chords for the bridge, and it fit like clockwork. But it felt flat. Plus, it wasn't really an ex hex. I didn't want anything bad to happen to my ex. It was a spell of protection.

Ah! Just like that, I glimpsed how the pieces of the bridge could jigsaw together: "This is an ex hex / This is an ex hex / A spell to protect us / And make you stay away." That felt freeing. I just wanted safety. The idea of broadening it to protect "us" felt good, like this was a collective spell of protection for everyone who wanted to be shielded from their exes.

—

I keep thinking I'm healing, that I'm letting you go, and then I'll realize that I've been talking to you in my head for the last few hours, trying to explain how much you hurt me. I feel like I stumbled into a steel trap, and its teeth clamped down on a delicate part of me. I struggled and squirmed and failed to get free, until, finally, I gnawed through that part of myself and left it behind. I'd never had my brain turn off like that, like a safety valve, probably to save me, probably because I was overwhelmed with panic and confusion and adrenalin. I wish I could climb into a time machine and end things between us when we got back from Prague. Or I wish I had swiped past your profile on that dating app.

—

I sent an MP3 of "Even Your Charms" to Marta.

Ten minutes later, she pinged me with a text: *hells yeaaah!!! ex hexxx! u r gettin witchy n i luv it!!!*

I'm glad you like it! Let's play it next time we jam! :)

yeeeesssss!!! when r u comin back? She added an emoji of a chick hatching from an egg.

I sent back a shrug emoji. *Any leads on Algy and Eloise?*
She sent me a GIF of a panda shaking its head.

—

While walking through Glass Alley this afternoon, I remembered a conversation I had with a friend about what happens when you experience
something devastating. A part of you breaks open. The plot of your life
feels as though it's been razed, like a forest razed by fire. Then, there's a
span of numbness and sadness. It can last for weeks or months or years.
As much as I'd like to speed up the film of my life, time-lapse style, I
know that I have to endure this blank stretch of hurt. My friend talked
about how, in the empty spaces where things have broken open, seedlings
eventually appear. At first, it's all emptiness. Then, small, soft things start
to sprout. "Even Your Charms" feels like a little green stem sprouting from
a nurse log.

—

I texted Marta: *So, I did something kinda crazy.*
She replied, *???*
I shaved my fucking head!
dude what??? lemme see!!!
I sent her back my cutest shaved head selfie. I thought I looked kinda
badass with a shorn skull, blood-red lipstick, and silver skull earrings.
She replied, *omfg, I luv luuv luuuv this look 4 u!!! 2 cute 2 scoot!!!* ("Too
cute to scoot" is something Marta often says to her tuxedo cat, Pandan,
when she scoots like a fuzzy little vaudeville performer, dragging her ass
across couches and duvets. Pandan stares straight ahead while noncha-
lantly grinding her butthole. It's hilarious and disgusting. Marta does not
find Pandan's scooting funny. According to the vet, there's nothing wrong

with Pandan. It just feels good when she rubs her asshole on stuff. The vet might have used the phrase "anal pleasure." Relatable content.)

Haha. You wish. I rub my ass wherever I want, bitch. Shaved head is pretty fucking cute, right?!

She texted back an exploding head emoji, followed by, *sooooo cute, bish!!! haha, this is yr 2nd britney phase! peach horizon, bb!!!*

Oh fuck, you're right! I pulled a Peach Horizon.

Marta joined my band when I went on my first tour after transitioning. It was the summer, and I decided to play the shows topless. It was my infamous Sun's Out, Guns Out tour.

My bass player, Billy, had quit the band a few weeks before we were slated to go on tour. He said he didn't like the new songs I'd written and blah blah blah. Okay, dude. Anyhow, I started auditioning bass players. Most of them blanched when I told them I was going to play topless. Marta, on the other hand, was stoked. She'd played a few topless shows with Clitoris-saurus and loved the freedom of being naked onstage. When I told her I was thinking about wearing a bondage harness, her eyes lit up. Fuck yes! she said. I love that!

When I'd first started reading about transitioning, I stumbled on the idea of a Britney Spears phase, which was shorthand for when a trans girl started wearing things to show off her body and her partner would say, Oh hell no, you're not leaving the house in that! I'd really wanted to avoid that phase. But, well, after two years of HRT, I was starting to love my tits and just wanted to say, Fuck it, I'm trans, I'm cute, and I'm available, so come and get it.

Marta used to live in Los Angeles. A friend of hers had actually worked in the hair salon in Tarzana, California, where Britney Spears went to get her head shaved. Apparently, Britney kept asking people in the salon to call her Peach Horizon. That tidbit never made it to the mainstream media. Instead, they focused on her bald head and how she bashed a car with an umbrella. But, yes, it looked like I'd just pulled a Peach Horizon. And it looked like this was, in fact, my second Britney Spears moment. Don't get me wrong. I have a lot of love for Britney. I'm not making fun of her. I'm in awe of her. She's weathered an avalanche of injustice.

I shaved my head because I need to heal, to get unstuck. I feel like I'm caught in a trauma trap. I want to wiggle loose. I want to do something that will get me out of this rut. (I kept thinking about how I used to rest my head in your lap when I'd had a hard day, and you would stroke my hair. I miss that so much. I don't want to feel your phantom fingers in my hair. There's a Yoko Ono song called "I'm Moving On" where she tells John Lennon to keep his fingers out of her pie. I feel the same way about my pie, but I also want your fingers out of my wavy locks, forever.)

—

I set up a Bandcamp page for myself as a solo artist. It felt strange, but these aren't Static Saints recordings. I uploaded the WAV files for "Deep Wound" and "Apples & Oranges." I copied and pasted the lyrics and gave credit to "Algy Suriya + Eloise Visser" and noted that the songs were "© Transsexual Riot Grrrl Music." I linked to the video with audio of the original demos and images of their DIY artwork and liner notes.

I agonized over the album art. Static Saints album covers have a minimalist design aesthetic. At heart, I'm still an unrepentant art fag. I didn't want to ape Ink Moon's "legendary" cassette tape, with its pink cover and black cartoon heart with the words "Ink Moon" in the middle. I dropped the snap of me with my shaved head, blood-red lipstick, and silver skull earrings into Photoshop. I fucked with filters and put some handwritten text here and there. I'd always loved the cover of Sinéad O'Connor's first album, and when I was done, my cover had a similar punk-grrrl-with-shorn-skull, rough-around-the-edges look. I called this release *Ink Moon Is Still Legendary*, OK. For pricing, I made the songs pay-what-you-want. I listed Jay and Sam in the credits.

I wanted to convey what Ink Moon means to me, but I knew I had to keep it brief. I mean, I was filling in the "about the album" field in Bandcamp, not writing a profile for *The New Yorker*. But I wanted to point to Algy and Eloise as two women who had made my life possible. I'd heard from so many trans fans about how much Static Saints meant to them, and I dearly wished for Algy and Eloise to know that they had been the catalysts. I wondered where they were and how I could find them. Or maybe they wanted to stay in the shadows.

Here's what I wrote:

Ink Moon changed my life. That's not hyperbole. It's reality. They showed me how to be trans and how to be creative. Algy and Eloise are two of the coolest women who ever lived. I have eternal love for them. As they wrote in the liner notes to their *Legendary Ink Moon* EP, "We are transsexual women. We are your worst nightmare. We are your wettest dream." Fuck yeah. Ink Moon still rules, OK.

I hit "Publish."

—

I've always felt uneasy about being a spokesperson for transness, but avoiding the spotlight entirely feels like an abdication, like I don't want to protect trans folks. But sometimes being interviewed feels like defusing a bomb. Do I cut the red wire or the blue wire first? Did I neglect to mention housing, health care, legalizing sex work, or prison abolition in my *Pitchfork* interview? I believe deeply in all those things, but it's exhausting to be seen as an expert on all things trans at all times. I'll be talking to a reporter about my latest album and suddenly be asked to justify why trans kids should be allowed to use the right toilet. If I call them on their shit, my words will be stripped of context, magnified, and exhibited in the court of clickbait.

Shortly after transitioning, I made the tragic mistake of talking shit about another trans girl in an interview. As soon as my words hit the internet, I knew I'd fucked up royally. I learned the hardest way possible that you should never talk shit in public about other trans folks. That's when I stepped away from social media and handed the reins over to Albertine.

—

I emailed the link to my Bandcamp page to Marta, Poe, and Albertine along with a brief *hey, it feels weird doing this without you* message.

Marta was the first to reply. She seemed to live online, like a queer cyborg with spiky pink hair.

Her reply opened, *You fkkking bitch!!! I'm going so-low toooo!!* I scrolled down to a GIF of a farting dinosaur. *No, it's fuckin kool! I luv u!* <3

After I sent a reply to Marta, I saw the first *Cha-ching!* message from Bandcamp waiting in my inbox:

Greetings tracy st. cyr,

Albertine Albertine (albertine@staticsaints.com) just paid $10.00 CAD for:

Ink Moon Is Still Legendary, OK, by tracy st. cyr,
Digital album $10.00 CAD

Order total:	$10.00 CAD
Revenue share (15%):	-1.50 CAD
Payment processor fee (credit card):	-0.55 CAD
Your share:	$7.95 CAD

I sent Albertine a quick *thank you!* message. They said the songs were
exactly what they needed in their life at that moment, that they really
hoped I was doing okay, and that I should let them know immediately if
I needed anything. They asked if it was okay to mention the EP on social
media and added, *I think your fans will love these songs as much as I do.* And
I knew they meant it. I replied, *Yes, please—thanks!* Albertine is the best
effing manager on the planet.

After the twentieth or thirtieth *Cha-ching!* message from Bandcamp and
a couple of DMs from fans, I messaged Albertine sheepishly to ask if they
could take over my Bandcamp page. In an instant, Albertine was on it.

I never heard from Poe, but I never expected to. That tall drummer girl
is a tough nut to crack.

—

On the rare occasions when you were unkind to me, I tended to cut you
slack. Yes, my childhood, teen years, and twenties were terrible, but my
trauma paled in comparison to yours. You rarely talked about your life
before you found queer kin and became a beloved bartender. I knew you'd
been pulled from your family by police and spun through a revolving door
of foster homes until you finally fled, hitchhiking from the Maritimes to

the West Coast. After a few hardscrabble years, you finally found your people. They introduced you to rock climbing, scuba diving, and weight-lifting. And you found your calling bartending at a queer pub. You were known for your strength, your loyalty, and your handsomeness.

The first love song I wrote for you was "Tigerfish Kisses," about your prowess in giving me orgasms and your love of marine organisms.

> I used to live in a basement suite
> Now I live for sweet debasement
> Oh, now I live for sweet debasement
> I come alive like Frampton for you, for you
> I shimmer like sea-fire plankton for you, for you
>
> I adore your tigerfish kisses
> I want more of your tigerfish kisses
> I love when your trigger finger squeezes
> I melt into jelly around you, around you
> Oh, how my knees buckle for you, for you

After we started dating, you added a drink to the menu as a tribute to me: the Ecstatic Saint (Old Forester bourbon, Bénédictine, Yellow Chartreuse, lemon, ginger, and egg white). You became the handsome tomboy of my wettest dreams, the dyke in leather overalls who wooed me by lugging my gear to gigs, who whisked me to a weekend sex cabin, and who tried to make a life with me. For quite some time, you put the "tender" in bartender.

After I got FFS, your tenderness started to taper. But I knew how much you still loved me. I knew you'd do anything for me. So, I tried to make it work. We saw a few therapists. Things would get better for a bit before reverting to how they had been. Once or twice a year, I'd go on tour, and we'd get a hiatus from the malaise.

Occasionally we'd have phenomenal sex, and all our troubles would dissipate for a spell. I finally resolved to break up with you. I was working up the courage to tell you one night, when you pounced on me like a mountain lion. We made out on the leather couch for a while. Then, you carried me to bed. In your arms, I turned into putty. You put me on the bed, peeled off my summer dress, my bra, my panties.

I want to take my time with you tonight, you said. Is that okay, honey girl?

Yes, please, I said.

And then you went down on me for what felt like forever. After a while, I couldn't tell what you were doing. You were swirling, you were sucking, you were fingering. Your lips, your tongue, your fingers were everywhere. Suddenly, my entire body started trembling. Time stopped and stretched. I heard myself sobbing. You slowed down, but I asked you, told you, begged you to keep going. I felt nervous and excited, because I wasn't sure what my body was going to do, but I wanted more. I was weeping and trembling. You paused. I told you through tears that it was okay, that I'd never felt so good. You kept going, nudging me upward and upward. I saw myself at the edge of a precipice. Teetering. Swaying on the blade of a knife. And then, in a drawn-out whoosh, I let go. I let myself tumble.

When I finally came, my orgasm flowed in endless waves, gushing and rippling, my skin an ocean of pleasure. My fingers pulsed with pleasure. My legs pulsed with pleasure. My pussy pulsed with pleasure. I felt warmth and love for you flowing through me again. My cunt was a flower in bloom, and I watched your lips and tongue milking pleasure from me. I saw honeybees buzzing in loop-de-loops nearby. I turned into water. I turned into steam.

Eventually, I asked you to stop. You kissed me, your face slick with my pleasure. I was transfixed by your dimples and your freckles. I was a puddle. It's impossible to forget a night like that. It's seared in my brain.

But now that night is tinged with sadness. Sadness that I can never trust you. Sadness that I never want to see you. Sadness that I miss you. Love is fucking messy.

—

Albertine messages me to check in now and then, mostly about Static Saints stuff. They understand that I need to lie low for a while, so they only pass along things they know I'd want to see. The two hardest offers to turn down have been a co-headlining tour with the Kills and playing at Coachella on a bill with IDLES (!), Run the Jewels (!!), and Frank Ocean (!!!). I was so tempted, but I knew my head and my heart weren't ready for it yet.

Today, Albertine texted about a rambling, detail-laden email they'd received from someone named Kathleen, who said she'd been my partner several years ago. It took a moment to remember her, even though we were together for a couple of years. So much of my past—especially my pre-HRT past—feels blurry.

Kathleen was my second bona fide girlfriend, the woman I dated after Astrid. I met Kath in an acting class at a community centre. I'd thought studying acting might teach me how to pretend to be like other people. Maybe I'd find out what my motivation was. I was paired with Kath for a scéne from *A Midsummer Night's Dream*. It was a strange scene. Her character was pursuing me, telling me that I could treat her like a spaniel. That line is still clear in my mind. Maybe she said I could kick her like a sleeping dog and she would still adore me. I asked her if we should ask our acting teacher for a different scene. This one seemed sort of fucked up. But to her, the scene wasn't about sexism or misogyny. It was about that feeling of being willing to do anything for someone you love, that feeling of being completely smitten. We rehearsed the scene a few times in her apartment. She kissed me. We started dating. We became a couple. I still didn't know what I wanted, so I was swept into the undercurrent.

We moved in together. We read a lot of Shakespeare aloud, and Kath became fond of using Shakespearean expressions like "struth" and "zounds." She seemed so happy. I felt inert, like congealed bacon grease. *I guess this is life*, I thought. I knew she wanted to get engaged, so I proposed. She exploded with delight. I knew she wanted to get pregnant, but I knew there was some flaw in my genetic code, so I wavered. We got a cat, Snug. Then, we got a second cat, Puck. I'd been having tummy trouble for months. I went to a doctor. I cut caffeine. I swallowed barium and got X-rayed. I saw a gastroenterologist. Nothing helped.

One day I finally told Kath that I wasn't sure we should get married. We talked and talked. Kath sprang into action. She found me a therapist who helped dig me out of a snowdrift of bleakness and blankness. My tummy trouble went away. I started to feel things. Mostly, I felt sad. I ended things with Kath. I was a holding pattern. I was holding her back.

As Albertine promised, the message from Kath was long and meandering. She'd always wondered how I was doing, and one night she "googled the snot" out of me and discovered that her ex was now Tracy St. Cyr. (Mercifully, Kath avoided my deadname.) She listened to my music and said, "it flipped my wig." She wondered how I was doing and how I looked so young. She added, *Maybe I should ask my doc for some Sex and the City hormone therapy. You look good, girl!*

I started writing a reply. I wondered how much to tell her. I tried googling the snot out of her, but it didn't lead me anywhere interesting. I told her I'd travelled overseas to write songs for my next album, which was vaguely true. I tried a few times to throw in a Shakespeare reference, but it felt forced. I tried different ways of ending my message, finally settling on "Bye for now, Tracy." I added a PS and a PPS, but I deleted them and hit "Send." A brief opening gambit was best.

Later that night, I felt an urge to explain to Kath what had happened during the years we'd been out of contact. I started a note on my phone to trace the dots.

How I stumbled around in a fog of confusion for so many years.
How I broke this stasis by starting a PhD program in art history.
How I was going to study trans artists, including Sadie Tang.
How I dropped out after a couple years.
How my gender shit kept bubbling up.

How I got married.
How I eventually told my wife that maybe I was trans.
How she and a therapist convinced me that I wasn't.

How I stopped painting.
How I bounced aimlessly between jobs.
How I got really into hot yoga.
How I grew one denial beard after another.

How I picked up the guitar again when a friend invited me to jam.
How we started jamming every week.

How we started a band.

How it was so fucking fun.

How my wife discovered me wearing her vegan leather corset, liquid leggings, and too-tight ankle boots.

How she told me to choose between my "fetish" and her.

How I tried so hard to explain my gender stuff with metaphors—that it was like a heavy-duty girlish albatross or an atomic element (I think I called it "genderium") that seemed to weigh more than anything in the universe—but her eyes were awash in hostility and pity.

How I flashed on Sadie's trans friend Em and audiences in movie theatres howling at films with dudes in dresses.

How I couldn't imagine living that life.

How I said I was confused and ashamed.

How I chose my wife.

How I tried really fucking hard for a few years.

How I formed a new band and started writing songs.

How my band put out a few good albums and toured.

How I realized in a hotel room in San Francisco that I was trans and needed to transition.

How my wife exploded with rage when I told her.

How she said I was selfish and mentally ill.

How she kicked me out of our apartment and her life.

How I was alone and afraid.

How I found a "trans friendly" therapist who asked some fusty, fumbling questions.

How she referred me to an endocrinologist, and I got access to hormones.

How I found other trans women online and in my city.

How when they asked what my name was, I said, I'm Tracy.

How I transitioned in public, which super sucked.

How I went into hiding for a while.

How someone I loved melted my circuitry with an act of psychic warfare.

How I returned to this serpentine city.

How I wish I'd known who I was back when I knew her.

How I'm sorry that I asked her to marry me and then bailed on her.

How I hope Snug and Puck lived good lives.

How I hope she found someone who was good enough for her.

The next morning, I scrolled through my long-winded note. Melancholy washed over me. The trans lady doth protest too much. Let the past be the past. I deleted the note.

—

After being on HRT for a while, I started feeling strangely fecund. I felt like a piece of ripe fruit waiting to be plucked. It was bananas. I remember being on a great date and worrying that I might get pregnant when we fucked later. To be clear, I didn't even have a pussy at the time. But my body and my brain were sending me signals that I was super fucking fertile.

Even though I ache everywhere, I've been having that familiar fecund feeling lately. My body is a jukebox stuffed with Joy Division and Prince.

I wonder if this fecund feeling is my body's way of telling me it's time to start dating cute queers. Maybe that's yet another way I can let you go.

I just joined a few dating apps. Actually, I didn't join them so much as I reactivated my accounts. I changed the main snap on the apps to my cutest shaved head selfie. I made my second photo the one of me backstage, wearing that unbuttoned white dress shirt with my leather bondage harness (and tits) peeking through. (Yes, you took this photo after a gig in Portland, the one time you went on tour with us. As soon as I activated my profiles, I immediately blocked you. It's weird to be back on the dating app where we first connected.)

—

After breaking things off with Kathleen, I spent the rest of my twenties living with a string of different women. When I lived alone, I always spiralled, so I rarely lived alone. I sought out kind, bright women to keep me afloat. I pinned my hopes on finding stability through domesticity. It didn't work.

In my thirties, I went to grad school and became a slut. Mostly, I became a slut for boys because it was terribly easy. I knew what they wanted, and I gave it to them. It started simply enough. I gave a blow job in a bathroom stall at the grad school pub to a cute flannel-clad philosophy student with a wispy beard. Word spread, and things snowballed. Soon I was going down on random smart dudes in bathroom stalls, cars, and campus offices. My favourite was office sex. I drew the line at business and criminology students. I mean, we all need standards.

In retrospect, I wonder if I was using their cocks to scratch a girlish itch in my brain.

—

I keep flashing on all the small things that I miss. Your staccato laugh. The small of your back. The furnace of your body warming mine. You purring "I love you" before I sank into sleep. The tangle of marine life tattoos that cover so much of your body. Being beneath you or on top of you was like being in an aquarium, surrounded by octopuses, seahorses, seaweed, jellyfish, anemones, and starfish. It was like being in a bathysphere, your skin teeming with aquatic life.

You always wanted us to get matching tattoos, but I begged off. Not getting a tattoo is more rebellious than getting one, I argued. Plus, I knew you'd gotten matching tattoos with a couple of former partners. A butterfly and an umbrella.

You seem obsessed with bats, you said. I had a few books on bats, which you found adorable. Let's be hot bat girls together. Oh, let's get Meat Loaf motorcycle tattoos and be *Bat Out of Hell* girls together!

I laughed. I want you, I said. And I need you. But I'm never gonna let you tattoo me. Now two out of—

Aw, come on, you said. I want three out of three. Two out of three stinks. I want the jackpot. I want three cherries on the slot machine, baby. I want the whole enchilada. Oh, what about a taco tattoo right above your pretty pussy?

—

The first date I went on seemed promising. She worked in the arts and looked incredibly cute in her unicorn onesie selfie. We met in a park. Within five minutes, she said a recent lover had broken up with her because she "fucked them too good." Uh, what. She added, I fucked them how they wanted to be fucked, but they can't admit it yet. Oof.

My second date was studying to be a massage therapist. She'd recently started riding motorcycles, and her profile featured several snaps of her in leather. I was pining to meet her because we had plenty of textual chemistry. While messaging the night before our first date, I mentioned my almost Pavlovian reaction to hearing a lover say the word "cunt." It can make me quake like jelly. My phone started buzzing. I answered. It was my date. She said four words and hung up: Goodnight, cunt. Sleep tight. I was abuzz and barely slept. So far, so great.

As soon as we started walking down Glass Alley with our cups of coffee, she leaned in and told me she was trans. She didn't have a lot of trans friends. Actually, she had no trans friends. So, we talked a lot about being trans, which was dull. She was stealth, and she needed to process. I got it, but, gosh, that date was a slog. She was super cute and had good energy, so I was willing to get through this date to get to a place where she could dial down the trans talk. Maybe on our second date she could give me a massage, bang me out, and take me for a spin on her motorbike. Then, in the middle of one of her monologues, she misgendered me. That was the rotten cherry on the shit sundae. At that point, I begged off, wishing her good luck with her massage therapy and her motorbike.

For my third date, I met a cute enby for cocktails on the rooftop patio of a tall building. The clouds were billowy and beautiful. We talked about books and music. We had zero chemistry.

My fourth date was with a self-professed sexologist. Over bowls of ramen, she told me that she'd fucked trans women with pussies and trans women with penises. I slurped my noodles and broth, waiting for her to stop talking for a minute. She kept going. Sometimes, she said, I really wish I had a cock. That must be amazing. I blinked back. I sipped my green tea. She told me she once tried to write a novel about a trans character, but she got confused about the character's pronouns. When we were saying goodbye, she leaned in for a hug. I took a step back and said, Sorry, I don't feel like hugging right now. I half waved, turned, and walked away.

My fifth date was perfect. We met at a quaint coffee shop and had a great chat. Her name was Charlotte. I found myself tilting toward her. We walked to a nearby park, where a queer couple happened to be getting married. I told her all my dates so far had been a bit of a bust. That's too bad, she said. I hope you eventually meet someone you like. Oh, I said, I think you're pretty great. Same, she said. And you're cute as hell. She leaned in and kissed me. In the blink of an eye, our lips and tongues got to a place our words couldn't touch. After kissing, we exchanged that delicious look that says, "We're going to fuck later, and it is going to be spectacular." She pulled me toward her. I felt something inside me bloom as I nestled my head on her shoulder.

After we cuddled in the park, Charlotte led me to an art gallery that used to be a bank. She kept commenting on the frames they'd selected to display certain paintings. Good choice. Bad choice. Oh, worst choice.

Eventually, I asked, What's with the frames?

Oh, she said, I thought I told you. I work in a frame shop. It's my job to frame things.

Right, I said. Sorry. I think you told me in the coffee shop, but I was kinda dazzled by you.

Appropriately, the gallery housed its most pricey paintings inside the bank vault. I whispered to Charlotte, This makes so much sense, because art is basically money in a picture frame.

Yeah, she whispered back, don't forget the frame, baby. She kissed me, furtively touching her tongue to mine before pulling away.

In the room with safe deposit boxes, there were a few video installations, including Sadie Tang's piece *Detachable Penis*. I'd seen it only once before, at a retrospective of hers in New York. We were playing a couple of shows there and I went to the MoMA with the other members of Static Saints.

Sadie's piece was first shown in 1993, a year after King Missile's left-field alternative rock hit "Detachable Penis." It's a disposable song, but Sadie's playful video has stood the test of time. It features famous actors whose scenes from Hollywood films have been spliced to make them say things like, "It really floats my boat when I find a lover with a detachable penis" and "Would it be okay if I touch your detachable penis?" It also contains several clips from films of the late sixties and early seventies with split-screen sequences. In each of the scenes, one of the split-screen frames has been replaced with footage of a brightly coloured dildo. My favourite is the scene from *The Thomas Crown Affair*. There's something delightful about Steve McQueen smouldering on screen while an enormous bubble-gum pink double dong waggles beside his face, threatening to break the frame and tickle his square jaw.

While walking around in the former bank, I couldn't help remembering that on my first album, I'd included a song called "(Let's) Nationalize the Banks!" I debated whether or not to tell Charlotte that I was a semi-famous musician. Finally I decided to say nothing, because that knowledge can make people self-conscious around me. It can feel a little like I'm saying, Oh hey, just so you know, I'm kind of a big deal.

I haven't played "(Let's) Nationalize the Banks!" in years. The only song from that first album that I still break out at shows is "ACAB," which includes a rallying cry that audiences love to shout along to:

> All cats are beautiful!
> All cops are bastards!
> Cuddle the cats and fuck the cops!
> Cuddle the cats and FUCK THE COPS!!!

A few years ago, we played "ACAB" during an encore in Amsterdam. Halfway through the song, three girls stormed the stage in sexy latex cat costumes and led the audience in a drunken singalong of "Cuddle the cats and fuck the cops!" that kept going and going. At some point, the sexy latex cat girls started grinding on Cookie, Marta, and me. We all shared a look that said "holy fuck this is so weird and hot and rock and roll and super fucking gay." Eventually, I had to grab a mic and yell, "Thank you! We love you! Goodnight, Amsterdam!"

After leaving the art gallery, we ended up in a tiny restaurant tucked away in a courtyard. Charlotte seemed to know every nook and cranny in the city, which was exhilarating.

The name of this place, she said, translates to something like the "Slippery Pearl." It's a sexy name. This is an oyster bar for queers. You like oysters?

I love oysters. It seems like queer oyster bars are a thing here, I said, flashing on how I learned the art of oystering in another queer oyster bar a lifetime ago.

Yes, the queers here love oysters. Oyster bars are one of the main places where queer women cruise for sex. I can take you to a bar after that's another cruising place.

Sure, I said.

We had cocktails, oysters, and a fish dish that Charlotte liked. The fish was covered in basil and zucchini and swimming in a fragrant sauce. The servers at the Slippery Pearl seemed to know Charlotte quite well. She was a gifted flirter, straddling the delicate line between overt and covert flirting.

The next thing I knew, Charlotte and I were in a cab, groping each other and zooming out to the industrial part of town, beyond the Old Quarter. We stumbled out, smoothed our skirts, and walked into a gay bar with an English name: Kiss and Bang.

We ordered a couple of cocktails. Charlotte got a Blue Utopia, and I got a Fucking Utopia. Hers was blue; mine was pink. They tasted identical, so either they added artificial colouring to the basic Utopia cocktail, or we were already pretty drunk.

We sat on tall stools, sipped our drinks, and took in the room. Clusters of flirty, tipsy queers were scattered here and there—at the bar, at tall tables, and in booths. At a nearby booth, an androgynous babe with a smile as sharp as a dagger and tattoos swirling up and down both arms was fingering a red-headed femme in a silver dress and silver heels. The silver femme was arching her back and gripping the back of the booth. The androgynous babe was fucking her hard with two or three fingers, oblivious to the rest of the room. In another booth, a petite babe wearing pink knee pads and a pink leather collar was kneeling under the table, giving a slow, sensual blow job to a fat babe wearing horn-rimmed glasses, royal-purple lipstick, and a black latex bra. The fat babe was gripping her lover's ponytail like a handle, using it to guide her lover's mouth up and down, from her glistening head to the base of her shaft. There was a small puddle of drool on the floor.

This place is interesting, I said.

It has a good feeling, Charlotte said. She leaned over and kissed me hard. She cupped my throat with her hand. Is this okay? she asked. Yes, I said. So okay. My cunt ached. She slid her other hand under my skirt and cupped my pussy. It's good? she asked. Fuck yes, I said. It's good.

She leaned in and kissed one of my earlobes. So, she whispered, what do you want? She tightened her hand on my throat. I felt my brain sputtering. I wanted her fingers to fill me. I wanted her to choke me. I wanted to grind my cunt against her soft wet lips and tongue, cradling the base of her skull, until I came in her mouth. I wanted to bury my face in her cunt and make her body quiver with pleasure. I wanted to be her fucktoy. Then, I wanted her to be my fucktoy. And I wanted to ride the joy of that fucktoy tug-of-war until we'd both had our fill, until we were both spent and exhausted, two banged-out femme fountains overflowing with endorphins.

Can you, I said. Can you put your fingers in me?

Yes, she said, nodding. But I think you should be a good girl and take off your panties. She let go of my throat and my pussy.

I sipped my Fucking Utopia. Then, I stood up, pulled off my panties, and dropped them into my handbag. See, I said. I can be a very good girl. I took another sip of my cocktail.

Charlotte smiled and sipped her Blue Utopia. Then, she let some spit drip from between her lips onto her hand. I felt her wet fingers against the hood of my clit. One of her fingers slid into me, so slowly.

How is that? she asked. She was easing one finger in and out of me. It felt like another finger was nudging my clit.

That feels good, I said. Like, so, so good.

She grinned and lowered her stool.

That's so smart, I said. Adjustable stools. Nice.

Uh-huh, she said. So nice. She slid her finger all the way inside of me. Oh fuck.

Add another finger, I said.

She pulled out and slid two fingers into me, slowly and deeply. Stars flared behind my eyes. That Peaches song was playing, the one where she keeps saying she can't talk because some chick's dick is in her mouth. I glanced over at the fat babe whose dick was filling the knee-pad-clad babe's mouth. The fat babe seemed somehow regal. Maybe it was her royal-purple lipstick or how comfy she looked receiving pleasure, as though she were seated on a velvet throne while an eager-to-please lady-in-waiting gave her head. I looked down at Charlotte, who was grinning up at me, sliding her fingers in and out of my cunt.

My fingers like you, she said. Very much.

Uh-huh, I said.

She got off of her stool so she could fuck me from a better angle. She started fucking me a little quicker and a little harder.

That's, I said. Oh fuck. I felt myself being banged into oblivion. Her fingers were steadily nudging me up the roller coaster. I reached down and started rubbing my clit. After a while, I found myself at the top of the coaster, knowing I was going to come. I looked at her, felt everything widening and narrowing. Oh fuck, I said. And I tumbled down and came as she kept fucking me. Oh fuck, she said, echoing me. Her brow furrowed, and her eyes widened as she watched me come. She reached up to cup my throat. When I pulled my fingers away from my clit, she slowed to a stop and wiped her hands with a napkin.

She adjusted her stool to return to my height and then sipped her drink. That was fun! she said. I nodded, still catching my breath. I flapped my hand like I was fanning myself and smiled at her.

When I finish my drink, she said, I'd like to fuck you with my mouth. And then you can fuck me. Do you agree?

Yes, I said. I agree. I definitely agree.

We sipped our pink and blue cocktails. I noticed "Ponyboy" by SOPHIE was playing in the background. I asked Charlotte if she liked the song. She tilted her head and listened. It is a strange song, she said. It feels sexy and scary. I enjoy the metal elephant sound. Horses are a good subject for a song.

I tried to remember other songs about horses. "Wild Horses" by the Rolling Stones, of course. And "Swimming Horses" by Siouxsie and the Banshees. That was probably my favourite. It's hard to top Siouxsie Sioux singing about a guy giving birth to swimming horses. I made a mental note to google "best horse songs" later.

As soon as Charlotte finished her cocktail, she knelt in front of me. I hiked up my skirt for her.

A voice said, Can I get you another Fucking Utopia?

I turned toward the voice. It was a cute server with a long fringe of dark hair with faint streaks of pink sweeping across her face. I felt Charlotte kiss my cunt. I imagined our server on her knees in front of me.

Oh, I said. Maybe. Yeah. Please.

How about you?

The server was half bending to talk to Charlotte, who took her face out of my cunt. I will have a Fucking Utopia too, she said. Thanks. And can we get a pair of gloves? Large. And a bottle of lube. Medium. Thanks.

Cool, the cute server said. Very cool. She swept her dark hair away from her eyes and smiled widely. Back soon, she said. She carried our empty cocktail glasses away with her.

I felt Charlotte's lips and tongue on me again. She gripped my ass with one of her hands. I was flooded with warmth and desire and felt myself opening for her. I reached for the counter to steady myself on the stool. She must have been humming, because I could feel vibrations thrumming through me. She slid a finger into me, and it felt like she was making a come-hither gesture. It felt lovely. Her lips and tongue were on my clit. And that felt heavenly. I started to get worried, because sometimes it takes me a long time to come unless I use my own fingers.

I saw that the babe in knee pads was now rimming the regal babe, who appeared to be texting someone. Her phone case was the same colour as the waterslides I used to whip down as a kid. What shade was that? Baby blue? Faded blue? Powder blue? Suddenly, the regal fat babe looked up from her phone and saw me looking at her. She smiled widely, made an "okay" sign with her fingers, and nodded her head vigorously. I smiled back and made an "okay" gesture with my fingers. I felt energy spreading through my body, felt it flooding my arms and legs, felt it clearing my mind. Then, just like that, I felt myself on the cusp of coming. I grabbed the back of Charlotte's head, pushing her down onto me. I blinked wildly and looked up at the ceiling. I noticed a chandelier fashioned from dozens of empty wine bottles. The light shimmered. My body shimmered. I turned into something soft and billowy, like a cloud or a wisp of smoke. And then I was back in my body, back on that tall bar stool.

Out of the corner of my eye, I saw the regal babe grinning and clapping. She'd been watching me come. I blushed and shrugged. I felt a strange affinity. We were a couple of hot queer babes getting fucked by our hot queer lovers in a cozy queer oasis. I wanted to hug the regal babe. The knee-pad-clad babe was still worshipping her lover's ass with her tongue. I sort of wanted to take the kneeling babe's place. The regal babe was just so fucking hot. I wasn't even that into rimming, but she seemed greedy for pleasure, and I felt like she deserved to have her ass tongued anytime she wanted. She didn't look like a queen or a princess, but perhaps she was a countess or a baroness. Or maybe a duchess? Ah, that was it. The Duchess of Bodily Pleasure. I remembered that Bo Diddley's band in the late fifties or early sixties had included a girl named the Duchess who wore shiny, skin-tight clothes and played rhythm guitar. Maybe rock music and sex are both about finding pleasure in rhythm and repetition—being present in the moving moment.

Once I'd brought in a new song to the band, and Poe started playing a Bo Diddley beat. We just locked into a deep groove that felt somehow light and heavy. It was like sonic levitation. It was so rhythmic and repetitive, but with slight variation. Poe would ting-ting-ting the bell of her ride cymbal here, and Cookie would unfurl a slinky riff there. It had a hypnotic beauty. But when we tried to record the song in the studio, we couldn't capture that sense of defying gravity. We tried to reproduce the mercurial energy of the first time we played it. But all we caught on tape were faint fumes of that initial energy. It reminded me of a Replacements bootleg where Paul Westerberg stops the band midsong and says something like, "Someone on this stage is faking it. Maybe it's me. But it's not happening."

Our server materialized. She nodded at me and set down two pink cocktails, a pair of gloves, and a tube of lube. There you go, she said. Drinks, gloves, and lube. Is there anything else you need?

Thanks, I said. I think that's everything for now. Can we settle up when we leave?

Of course, she said. I haven't seen you here before.

This is my first time, I said. Just then I felt Charlotte's smooth, warm tongue sliding along the crack of my ass, easing into the opening, retreating, and licking up and down again.

It's nice to meet you, our server said. I hope you're enjoying yourself. She smiled and glanced down at Charlotte, whose face was buried in my ass. Then our server walked over to deliver fresh drinks to the booth with the androgynous babe and the silver femme, who had finished fucking and seemed to be arguing about something.

I tilted back on the stool slightly and tried to open my ass a bit more for Charlotte. I felt some vibrations inside me and guessed that she'd murmured uh-huh when I'd shifted in my stool to let her tongue go deeper. I looked down and saw that her skirt was hiked up and that she'd slipped her fingers under her panties to rub her clit. I watched the Duchess leaning back in her booth, sipping a cocktail and checking her phone while being rimmed. The phrase "plum bum" came to mind. Maybe it was because of the Duchess's purple lipstick and her ass. "Plum bum" was something I was taught in school, maybe in science class. I saw an image of a lead pipe. Oh right. *Plumbum* was the Latin name for lead. That's why Pb was its chemical symbol. I wondered how the Duchess's ass tasted. I wondered if she tasted like a salty plum, like umeboshi.

I looked up at the glass bottle chandelier again and felt Charlotte's tongue gliding inside me. It had been at least a few months since I'd felt that soothing sensation. I felt almost like I was floating. Above the chandelier, I spotted a few silver helium-filled balloons. I wondered how long they'd been up there. I looked over at the Duchess just as she was feeding the lady-in-waiting her cock again. She was saying something too. I didn't catch most of what she said, but I did hear the word for "more" a couple of times. I loved the idea of a lover simply saying "more" to communicate, What you're doing feels good, so you need to keep doing it to keep making me feel good. I wanted to be the one the Duchess was saying "more" to. I wanted to be the one drooling with her cock in my throat, feeling useful and used. The Duchess looked over at me and winked as she grabbed the kneeling babe's ponytail tightly with one of her fists. I smiled back and sipped my Fucking Utopia while I watched her guide her lady-in-waiting's mouth up and down, up and down, slower, faster, now even faster, smirking at me while she face-fucked her eager servant. There was a puddle of drool on the floor so large that our server had to put down a few paper towels to sop up some of it. For some reason, I remembered a couplet from our abandoned song with the Bo Diddley beat: "I swoop in quick / Like Marlene Dietrich." The Duchess of Pleasure had a Marlene Dietrich-ness to her. She had that power and assuredness. Unlike Marlene Dietrich, the Duchess also had a cute cock.

Truth be told, I miss having a cock sometimes. There's something so glorious about having this dowser wand of pleasure stemming from your body. And it spurts when you orgasm, which is rad. But, also, it kinda fucking sucks. If I could have a detachable penis, that would be perfect. Sure, a strap-on is a detachable penis, but sometimes it felt so good to have all that sensation, to feel myself throb with want and desire, to empty myself into a lover's mouth, to watch a lover swallow a mouthful of my cum. And my cock was kind of gorgeous. Just so pretty. Now the Duchess was looking at me, her face contorting as she came into her lover's mouth. A little of her cum burbled over the kneeling babe's lips and onto the floor. Then, the Duchess closed her eyes and let go of the ponytail.

Suddenly, Charlotte was standing beside me, wiping her hands and her face. She took a sip of her cocktail. She put her lips to my ear. You are still going to fuck me, right? she said.

I nodded enthusiastically. Yes, I said. I am down to clown.

She laughed. I don't know that expression. Down to clown? It sounds strange, no? Who wants to be fucked by a clown?

I laughed. Good point. Okay, I am down to fuck you. Very down.

Are you down to fist me? she asked.

I'm down, I said. But I've never fisted anybody before, so I kinda don't know what to do, exactly.

No problem, she said. I can show you. I need to pee. When I get back, I will teach you to fist me.

Okay, I said. I am down. Down to fist you like a rodeo clown.

You are weird, she said. Don't steal my drink, you hot fucking weirdo.

Our cute server appeared. These shots, she said, are for you and your friend. She put down two shot glasses. From your admirer over there, she added, gesturing to the Duchess. She was now sitting with her legs crossed, wearing a leopard-print silk blouse, her black leather skirt no longer hiked up to allow easy access to her regal asshole and cock. She looked as if she'd just arrived at the bar, her makeup immaculate. Her lover now looked surprisingly demure, her knee pads gone, yawning and leaning against the Duchess. The floor under them looked like it had just been polished. The Duchess gestured for me to come over. I thanked the server and walked over to the booth with one of the shot glasses.

Hi, said the Duchess. We wanted to say we have enjoyed sitting close to you. I like your shaved head very much. You have a nice skull. And you have amazing lips. Very sensual. Her sleepy lover nodded. Very good and very hot, she said.

Thanks, I said. I wondered if she was saying I had amazing lips because she wanted me to give her head. That was fun, I added.

Yes, very fun, agreed the Duchess. We are leaving now, but I would like to give you my telephone number. She paused. You can say no, if you want to say no.

Oh no, I said. That would be great. She told me her number. I texted her right away: *hi, it's Tracy :)*

Her phone pinged. I'm Tracy, I said aloud.

I'm Exie, she said. E-X-I-E. This is my friend Polly. Her lover blinked and nodded.

Exie raised her glass. Please drink your drink with us, she said. She smiled crookedly and gulped down her shot. I did the same, and so did Polly. It burned and tasted like licorice and gasoline.

I hope you and your friend have more fun, Exie said. She stood up, gave me a quick hug, and walked away. She smelled like licorice, sweat, and sperm. Polly waved as she walked past me.

As I watched them walk out of Kiss and Bang, I wanted Exie to turn back, to spit in my face and push me down on the ground, to take out her cock and say, More, I need more, then to turn me into a wanton thing, turn me into a drooling, greedy hole. I wanted her to debase me, to defile me, to come inside me, to come on my face and on my shaved head. I wanted her to make me her fuckdoll. And then I wanted her to get up and walk out the door when she was done using me, to leave me kneeling on the floor, drenched in cum, drool, and spit.

I walked back, climbed onto my tall stool, sipped my pink drink, and tried to lose myself in my phone.

—

When I was about ten years old, I found an abandoned doll in the woods near my house. It was a bit ratty, but I stuffed it into my backpack and sneaked it into my room. It smelled musty, but it could blink its dark-brown eyes, and it wore a fur coat. It was about two feet tall. I hid it under some blankets. For some reason, I kept thinking about this dark-eyed doll shitting in my mouth. Maybe I thought that I could prove to this doll that

I loved her by eating her shit. I remember wanting to do something for the doll to show that I could be useful, to show that I could worship her. After a long spell of spiralling down into this fantasy, I felt a surge of deep shame, because I knew something was wrong with my brain. I shoved the doll into my backpack and returned to the woods, where I buried her under a mound of dirt, rocks, and dead leaves. I had to bury her face down because I felt monstrous with her staring up at me.

—

I'm sorry it took so long, Charlotte said. There was a line. She kissed me. Her tongue tasted like peppermint and smoke.

How did you describe your pussy? she asked. I'm forgetting. Is it a handmade pussy?

I laughed. That's good, I said. I like the sound of handmade pussy. I think I called it a bespoke pussy. That's usually what I say. (I remember the first time I used that phrase. A lover said it sounded like I had a hipster pussy. After that, she sometimes called it my artisanal pussy, which made me laugh. One time after she gave me head, she said, Your snatch is so delish it could be an artisanal ice cream flavour. Gimme a waffle cone with two scoops of Trans Girl Rock Star Pussy, please. She was the same lover who once said, Every time you go down on a trans girl, an angel gets its wings. Too bad she moved to London.)

Bee-spoke, Charlotte said. That's right. This was a new word for me, so I had to look it up on my phone. I like your bee-spoke pussy. It means made by a tailor or a seamstress, right?

Yes, I said. Exactly. My bespoke pussy likes you too. Oh, I almost forgot. This is for you. I pointed to the remaining shot glass.

Thanks, she said, but I don't drink shots. She shrugged and handed me two black nitrile gloves. You can probably wear just one, she said.

Unless you want to double fist me. But maybe that's too advanced. Today is Fisting 101.

Fisting 101, I repeated. All I could think about was getting fucked by Exie. Now I had her number. I could text her tomorrow. I felt giddy. Time to get back to the present. Be mindful, Tracy. Get back inside your body. Time to learn how to fist. Good thing no one was watching. I looked around. There were still about a dozen people in Kiss and Bang.

Should we go to a booth? I asked.

Absolutely, Charlotte said. We grabbed our bags and drinks, and she led us to an empty booth. It was the same booth where Exie had just gotten sucked and rimmed. I gulped down the remaining shot of licorice and gasoline. I coughed.

Good girl, Charlotte said. Are you okay? I nodded, covering my mouth. I cleared my throat. I'm okay, I managed. Fisting 101.

I fitted my fingers into the black gloves. Are you ready? I asked. Uh-huh, she said. Very ready. I bent down and kissed her cunt. She grabbed the back of my head roughly and pulled me into her. I shivered. I still wasn't used to my shaved head being touched. I felt like a hot aging punk dyke and realized that maybe I was a hot aging punk dyke.

I pulled myself away from Charlotte's cunt, spat on my hand, and grinned up at her.

Okay, I said. Buckle up, fucktoy.

Her eyes lit up. You are so fucking hot, she said.

I laughed and said, I know, right?

I slid one of my fingers into her. It went in so easily that I slipped another finger in right away. I felt her opening up for me. I wanted to take one of her nipples in my mouth and realized that nobody in the space had their tits out.

So, I said to get Charlotte's attention. She looked down at me. So, nobody has their tits out. Is that not allowed here?

She looked down at my two fingers moving in and out of her cunt. Yes, she said. It is. Frowned on. Harder, please.

I fucked her a little harder and started rubbing my thumb against her clit. Do you want another finger? I asked.

Yes! Yesssss. Pleeease.

I added a third finger, bent down, and took her clit into my mouth. I thought about Exie splayed in the booth, using Polly's ponytail like a handle. I thought about Exie's cute cock filling my mouth. Charlotte gripped my head between her hands and pulled me toward her. Mm-hmm, I murmured. I started sucking her clit like it was a tiny cock. I kept giving her head and fucking her for what felt like a long time. I was doing my best to gulp air without breaking my rhythm, but it was tricky to keep it up. A snippet from a song floated into my mind: "I wanna see you / I wanna see you on a horse." I imagined Exie astride a horse, naked except for knee-high riding boots and a riding crop. Charlotte's legs started trembling, and she made a guttural noise that sounded like Fuck fuck ooooh fuuuuck. It was hard to tell because she'd started pulling on one of my ears. I felt another shiver down my spine as she ran one of her hands over my shaved head to the base of my skull.

I looked up at Charlotte. Her eyes were shut tight and her mouth was open. How are you doing up there? I asked.

I'm great! Wow wah wow wow.

Charlotte the Great, I said.

She laughed. I like it! she said. Charlotte the Great!

Would you like me to keep fucking you, Charlotte the Great?

Yes! Charlotte. The Great. Will teach you. How to make. Uhhh. Your fist. Disappear.

You look so good, I said. Do you want another finger?

Yes! But we need. Some lube.

I slid my fingers out of her. She looked down, slightly disappointed. I spurted some lube onto my gloved hand, spread it around, and slid two fingers back into her. They glided in easily. I added a third finger. Easy peasy, fresh and squeezy.

How's that? Do you want another finger?

So good! she said. Fuck. Yes, another. Finger.

I slid a fourth finger into her. There was a little resistance for a sec, and then she opened up. A lyric coming out of the speakers caught my attention. It was Janelle Monáe's "Make Me Feel." Until now, I hadn't realized that it echoed the final line of Eloise and Algy's "Deep Wound"—"You make me feel so fucking real." I wondered if I should put together a band and play a few shows here. I really missed performing.

Now, Charlotte said, now it gets tricky.

I stopped spacing out and got back in my body. Okay, I said. Tell me.

You do this, she said. She smooshed her fingers together so they all ended at the same spot. It looked like a duck bill. It was a shape I remembered making as a kid in a darkened room with a flashlight, casting a duck silhouette on the wall. You used the thumb as the bottom of the beak to make it talk.

Like a duck bill, I said.

Uh-huh.

You want me to fuck you with a duck bill. Got it.

But, she said, inside. Uh, fuck. Inside. You make a fist.

Oh, I said. How does that happen? How do I get inside?

Just … just keep fucking me.

I slid in my thumb and started fucking her with the duck bill. She bore down on my hand and started opening for me.

More lube, she said.

I slid my way out and spurted a lot of lube onto my hand. Added a little more for good measure. I worked my way from two fingers to three to four to the duck bill. Charlotte kept opening for me. My gloved fingers were in past my knuckles. I was disappearing into her. I was amazed and excited by how she kept opening and opening, how much of me she could take into her. I felt more pressure and felt myself being pulled, almost suctioned into her. I imagined a whirlpool or a black hole. Her pussy was greedy. Then, just like that, I felt her clamp down on my wrist.

What do I do now? I asked.

Tuck your thumb under and make a fist, someone said.

I turned. It was our server. Hi, she said. She tucked a few strands of pink-streaked hair behind her ear. Now you should fold your thumb under and make a fist. She demonstrated with her own hand. I moved my hand to make the shape our server was showing me. My entire fist was inside Charlotte. It was astonishing.

Oh, Charlotte said. Oh fuck.

Are you okay? I asked.

Uh-huh, she answered.

Do you want her to twist her wrist? our server asked Charlotte.

Yes! Twist!

I slowly twisted my wrist inside of her.

Oh fuck. That! That's good. I liiiiiike it.

For the next several minutes, our server gave me a hands-on crash course in Fisting 101. She kept checking in with Charlotte about what felt good for her and used that feedback to tailor how I fisted her. Our server would show me a technique with her own fist, and I would do the same thing inside of Charlotte. It was so fucking weird and hot. It was like she was using me to fist Charlotte, like I was her fisting marionette. And I was deeply into it. I found myself wondering if I was a latecomer to the fisting party. Had everyone else been doing it all along? It reminded me of when I was eighteen and my first girlfriend asked whether I'd be open to her fucking me in the ass with a strap-on. I was. Afterward, I wondered if all the girls were wearing harnesses to fuck their boyfriends in the ass. I sure hoped they were.

After a while, Charlotte said she'd had enough, which was for the best, because my hand was starting to tingle by then. Our server instructed me on how to smoothly work my fist out, get it back into the duck bill, and, finally, slide my hand out entirely. I kissed Charlotte and profusely thanked our server.

My pleasure, she said. I'm Nisha.

Nisha? She nodded. Nisha, I'm Tracy.

Hi, Tracy, she said. I have to get back to work. Sorry. She walked away with her drinks tray.

I dropped the gloves in a nearby wastebasket and came back to cuddle.

Oh. My. God, Charlotte said. You did a good job. You passed Fisting 101. She kissed me and put her head in my lap, sighing. I ran my fingers through her hair.

That was amazing, I said. Amazing and super weird. It was almost like Nisha was my fisting instructor. She was walking me through every step. You kind of stopped talking.

Oh yeah, Charlotte said, looking up at me. Sometimes that happens. It's a lot. Just so much. Nisha knows what she's doing. You had a good teacher. Wah wah wow. A really good teacher. I think Nisha might like you. She's a tiger in bed. If she wants to fuck you, you should for sure fuck her. My pussy is, um. She opened and closed her fingers a few times. It's going whoom, whoom, whoom.

Uh, maybe "pulsating"? I suggested. Or "throbbing"?

Yes! she said. Wah wah wow. She exhaled and closed her eyes. Good job. Good throb? I asked.

She opened her eyes and squinted up at me. You are a funny one, she said. You did a very good throb. I like your fingers in my hair. It is very calming. She closed her eyes and yawned. Wake me up, she said, sleepily, when you want to go-go, funny girl.

—

I wish that I could be fisted in my bespoke pussy. I remember joking about fisting with the nurses in Montreal after getting lower surgery.

But seriously, I said to one of the nurses at the table after breakfast, when can I get fisted? A couple of the other trans girls at the table tittered.

Never, said the nurse. It would be so dangerous.

Oh c'mon, I said, it's me. Didn't I get a special pussy, one that can take just a little fisting?

Whenever I brought up fisting, the nurses in Montreal were never amused, except Lulu, who turned everything into a joke.

Well, first, you could have the fist, she said, with her pronounced French Canadian accent. Then, you could have the fistula. She burst out laughing. Lulu looked nerdy and unassuming with her oversized glasses and her frizzy hair. But, somehow, the way she found delight in every small thing made her strangely alluring. I mean, she was always so playful and energetic that I could tell she would be incredibly fun to make out with.

I was always glad Lulu was the nurse who taught me to dilate. To put it inside, she said, you squeeze the lube on the tip, like ketchup on your fries. She squeezed a blob of lube on the head of the smallest dilator, the one that was azure blue. Maybe a little more, she said. We like a lot of ketchup on our fries. She cackled.

Then, she walked me through how to insert the dilator into my new pussy. She explained the correct angle for insertion and told me to change the angle once it was a little ways inside. I slowly slid it into me and adjusted the angle when it wanted to swerve inside my body. It hurt.

You are doing very good, she said. I felt proud, like I was an obedient puppy that had just learned to shake a paw. When you slide it in right to the top, she said, you make a little tap-tap. She quickly slapped two of her fingers against a balled-up fist to demonstrate. When it was in as far as it would go, I tapped the base of the dilator twice, as she'd shown. Tap-tap. I felt a jolt inside of myself. Ever since getting surgery, I'd been feeling occasional bursts of what I'd started calling "pussy static" as my nerve endings came back online in their new locations.

Excellent, Lulu said. You are a fast learner. She smiled. Now, she said, you must hold it for ten minutes. I reached over awkwardly, unlocked my phone, and started a timer.

As I held the dildo in place with my legs spread widely on the bed, Lulu launched into an enthusiastic discussion of her favourite glam metal bands. (At lunch the day before, I'd been the only trans girl who recognized the Accept song "Balls to the Wall," which Lulu had been singing while bopping around near the communal ice machine. While she namechecked long-forgotten glam bands like Slik Toxik and Harem Scarem, I couldn't help thinking "Balls to the Wall" was a hilarious choice for a nurse to sing in a recovery centre for trans women who'd just had vaginoplasty. As far as I knew, my balls were likely sitting on ice at a nearby university, waiting to be poked and prodded by med students.) Halfway through the ten minutes, Lulu got me to do another tap-tap to make sure the dilator hadn't started to slide out. Then, she chatted a little more about eighties glam metal until the timer on my phone finally dinged.

Now, you let it slide out, she said. You might have to be its little helper. A gentle little helper. It wants to come out. The dilator felt strange coming out of my body. I helped it gently and slowly. Caring for my tender pussy felt like tending to a newborn. I kept feeling like I might do the wrong thing and permanently fuck it up. Finally, the bright-blue plastic dilator slid out. I held it with the lube-drenched tip pointing at the ceiling. Careful where you put that thing, Lulu joked.

She handed me a paper towel. Now, she said, you wrap it with this to make a little burrito sandwich. I laughed. But her description was accurate. She watched as I wrapped the paper towel around it to make a lube-and-dildo burrito, which I then placed on the serving tray on the bedside table.

Good job, Lulu said. You get a gold star. Now you get to slide the green one right to the top.

—

I texted Exie: *hi, it's tracy again. do you wanna hang out sometime?*

I stared at my phone, willing her to ping me back immediately. Then, I turned off my ringer and tried to read. Every fifteen minutes or so, I kept checking to see if she'd replied.

A day later, there was still no reply. I checked to see if my message had been delivered. It had. Maybe she'd given me the wrong number. Although when I'd texted her in Kiss and Bang, I'd heard her phone ping.

After a few days, I deleted my message to Exie from my phone so I wouldn't have to be constantly reminded that she'd already lost interest in me.

—

Marta was the only member of the band who was into the Sun's Out, Guns Out tour.

Poe opted to wear a see-through bra, which was hot. She sulked behind the drum kit as usual. I could never tell where I stood with her. She's been in the band for four years now, and whenever I ask her what's wrong, her standard answer is invariably, No, it's fine. But she's a monster on drums. Plus, she's trans.

And Cookie really wasn't into my topless tour. I didn't understand her reticence until she finally illuminated me.

You're a baby queer white trans girl, she said. It's great that you like your tits. I'm a Black dyke. Sorry, but I'm not gonna play topless.

Cookie has always been the calm in the eye of the storm. When I told her I was transitioning, she didn't even seem surprised. She just said, That's it? I thought you were gonna tell me something bad, like you had six months to live. That's awesome. Let's jam.

Sometimes I get frustrated by her quietness. I remember once during a recording session, I literally said to her, Cookie, use your words. She shot back: Why? Everyone in the room laughed. She tends to communicate by doing things rather than saying them.

A week or so before we were slated to start the topless tour, Cookie arrived for practice wearing a leather jacket over a T-shirt with a black-and-white photo of breasts.

Cookie! I exclaimed. That's the best shirt!

I'm so tired of white tits, she said. All the shirts have white tits. I finally found a shirt with black breasts.

Thank you, I said. Thank you.

I'll rock a titty tee for you because I love you. You're welcome.

For most of that tour, Cookie played with her back to the audience, Jesus and Mary Chain-style. She'd occasionally spin around, and the audience would catch a glimpse of her T-shirt under her leather jacket, but mostly she faced away. At the time, I didn't get how hard that tour was for her. I thought she was being coy by facing away. But no, she was doing me a huge favour, doing something I had no right to ask her to do. It was unfair of me to ask her to make herself vulnerable like that. At the time, I couldn't see that, because I was too tangled up with being a wannabe slutty trans femme rock star.

It reminds me of when Lou Reed declared he was going to make his next tour the No Sunglasses Tour. His go-to guitar genius, Robert Quine, always wore sunglasses onstage, so really it was a dipshit alpha move to put Quine in his place. Essentially, it was the Fuck You, Robert Quine Tour. But Lou Reed was pretty shitty to lots of folks. He also turned down Robert Quine's guitar on his next album after Quine had crafted meticulous guitar parts to thread through Reed's songs. What a fucking prima donna.

I impulsively sent Cookie a text message. *I'm so sorry I asked you to play topless. That was really shitty of me.*

Only after I sent the text did I realize that we'd been out of contact for nearly six months. I missed having Cookie in my life.

I sent a second text: *I miss you, C.*

—

I met up with Nisha from Kiss and Bang at one of her favourite coffee shops. Her lipstick was the same shade as the pink streaks in her hair. The dark slant of hair falling across one of her eyes was almost identical to my first cut after transitioning. I'd brought in some photos and asked my stylist for something "very femme and very queer." After an hour or two of snipping, I looked like I was ready to audition for *The L Word* or to join a trans femme Tegan and Sara cover band. After a few months, I got a different cut because I felt strangely shy with that curtain of hair sweeping across my right eye.

Nisha got a chocolate eclair. I've never been an eclair girl, but I got one too, because her description of them sounded delicious. I sipped my cortado and watched her pick up her eclair. She surprised me by gently tonguing the hole where the eclair had been filled with vanilla cream. I'd never seen anyone go straight for the hole, even though it made so much sense. She looked back at me, shrugged, and put her tongue even deeper into the hole. Clearly, her angular queer hairdo (what my stylist called "the fringe") didn't make her shy.

After a minute, she put down the eclair. So, she said, what's your deal, Tracy? All I know about you is that you fuck on the first date. She raised her eyebrows and laughed.

She didn't seem to have any shame, which was incredibly hot. I was glad I'd brought my deluxe slut kit for my first date with her. I hadn't been on a first date with another trans girl for a while (aside from my fucked-up date with the stealth wannabe biker / wannabe therapist), and I'd forgotten how direct other trans women can be right off the bat sometimes. My idea of what constituted TMI had shifted drastically as soon as I found a clutch of other trans girls. Suddenly, I was being dished all sorts of dirt. I was there for most of it, but I drew the line at anything with an abundance of blood, puke, or shit. In the whirl of my transitioning cyclone, I didn't think too much of it. Later, I wondered if it flowed from all the shame we'd kept bottled inside for decades. It felt good to release some of that pent-up pressure in a form that felt safe.

True, I said. I don't know much about you either. I know you work at one of the best spots in the city for queer public sex. And I know you could teach Fisting 101.

She laughed. Oh, I could teach the advanced courses too.

194 HAZEL JANE PLANTE

Good to know, I said. Why aren't we fucking right now? I mean, you know that I fuck on the first date.

She laughed. Let me finish my eclair first, she said. I live upstairs. You can meet my cat, Coco.

—

After two long days, I heard back from Cookie.

That topless shit was weird, she texted, *but it's okay. All is forgiven, t.*

A few minutes later, she sent another message: *Here's my unreleased* JPN *solo* EP. And there was a link, which took me to a page with one line of text:

how do you like your dark-eyed girl now, Mister Death

I guessed that was the name of Cookie's EP. Below the text, there were five sound files.

It took me a moment to puzzle out "JPN." Ah, right. Japan. A year or so ago, she'd fallen for a hot architect named Tomoko and U-Hauled across the ocean to settle in Tokyo.

I downloaded the sound files and put on my headphones.

For the tour we did following the topless tour, I bought everyone custom tank tops. I'd flashed on the idea after getting a tank made for myself that was styled after the T-shirt Sadie Tang was wearing the first time I saw her:

trans

sexual

artist

Mine was similar, except that I opted for a black tank with white lettering in a German death metal font:

trans

sexual

musician

One of the tank tops Cookie got made said:

how do you like your

dark-eyed girl now

Mister Death

I remember thinking it sounded badass. And now it was going to be the title of her first solo release.

I was floored by Cookie's songs. She might be the only musical genius I know. When she left the band, I had to audition for a replacement guitarist to go on tour. Nobody could play Cookie's guitar parts like her. Some guitarists could approximate her style, but nobody could elevate the songs like her. Nobody had her tone. Nobody was as subtle. Nobody made her guitar parts feel effortless. For the tour, I hired a guitarist who played around her parts rather than trying to xerox them.

After spending a few days with Cookie's atmospheric, poignant EP on repeat, I finally messaged her:

Cookie! I adore your songs. I can't stop listening to them!

I've attached a song I wrote a few weeks ago called "Even Your Charms." The drummer is a sweet trans dude named Jay. I don't know if you know, but after I broke up with Johnny, she spiralled badly. Everything went sideways. Hayley is okay. I'm okay. But it got super scary. I left town. This song is a protection spell against exes. Love you! <3

t.

xx

—

I just came across an image of you holding "our cocktail" in "our restaurant" with your arm around a trans girl with blue hair. Your new girlfriend is also brandishing our cocktail. You look like a gorgeous raven-haired lumberjack in your pink-and-black flannel shirt.

Now, I'm blasting Beyoncé's "Freedom" from a Bluetooth speaker in my tiny apartment. I'm dancing. I'm crying. I needed to get free, so I cut myself loose and crossed the ocean. I'm free, but I'm finding it hard to let go of this sadness and anger.

I made an appointment to chat with my therapist.

—

When we went on tour the first time, I let myself be seduced by fans in different cities. Okay, sometimes I did the seducing. It's tricky to play a show and feel so dialled up afterward and be imbibing and flirting with a babe who loves your music and not feel like it's a great idea to go back to the hotel and fuck like tipsy bunnies. I gave head to a lot of cute fans, which probably wasn't what they were expecting. I rarely let them make me come. Often, they wanted to give me pleasure, but I just couldn't open myself up to them, and the ways they wanted to touch me were never the ways I wanted to be touched.

I was semi-famous for kissing fans during shows. Because I kissed across genders, I got a lot of flak online.

When our lives collided, I told you that I had other lovers. You said you might be okay with me seeing one other person, as long as you were my "primary partner." I'd been living on my own for a while at that point. I was my own person, but my heart tilted toward you. You wooed me openly and tenderly. I swooned. We nuzzled and toppled toward one another. I stopped having sex with other lovers. After a few months of intense dating, we moved in together.

I went on tour, and you asked me to stop kissing my fans. I acquiesced.

After I got back from Europe, my mom died unexpectedly, and you were there for me through the muck of that. It unearthed a lot of grimy memories. All of those memories had sharp edges. Every day, new stems would sprout, each one with thorns and thistles. I tried to trim them, but I needed help. You suggested that I see a therapist, and I finally found one who helped me through that rough patch. A while later, I realized during a session with my therapist that I felt smothered, that I needed to change the configuration of our relationship, that I needed to open things up. Eventually, that same therapist would help me recognize that I needed to disentangle myself from you for good.

I told you a few times that I was planning to get FFS. You always told me how much you loved my face, that you didn't want me to get surgery. You're already so pretty. I love how you look. You just didn't get it. And I didn't have the energy to delineate the differences between our lives.

When a rich fan offered to pay for my FFS, I took him up on it. You thought I didn't care about how you felt. You thought I was being selfish, that I was conforming to misogynistic beauty standards. I told you to fuck off.

You apologized. You came to Spain with me. You helped me through the recovery process. You said you loved me more than you'd ever loved anyone, that you'd always love me.

When we started dating, we had fantastic sex. I loved being your fucktoy. Over time, that initial intensity tapered into erratic bursts of erotic energy. To reconnect sexually, our therapist suggested we put it in the calendar. We scheduled sex for Saturday nights. Eventually, I started dating Hayley. You never wanted to hear her name or to know anything about my relationship with her. That was the only way you said it could work for you. You'd let me see her one night a week, as long as it was a weeknight. Tuesdays became my night with Hayley. So, I'd have sex dates on Tuesdays and Saturdays.

Several times after we fought, I'd return to the bedroom after my nighttime skin care routine to find you naked, your legs splayed and a pillow placed on the floor at the foot of the bed.

More than once, you literally said to me, This pussy isn't going to eat itself, baby girl.

Much to my chagrin, I immediately shifted into good girl mode and got you off with my mouth and fingers every time. I was such a sucker for your hot mean girl shtick.

—

On our first date, you fucked me with such tenderness and intensity. I came; then, I wept. You'd called yourself a tear goblin and pretended to gobble my teardrops. I stopped crying and melted into you. Nestled in your arms, I felt fluttery and cozy. You flashed me a dimpled smile and said, Tell me something you've never told anyone. Make me feel special. Right then, I decided to trust you, and I opened up about things I'd never shared with anyone. Years later, you used some of those things against me. I'd handed you a bejewelled dagger.

We live, we learn. We wrap our throbbing hearts in chain mail.

On our third date, you handed me a copy of *The Good Girl's Guide to Giving Bad Girls Great Head*. My skin prickled when I saw the book's title. I felt ashamed and aroused by your boldness. I studied that book. I learned a few things. I became such a good girl for you.

—

I never felt more protected out in the world than when I was with you. I remember one time a guy in a fedora murmured something shitty to me in that cocktail joint in Chinatown, and you had him thrown out. When the bartender told him he was eighty-sixed, Mr. Fedora yelled to get our attention. Hey you! You spun around, eyes ablaze. Hey yourself, you said. This is my girl. Talk to her again and I will gut you like a fish. The man muttered something and left. I'd seen you cold-cock a racist shithead at a protest. By that point, I'd also seen your collection of knives, a sight that had frightened and thrilled me. You'd grabbed a butterfly knife, spun it with your fingers, the blade whirling so quickly I was sure you'd cut yourself. I begged you to stop. You paused, looked up. Okay, you said. I'll put it to bed. You kissed the blade. Then, you whirled it for a moment and slid the knife back into place.

Your protectiveness started to slide into possessiveness. You were jealous of my past lovers, but you also seemed jealous of my friends and the members of my band. You started texting more frequently to check in on me, even though we kept a shared calendar. I started feeling guilty whenever I hung out without you. As soon as I arrived for band practice, I'd text you a snap of our jam space. Looking back, I guess I was sending you ocular proof: See, I'm not lying to you. I'm being a good girl. It felt like the walls were closing in.

Eventually, I realized I needed an exit strategy. I spent months talking to my therapist about how to break up with you as painlessly as possible. We talked through all the moves I could make. It was like thinking through an imaginary chess game. If I said this thing or did that thing, how would you react? There were endless options, but so many of them seemed likely to provoke a messy endgame. I needed to figure out how to gently lay down my queen and forfeit.

After we broke up, I felt like I could breathe deeply again. I was a falcon no longer tethered to her falconer. I found myself a bright two-bedroom apartment with hardwood floors. It was near the water, got plenty of light, and I could afford it. I hired movers and settled into my new place. You came by and said you were jealous, that I'd found the perfect apartment. You fucked me hard on my new bed. When I was on the cusp, you cupped my throat and told me to look into your eyes. I stared in your eyes and came and remembered how profoundly fragile and vulnerable you could be, remembered the soft, sad aspects of yourself that you shared with me but kept concealed from the wider world.

While you spooned me, I thought about how you'd patiently and lovingly helped map my bespoke body, lingering over my pleasure points with your mouth and fingers. At times, you made me feel like a glorious and holy thing. I'd become like the special drink you'd concocted when you fell for me: an ecstatic saint. I'd had sex with plenty of people before you, but none of them had co-written a user's manual for my body.

After a while, you asked if it would be okay if I made you come. I nodded and kissed you. You asked me to use my bare hands. You were greedy for pleasure. Afterward, you sprawled in my bed, looking spent and content. You said that we should stay lovers, that we had incredible chemistry, that there would always be something special between us, that you still loved me so much and would never do anything to hurt me.

We'd been living apart for a couple months and had settled into the friends-with-benefits phase of our relationship. Everything seemed okay. Then, I started seeing a tender sadist who left bruises on my body. The first time you saw marks on me left by another lover, you refused to touch me and sent me away. You later apologized by text with soft sentences and a few well-chosen emojis. You said you wanted to keep seeing me, but you wanted me to have "pristine tits" for you. I loved the idea of pristine tits (what a great name for a band!) and the ways you worshipped my tits, so I agreed. I messaged my tender sadist to say that from now on my tits were going to be off limits, but they could continue to smack me up and mark me up in other places. *Yes, of course,* they replied. *Only too happy to keep smacking you up and marking you up.* They added a sneering purple devil, their emoji of choice.

—

After I got FFS, you seemed less attracted to me. You started telling me which of my trans friends you thought were cute, which you'd seldom done before.

My gender dissonance, the reason I sometimes spat at my own reflection in the mirror, seemed to turn you on. That was hard for me.

I think your friend Clarice is into me, you said.

Why do you say that?

She kept locking eyes with me, you said. That thing you do when you like someone.

I don't think so, I said.

I dunno, you said. You should keep that one on a leash.

The truth was Clarice loathed you. She never thought you were good enough for me. We had a flirty friendship. I wasn't into her, but she dropped hints that she liked me. We made out on dance floors a few times, fuelled by BPM and MDMA, but that was it. I remember Clarice messaged me when she was applying to get vaginoplasty. She asked if I could send her a snap of my bespoke pussy. I did. She texted back, *Sweet snatch! It looks delicious.* She added a watering mouth emoji. I sent back a GIF of Hari Nef eating a peach. It was that kind of friendship. We were a couple of trans girls. NBD.

The day after you told me you thought she was into you, Clarice texted to say you were trying to connect with her on social media.

—

When we moved in together, I was surprised by the intensity of your periods. Until then, I'd never seen you waylaid by anything. But when your period arrived, it was so intense that you'd often spend entire days on the couch in your pyjamas, dampening the ache with a steady diet of bourbon, popcorn, and painkillers. Breakfast was always French toast. For lunch and dinner I'd try to make whatever you requested. Mostly, you asked for comfort foods that I assumed you'd had as a child: mac and cheese, chicken soup, shepherd's pie, and meatloaf.

And there was always TV, that ubiquitous anesthetic. You'd gorge yourself on shows from the seventies and eighties that we'd both grown up watching. You'd spit out the name of a show, and I'd be your obliging streaming DJ. In the early days, you tried to surprise me with obscure shows, but we'd both been TV babies, so nothing stumped me, aside from the odd regional show. We spent endless hours together watching grainy shows that sometimes activated vestigial memories in our brains.

WKRP in Cincinnati Silver Spoons Brady Bunch Punky Brewster Jeffersons Diff'rent Strokes Gilligan's Island Good Times Taxi B.J. and the Bear Sanford and Son Happy Days Love Boat Laverne & Shirley Magnum, P.I. ALF Hart to Hart Three's Company Fantasy Island Golden Girls Dukes of Hazzard Alice Gimme a Break! Bewitched Benson I Dream of Jeannie 227 Beachcombers King of Kensington Danger Bay Littlest Hobo Degrassi High A Different World Fraggle Rock Facts of Life 21 Jump Street Hortense in New York Growing Pains Red Dwarf Eight Is Enough A-Team Fall Guy Knight Rider Family Ties

Curled under the blankets with a hot water bottle or a heating pad, you occasionally showed glimpses of the girl you once were. I was astonished to discover you knew the words to every theme song. The show you kept returning to was *The Facts of Life*. I got it. I could imagine you as an angry, traumatized kid being dazzled by Jo, the motorcycle-riding tomboy.

For the first year or so, we'd cuddle and sink into those corny shows together. Over time, your snarky comments would sometimes turn toward me rather than the TV shows, especially after several drinks. It first escalated beyond isolated barbed words during *School's Out*, the controversial made-for-TV movie that concluded the *Degrassi High* series. You repeated Caitlin's infamous line to Joey: "You were fucking Tessa Campanelli?!" Then, you repeated variations on the line, inserting the names of everyone you thought I may have fucked. You were laughing like it was hilarious, but I could see the anger and anguish in your eyes.

And then I met your monster. You started screaming and throwing things at me. You don't love me! Why are you even with me? I tried to calm you and reassure you that I loved you, but you kept yelling at me. You think you're better than me, don't you? You're going to leave me for someone else, aren't you? My body started shaking. I found myself yelling back at you. It was like watching a car crash. I knew it was happening, but I couldn't stop it. Looking back, I can see that my monster came out to meet your monster. It emerged to protect me. It was like an inevitable battle in a superhero movie. Those scenes never make sense to me because of the frenetic editing and shifting angles. It's all too much. I get disoriented. And our fight was like that for me. I lost myself. Finally, I fled. I got an Uber and stayed the night at Clarice's place.

After that, your monster surfaced from time to time. I always tried to leave before my monster appeared to confront your monster. I often failed. My monster was so alert and protective.

—

Sometimes someone says something that shifts a shitty situation into an okay situation. My therapist just did that for me. I'm still dazed and amazed by how she did it.

I told her how bogged down I'd been feeling. She used terms I didn't feel comfortable using to describe what had happened. Harm. PTSD. Dissociation.

It's been a few months, I said. I just want to move on. I don't want to keep being walloped by panic. It's exhausting. I don't want to have her in my life anymore. I want her out of my head.

She is out of your life, she said. You might run into her, but she's not in your life any longer. But you're still left to deal with the aftermath of what she did. It will take time to heal. She's gone, but she left you with a wound. And sometimes your wound hurts. Sometimes it shakes and it cries. You need to tend to your wound. If you could talk to it, what would you say to your wound?

I was alone in my apartment, wearing headphones and talking to her pixelated face on my laptop. It was dark outside. I imagined cradling my wound, like it was a fussy baby swaddled in a blanket. I'm feeling a lot right now, I said. I think I would say to my wound, I see you. I feel a little silly. Okay, I'd say that I see you. I know you're there. I can take care of you. I can be gentle and patient and help you heal. It's going to be okay.

It is going to be okay. You're healing, Tracy. Being gentle and patient with yourself sounds wonderful.

—

Cookie isn't much of a texter, so I was surprised to find two messages from her when I awoke.

Her first text may have been one of the longest she's ever sent me: *Even your charms is razor sharp! I'm sorry you went through that. Glad you're coming out the other end, tho. And I'm so pleased you like my instrumentals.* Thirty minutes later, she'd texted: *I'm here if you need to talk. I love you, t.*

—

I couldn't go out last night. I was smacked by sorrow, so I stayed in to care for my wound, soothing her until she became still and silent. *It's okay, baby girl*, I thought. *I see you.* I fed her a pint of sour cherry ice cream, and we watched a saccharine romantic comedy about a bank teller who falls for a jewel thief.

—

Sometimes I worry about how cis women will react to my pussy, I said.

Oh? Nisha asked. Did some cis girl complain about your pussy or something?

I shook my head. For some reason, I felt like I might cry, so I stared ahead at the *Kiki's Delivery Service* poster on her wall. It showed Kiki and her black cat Jiji riding a broomstick above the rooftops of a coastal town. The poster was in a bright-red frame, which foregrounded the red bow in Kiki's hair. I remembered Charlotte saying a frame shapes how you see the work.

Nah, bitch, Nisha said. Your pussy is great. I might even like it better than I like my own. And your clit is perfect. It's like a Goldilocks clit.

I laughed. Nobody's ever said that to me before. Your clit isn't too shabby either.

She laughed. I do okay. Look at us with our Goldilocks clits. Lots of cis women would fill wheelbarrows with cash to get magical pussies like ours.

I can see a team of Scrooge McDuck soccer moms, I said. Their wheelbarrows are overflowing with gold doubloons. They are—

Nisha put her finger to my lips. Shhh, she said. You are too funny for your own good. I want to give you a blow job. Is that okay? I nodded. I got weak in the knees when she said "blow job."

She took her finger from my lips and reached down to cup my cunt. All my thoughts evaporated. She got her fingers wet and started moving them in circles around my clit. She was humming a song. After a while, I recognized it as "Half a Person" by the Smiths. I heard Morrissey's voice in my head, singing from the POV of an introverted girl hoping to become a back scrubber at the YWCA. For a moment, I felt the emotional dissonance of a hot brown trans girl moving her fingers against my clit while humming a song sung decades ago by a racist twat. Then, Nisha started moving her fingers more quickly, and I lost the thread of the song. She kept humming as she lowered herself to the floor and slid a finger into me. She got me to scooch a titch and knelt to put her vibrating lips on my pussy.

—

I've been listening to Cookie's instrumental tracks endlessly, and I found words coming to me for one of them. It's called "Late Spring" and sounds like Jesus and Mary Chain meets Galaxie 500.

During one part of the song, I flashed on the tide pools I used to visit as a kid. I remembered driving with my dad to the beach and spending hours transfixed by the sea creatures in those tiny pools. I found myself singing the line, "I see the tide pools in your eyes" over Cookie's shimmering chords. It sounded strange, but also sort of beautiful. Like gazing into a lover's eyes and seeing a small universe there. Tide pools are really their own tiny worlds. Sequestered. They don't last forever, because the waves crash onto them, or they dry up. But there's something about their temporariness that makes them special. This watery world shall pass, but it's gorgeous while it lasts.

I stretched out the word "see," so I was singing, "I see-eee-eee the tide pools in your eyes." My voice would waver on the second and third "eee," and that wavering felt right.

On my laptop, I broke the three different sections of her song into separate files. Then, I made loops for the parts so they could play endlessly while I found words for them.

I looped a fuzzy, chiming riff. I let myself drift. I knew the narrator for this song had been through some shit. Like Britney Spears. Like me. I jotted down a number of things she might have put behind her, things she'd weathered to get to a place where she could lose herself in her lover's eyes. Tsunamis. Dust clouds. Wildfires. Tiger traps. I sang, "I see the tiger trap behind me," with Cookie's ringing chords. I tried a handful of different things and finally settled on four things she'd put behind her before reaching those calm tide pools:

> I see the tiger trap behind me
> I see the broken jaw behind me
> I see the crashing waves behind me
> I see the dust and ash behind me

They were things that were broken or that could break you. For the next part, I sang, "I see the tide pools in your eyes." I felt something ache in my core. Maybe it was the wound. This song almost felt like a healing spell for my wound. I'd been broken, but I was opening up again, somehow.

After singing "I see the tide pools in your eyes" a few times, I wanted something about being broken and being open. I played the loop for the third guitar part. It had three chords and felt inviting and spacious, like a room with a vaulted ceiling. I heard myself singing, "I am broken," with the first chord. For the next two chords, I sang "broken open" twice.

> I am broken
> Broken open
> Broken open

I sat there stunned, because it felt like the song had tumbled out of me painlessly. I was broken, but I was unbowed. And now there was beauty sprouting. "Even Your Charms" had a defiance that I loved, but this song was profoundly vulnerable. I'd never written such an honest, unadorned song before. I tend to obscure my meanings.

Now I wanted a second verse for the fuzzy Jesus and Mary Chain chord loop. It should be about feeling tender, wounded, and wanted. The next four lines gushed out of me almost fully formed.

I feel a tenderness inside me
I feel a wound healing inside me
I feel you deep and warm inside me
I feel you rough and soft inside me

And, like that, I had a song. I called it "Broken Open." It felt softer and rawer than anything I'd ever written. I made a lo-fi recording of me singing "Broken Open," over Cookie's chiming, ethereal chords.

I put my guitar back in its case, climbed into bed, and held myself. I felt my body relax while I sobbed. Something inside of me, something delicate and fractured, was mending.

—

Nisha had other lovers and her own life, which was perfect for me. She seemed to know everyone and introduced me to a bunch of cool trans folks, including another lover of hers, Luna.

I met Luna for our first date in a coffee shop. Our chemistry was frothy as fuck. Her goofy, toppy energy undid me. Before long, we were back at her place, our clothing strewn on the floor from her front door to her bedroom. Before I knew it, I felt myself opening up to her as she eased a finger into me, felt her stroking me inside, felt myself start to pulsate with want.

I felt swoony, like a chaste woman in a Victorian novel being seduced by a mysterious stranger with a crooked smile and a sultry voice. She kissed a tingly spot near my ear. She said softly and slowly, How do you want me to fuck you?

I settled back into myself. Oh, I said. Well, um, how would you feel about wearing a harness?

I feel good about it, but I am not sure how my aubergine will feel. Let me see the harness.

She'd already told me she wanted me to refer to her genitals as her aubergine. Another lover had come up with the term, and she adored it. What's not to love about the slippery, soft sound of the French word for eggplant?

She slid her finger out of me, and I dug out my leather harness, along with a dildo.

I totally get it if this doesn't work for you or your aubergine, I said. My harness can be a bit fiddly, but it's pretty good for all sorts of anatomies. We'll see. And this. This is a special dildo. It comes from a mould of my aubergine before I got a pussy.

Are you serious?! I love that!

I had an artist friend make a mould, and I got a bunch of them made up. It's cool, right?

Wow! Now I really want to fuck you with it.

Luna stepped into the harness and started cinching the straps. This was clearly not her first strap-on rodeo. Her rounded tummy looked really hot above the leather straps and the dildo. She used one of her fingers to pull down the head of the dildo before letting it go. It sprang up, and she laughed. Boing! she said. The harness feels good.

She went down on me for a while before kneeling and resting the head of the dil against my pussy. How's this? she asked. I nodded enthusiastically, grinding myself against her. Do you want some lube? I shook my head. She laughed. Yeah, she said, you seem pretty wet.

I was getting impatient to be fucked. I said, Can you just, uh—

I felt her sliding in and filling me. Oh fuck. I felt myself opening up for her. She pinned my hands above my head. I felt her weight as she started moving inside me. Oh goddamn, oh fucking goddamn. I adjusted myself so she could fuck me a bit deeper. I wrapped my legs around hers. She let go of my hands, held herself aloft, somehow managed to take one of my nipples into her mouth and bite me gently. I imagined her standing in front of me, imagined kissing her aubergine from its base to its head, imagined taking it into my mouth, sliding my tongue along the underside to that soft, sensitive spot near the head. I reached down and applied a little pressure to my clit with my middle finger and started toggling back and forth, back and forth. Oh fuck, oh fuck. Luna started fucking me harder. I looked up and saw her grinning down at me. I pulled her on top of me so I could feel her weight bearing down on me as I came.

Afterward, she undid the straps and dropped the harness and dildo on the floor. I did all the work, she said, so I think you can wash that. I laughed. I can do that, I said. Can you hold me now? I pressed my back up against her and she spooned me, cupping one of my breasts. I loved that, I said. She dotted my back with kisses. Mmm-hmm, she murmured.

What can I do for you? I asked. What would feel good for you? I turned my head slightly to try to make eye contact.

Sometimes I like being muffed, she said. I can do it to myself or you can help, if you want.

Oh right. Yeah, I'm down to help. I turned on my side to face her. You'll have to remind me. It's been a while.

She rolled onto her back. I watched as she slowly slid a finger into one of her sockets. She started moving her finger. She moaned. Parts of my brain lit up. I'd fucked myself that way sometimes and had taught a few lovers how to muff me. I distantly remembered there was often a mixture of pain and pleasure that came from being fucked in my sockets. But I'd also derived a distinct trans femme joy from being penetrated there. I remembered one cis femme in particular who had a "holy fuck this is so amazing and hot" response when I showed her how to finger my sockets.

Luna slid her finger out and asked me if I was game to try fingering both her holes.

Yes! I said. I'm in. Or I'll be in soon. I laughed.

Sometimes you are funny, she said.

She talked me through it as I fitted my fingers into the sockets on either side of her aubergine.

Oh, that's good, she said. Just. Uh-huh.

It was coming back to me. Like riding a bike, except with orifices and orgasms.

Hey, I said, where are you? Are you in your body?

Yes, I'm here, Luna said.

Oh good. This is nice.

We were spooning. She was small spoon, even though she had a few inches on me. I kept glancing down at the stray hair spilling out of her armpit. It reminded me of the cover for Patti Smith's *Easter*, where she's raising one of her arms to reveal a small nest of hair in her armpit. In retrospect, that's the one spot where I regret getting laser, because a thatch of armpit hair on a woman is actually really hot. It offsets the softness.

Luna squeezed my hand, which was cupping one of her breasts, and pushed her ass against me.

I feel super calm here with you, I said. All soft and shimmery.

Yes, she said. So nice. I think I snore.

Oh okay. Me too. I kissed her shoulder. I think I do too. At least that's what I've heard.

—

For a long time, I hated the bits of my body that signalled I wasn't cis. I didn't want to be visibly trans. I didn't want thick fingers. (When I get my nails done, I'm invariably told that I'm lucky to have wide nail beds. Yay, me.) I didn't want to have broad shoulders. I didn't want to be over six feet tall. I didn't want to have scars on my vulva.

Lately, I'm occasionally happy that some of the history of my body is visible. It's like how I love being in an art gallery that used to be a bank. It's so fucking cool to glimpse parts of a structure's past peeping into the present, like a palimpsest.

For short-lived spells, I'm able to see my body like that.

—

Earth to Tracy, Nisha said.

Sorry, what?

I asked if you knew Bailey Jay, she said. She's a white trans girl. She does porn.

Oh right. Yeah, kind of. Not personally. Why?

I was just thinking about something she tweeted, Nisha said. She said how much CBT had helped her. And then she had a follow-up tweet explaining that when she said CBT, she meant cognitive behavioural therapy, not cock and ball torture.

I laughed. Wow, so random. Why were you thinking about that?

I'm not sure. Maybe because we were talking about trauma earlier.

Oh right.

I think she also said that if cock and ball torture helped other people, that was cool, but it wasn't the kind of CBT that worked magic for her.

That was good of her, I said.

Nisha's phone made a sonar ping. She reached over and silenced it. Oh damn, she said. Do you want to go bowling?

Like, right now? I said.

Yeah, I'm supposed to go bowling soon. You made me lose track of time.

Oh, got it. I dunno. I'm not very good at bowling.

I'm surprised, because you're so good at putting your fingers into holes. She wiggled one of her fingers and giggled.

Pah-toom-paaah!

Is that a drum sound? Like a rim job?

Rim shot?

Oh right. Rim shot. What did I say? Rim job? She cackled. If you want to come bowling, you're invited. Luna will be there. I'm not sure if it would be weird, because I know the two of you are fucking. It wouldn't be weird for me. It's mostly trans women and a few cool queers.

How long have you been bowling?

A few years. I got really into it when I got sober. Everybody in my bowling circle is pretty much sober. I'm not trying to convert you. But if you come, it would be cool if you don't drink alcohol. Mostly, we drink soda and gossip.

Nisha introduced me to a dozen or so queer hipsters in rented bowling shoes. I noticed a few of her friends exchanging looks that I decoded as, "Oh, so that's who Nisha's been fucking lately." Luna gave me a hug.

We settled into a low-key bowling routine—mingle, chat, flirt, sip some rhubarb soda, take a turn throwing a bowling ball, chat and flirt some more—and I found that I loved the easy camaraderie of being among some of Nisha's friends. I let my guard down. It reminded me of relaxing my limbs and letting myself float on my back in a swimming pool.

At some point, I found myself sitting beside Luna. It's good to see you, she said. Today has been a bad day. She nuzzled up next to me.

I put my arm around her and pulled her close. Aw, I'm sorry it's been a crappy day, I said. Do you wanna talk about it or just be quiet and sit together for a while?

My head is booming, so quiet, please.

Okay, I said. I kissed her cheek and the back of her neck and held her. I saw Nisha looking over at us, smiling. She touched her hand to her heart. She pointed and mouthed the words, "So cute." I nodded.

Two older women walked by, and I noticed one of them was staring at me. She looked a bit like Catherine Keener, but her angrier sister. She curled her lip and slowly shook her head. I've received similar looks countless times, mostly from older women. It's what I've come to think of as gender skepticism. She wanted to telegraph that she didn't see me as a woman. I felt something surge in me. I smiled back at her and slowly nodded. She rolled her eyes and turned her head. I watched her and her friend return their bowling shoes. Then, I watched their floral muumuus drift out the front door. I squeezed Luna and said, I love you, friend. She smiled and said, I love you too. Can you get me a root beer? I laughed and went to get her a root beer.

—

After I broke things off, you sent me a link to a playlist. You wrote, *These are the songs I cry to since you busted my bloody heart.* The playlist was called "Tracy is a heartbreaker," followed by three emojis: broken heart, broken heart, broken heart.

It stung, because I knew it was true. I was a heartbreaker. I'd been told that for years. I loved you and tried to make a life with you. Your love for me was heavier than I could handle. It was like tungsten or mercury. The weight of my love for you had less and less gravity. At first, it was quite heavy, like silver or tin. Back then, the scales almost balanced. We were somewhat centred. The teeter-totter didn't topple. When I started to drift, my heart became zinc or copper. I needed to be around other elements. Later, I was like sulphur, then neon, and, finally, oxygen. I needed to breathe. I'm sorry, but I needed to be free. In the end, my oxygenated heart broke your mercurial heart. No, by then, you'd also drifted, especially after I got FFS. By the time I broke it, your heart was cobalt or krypton. But its relative weight didn't really soften the blow. Your heart still broke.

And now, many months later, I'm listening to the opening track on your heartbreaker playlist on repeat. "Motion Sickness" by Phoebe Bridgers. Its opening couplet encapsulates the tug-of-war of opposing emotions I feel for you: "I hate you for what you did / And I miss you like a little kid." It's strange that the same song can resonate for both of us. You hate me because I broke your heart, because I drifted away from you, because I fucked other people. I hate you because of how you broke my brain that night, because you seemed so blasé and remorseless afterward, because you wanted to make me suffer. But you miss me. And I miss you. And today, I feel sucky, like a little kid.

After spending years with someone, how do you scrub them from the memories of things you did together while you were tethered, while they were beside you, in your head, in your heart, the entire time? So, yes, I hate you and I miss you. And I wonder if you're listening to this Phoebe Bridgers song right now, like I am.

I messaged Luna: *Can I come over and cuddle?* I added three emojis: spoon, spoon, spoon.

—

Violet, the first woman I lived with after transitioning, also told me I was a heartbreaker. I remember she got so drunk at our "we are shacking up" housewarming party that she could barely stand. She wobbled up to me in her kitten heels and leaned on me. I dubbed her the Leaning Tower of Violet. A few people in the circle around us laughed, and she thought I was making fun of her. Violet said to someone I used to date, She's with me now. She loves me. My ex looked away. Please be nice, Vi, I said to her. I am nice, Violet said. I am nice like sugar and spice. I apologized to my ex and tried to steer Violet toward our bedroom. She fucks me now, Violet blurted. Only me! Then, she bolted down the hall and puked in the sink. She had chunks in her hair, and her breath smelled noxious and sour.

I cleaned up her face and pulled her into the bedroom. I'm sorry, she said. I fucked up. Promise you won't fuck anyone else tonight. Please don't break my heart. You can fuck me. Just wake me up. Anytime. Do you promise? I nodded. Pretty please, she said. Don't break my heart. Yes, I said. I promise. I kissed her forehead, took off her dress, folded it carefully. It would need to be washed soon so it wouldn't stain. Goodnight, I said. She was already zonked on her pillow, her arms folded across her chest, sleeping the way she said she'd slept since she was small, the way Hollywood vampires sleep in their coffins.

After a couple more drinks, I broke my promise to Violet and went down on my ex, the one she'd yelled at. I knew that was what would happen if I kept drinking, but I let it happen. I was a shitty girlfriend, especially when I was drunk. And Johnny was blind drunk the night she turned everything upside down. Maybe my sober lovers, Nisha and Luna, were onto something.

—

I go for a brisk walk nearly every morning. Most days I trace a rectangular route through the alleys. Occasionally, I let my curiosity sway me this way or that, a caffeinated zigzag wanderer, letting myself get lost in the labyrinth. At the end of my walk, I often linger on one of the gleaming benches in Silver Park, which is humble and comfy with slender trees always full of starlings. Starlings are vicious birds, but I love the iridescent sheen of their feathers. Their nasty reputation doesn't stop me from being beguiled by their beauty. I wonder if they've evolved to make themselves more attractive to humans. I've always wondered the same thing about squirrels, with their bushy tails. You take away those tails, and they're like little rats. But those poofy tails make us ooh and aah and throw them snacks.

—

Today, after some encouragement from Nisha, I posted an ad on a queer personals app:

TRY A LITTLE TENDER FIST

Me: Playful, tender + cute white low-femme trans babe with a good-sized fist.

You: Cute, drama-free + very into being fisted.

I'm into other things, but lately fisting is my jam.

An hour or so after I posted the ad, Nisha messaged me: *Don't keep me in suspense. Who's the lucky queer you're fisting tonight?*
A handful of people have liked my ad, but nobody has messaged me yet.
Nisha: *A handful! Love it!* She added a light-brown fist emoji.

Haha. But, seriously, what gives. Should I start messaging people who liked it?

Wait and see if some eager beaver messages you first. She added two emojis: a white bunny and a toothy beaver.

I messaged Nisha: *I'm on my way to drink some tea, eat some pie, and maybe fist some guy.*

Nisha: *Fuck yeah! You buried the lead, girl.*

Me: Shrug emoji.

Her: *They serve pie in Fist City?!? Send the address and text me when you get there.*

—

Hey, are you Dex? I'm Tracy.

He stood and gave me an awkwardish hug across the small table.

Can I wet your whistle? he asked.

Uh, what?

Can I get you a drink? Do you like tea?

Yeah, but I can get my own.

No, it's okay. Please let me. I got here early, and my teapot is almost empty. You like oolong?

Uh, sure.

And how about pie? Their cherry pie is to die for. Wanna split a piece?

Uh, yeah, sure. Thanks.

Dex was back in a couple of minutes with a white teapot dressed in a Hello Kitty tea cozy. He set it down on the small table. Be right back, he said. He left again, returning a moment later with two small cups, two forks, and a slice of cherry pie.

Thanks, I said. What is this place? Is this where you take all the trans girls?

He laughed. Yeah, it's definitely a hit with the transes. My friend Barker runs it. Do you know Barker? I shook my head. It's the kind of business only a trans guy who's just started shooting T would have the balls to open.

Okay, so, your pal Barker started a tea shop called t4t, which is a genius name. Dex nodded and leaned in to pour us both some tea. How have I never heard of it before? I'm super fucking trans. Like really, really trans.

Yeah, I'm sure you are. I'm not gonna lie, you look. What can I say? He paused. I blinked. You don't look super trans to me. Is it okay if I say you're passable? Does that sound weird? I don't wanna be weird.

You're fucking weird, dude, I said. But, yeah, I guess that's okay to say. It makes me feel a bit embarrassed, because I'm lucky and I had FFS and I'm white and yada yada. Whatever. You also don't look super trans. You look good, though. So, there's that.

He laughed, rolled up his sleeves, and grabbed a fork. He pointed its tines at the cherry pie. You first, he said.

Oh, what am I? Your royal taster? Ist thine poisoner still on the loose, my lord?

On the loose. Gotta love those Elizabethan phrases.

I rolled my eyes and sampled the cherry pie. It was flaky, gooey, and delicious.

Holy fuck, I said. He nodded, a sly smile filling his face. That's some really good cherry pie.

He took a forkful and closed his eyes to chew it. Finally, he opened them. So scrummy, he said.

Shit, that's what I should have said. What did I say? Holy fuck? I laughed. So, this place has killer cherry pie and every type of tea you—

The peanut butter chocolate pie, he said, might be even better.

I frowned. Can I finish talking now, sir?

Fuck, sorry, he said.

Just joshing you, I said. Well, mostly joshing you. You look like a Josh. Sure your name is Dex? Anyway, as I was saying. What was I saying? I spotted a TCB lightning bolt tattoo on his forearm. No wonder he liked that peanut butter chocolate pie. Elvis, huh? I said. He reddened. So, anyway, this place is all t4t with its tea and its pie, but it also sells, like, packers and dildos and floggers. Was that your friend—what's his name again? Brock? Brockton?

Barker.

Right, Barker. Was that Barker's original idea? A tea shop that caters to trans folks, so you can get a slice of pie, a pot of oolong tea, a riding crop, a clit sucker, and a bottle of lube?

Yeah, that's Barker's kajillion-dollar idea. The rent here is dirt cheap. It's hard to find. If I hadn't told you exactly how to get here, I don't think you'd have found it. So, it's really by word of mouth, almost like it's by invitation only, like a speakeasy or something. Knock three times and say "my father is a pencil" and abracadabra, open sesame.

Dex was right, I'd needed his detailed instructions to find t4t. Even as I'd walked into a dark side alley that branched off Glass Alley, checking twice that it was "between a fire hydrant and a phone booth," I wasn't sure that I was going the right way. There were scattered bicycles, someone selling pottery on a blanket, a couple of kids skipping rope, and then, as the note said, there was a spiral staircase with a small sign above it adorned with four blue teapots. I'd climbed the stairs and found the shop.

My phone pinged. Fuck, right. I needed to text Nisha to tell her I was okay. Sorry, I said to Dex. I sent Nisha a quick text: *Sorry!!! I'm good. Pie is great! Dex is hot as hell.*

I put my phone down. Sorry, I said again. My phone pinged. Fuck. I turned off the ringer.

Dex warned me that he had a slobbery St. Bernard at home. I said it was fine. Then, I went back to his place and, oh yes, his oversized dog was a slobbering mess.

He gave the dog a toy that looked like a disembowelled rag doll. That's his fave, Dex said. Isn't it, Anders?

What kind of name is Anders?

He's named after Anders Andersson, he said. Lionel is a huge fan. (Lionel was Dex's partner, who would be at work for a few more hours.)

I don't know who that is, I said.

Anders Andersson was a trans guy who lived like two hundred years ago in Copenhagen. You know that movie *Amadeus*?

Yeah, sure, I said.

Well, Dex said, Anders Andersson was like Salieri to Kierkegaard's Mozart. He was a philosopher, and apparently he wrote some stuff Kierkegaard copied or something. I don't know and I don't care. There's a world of people online who live for that shit. Lionel studied philosophy before he became a butcher, so I let him name our slobber-puss. Right, Anders? No, stay there, boy. All I know is Kierkegaard was an odd duck. And Anders was also really weird. For being a trans guy, it sounds like he was also a real pussy hound.

Did he say "pussy hound," Anders?

Anders eyed me, the rag doll still in his mouth. He looked up at Dex expectantly.

Uh-oh, Dex said. Is that okay? Did I fuck up by saying "pussy hound"?

Nah, it's cute when you say it.

Oh good. I thought I blew it with that. I don't know how you're feeling about things, but I can put up the baby gate and close the door so he won't come in the bedroom. If you want to fool around.

Yeah, I'd like that, I said.

He walked over to me. I was a few inches taller than him. Can I kiss you? Suddenly, he seemed like a timid boy, even though I got the sense that he hooked up with folks regularly, based on the quick rundown we'd done while walking back to his place.

After making out for a bit, he asked if I still wanted to fuck him. He was smirking, all his timidness gone. Uh-huh, I said. He could tell how much I wanted to fuck him. When we were in his room, he opened the curtains, and light spilled in from the huge window.

Can you make a fist for me? he asked. I did. He stared at my balled-up fist. I looked at the huge shadow it made on the wall behind us. God, he said. You have a beautiful fist.

—

Johnny keeps bubbling back into my mind. It's maddening because I don't want to be with her. My memories before I transitioned are quite hazy. They seem indistinct, like they're behind a thin fabric. If I concentrate, I can make out the shapes. But things after I transitioned are just crisper. It's not that they're better; they're just clearer. It's like watching a VHS tape with wonky tracking versus a brand new Blu-ray. I spent the lion's share of my post-transition life with Johnny, so it makes sense that she'd be hard to shake. My sense of time is haywire. The time before I transitioned feels collapsed, and the years since I transitioned feel elongated. So, Johnny's shadow looms larger than it should. A brain is a mysterious machine.

—

After visiting Dex, I found myself writing a song about a jilted woman who finds out her ex now has a St. Bernard.

I jotted down a few lines that came to me:

I heard you've got a St. Bernard
I feed a stray in my backyard
Living alone ain't that hard

I like songs where the listener knows more than the narrator. Here, I could tell the girl singing the song didn't like living alone. And there's a competitiveness to the second line, Oh yeah, I feed a stray in my backyard. It took me a while to find the next line, but when I did, I felt that "oh gosh yes" feeling in my tummy: "Abstract pain is avant-garde." I loved how it suggested both abstract painting and masochism.

I put a capo on the second fret of my guitar and fumbled around with chords, finally locating a simple chord progression: Bm D A E. This felt like the chorus.

For some reason, I flashed on the moment when I'd felt sure I was trans. I was in a hotel room in San Francisco, and the light was creeping in through the blackout curtains. I saw the dress I'd been wearing alone in my room the night before draped across a chair. That memory brought me back to Dex's bedroom and the moment when sunlight flooded into the room. I saw the shadow of my fist on the wall.

I found two chords that chimed nicely and felt bright and open, and then I added in a couple chords from the chorus, D and Bm, throwing in a Bm7 at the end to give it a little less resolution.

I sang a couple of lines that floated out smoothly:

Someone said you moved to San Francisco
Or maybe they said Los Angeles

I liked the way the narrator suggests that she doesn't even remember where her ex moved. It was a game of deception. All smog and mirrors.

I super don't care, she seemed to say. San Francisco, LA, whatever, it's all good. I hated the narrator, but I loved her at the same time. She'd clearly had her heart handed to her. Thinking about the names of the cities and the sunshine and shadows I'd seen earlier, I found the next couple lines:

> It was a city of saints or angels
> It was a city of sun and shadows

Now, I was at the point where I didn't want to fuck it up. Sometimes you can tell something is special, that you're really just a vessel for this special thing to come into existence. I didn't feel smart enough to write the lines that were coming to me. It was almost like I was picking up a faint radio signal from a parallel universe.

I popped across the street to the coffee shop and got a cortado and a croissant, perfect rocket fuel for songwriting. The sun had just set, and the sky was fairly glowing. Magic hour. I looked down at the silver cobblestones in the alley, which were refracting the buttery light.

When I got back to my apartment, I tried to pick up where I'd left off. All my phrases felt flat, so I gave up. I made some pasta. I tried to watch a movie. I kept pausing it and strumming chords. I mumbled some words, hoping to stumble on the right ones. I found a few okay lines, but nothing that really sang. Finally, I went to bed. Lying in the dark, words kept tumbling in my head, like the numbers on a combination lock. Eventually, I knew I had the next four lines. I turned on the light, threw on a T-shirt dress, and grabbed my guitar. I quietly sang the song from the start, went into my new lines, and moved into the chorus.

Someone said you moved to San Francisco
Or maybe they said Los Angeles
It was a city of saints or angels
It was a city of sun and shadows
I get lost in jump-cuts and magic hours
I get lost in a haze of whiskey sours
You left and I forgot where I was from
Your name's still tattooed on my arm

I heard you've got a St. Bernard
I feed a stray in my backyard
Living alone ain't that hard
Abstract pain is avant-garde
I heard you've got a St. Bernard

It was suddenly about cinema and how time moves. Then, it was about
drinking to tamp down the feeling of being left behind. I felt a pang at
the sad detail that she still had her lover's name tattooed on her arm. I
remembered a lover telling me she'd briefly dated a guy who always wore
a bandage on one of his forearms. She thought he had a cut that wouldn't
heal until she discovered the bandage was there to cover a blue-green
tattoo of another woman's name.

It was nearly 1 a.m. I didn't want anything to fade before I could capture it, so I set up a mic and made a very rough recording, singing softly
and strumming my unplugged guitar.

I turned out the light. Before I could drift off, a few more lines tumbled
out that I knew would go in the song somewhere, maybe at the very end:

The past fades like a postcard
You busted up my bloody heart
I need a locksmith for my heart
Maybe I should get a St. Bernard
Maybe I should get a St. Bernard

—

The next morning, I added a few more lines and a Sonic Youth–like guitar break after the verse, which gave the simple chords in the chorus even more springiness. I recorded a rough version and listened to it on my headphones. I badly wanted Cookie to add some of her guitar magic. Fuck it. I sent her a WAV file with the following message:

Hi, C!

I wrote a song called "St. Bernard" and I still don't know where it came from. It seems beyond my ability. Maybe I accidentally stepped into a parallel universe. I have no fucking idea. It's a long shot, but how would you feel about adding some witchy guitar magic? I'm thinking Rowland S. Howard meets Mary Timony, which feels right in your wheelhouse. No problem if you don't wanna add anything.

I'm also attaching a song called "Broken Open." I've been listening to your EP constantly, and the words for this track tumbled out one day. I've been hesitant to share it with anyone because it feels so raw and open hearted. I hope you don't mind that I sang over your song. For some reason, we never tried writing that way before. I really like it.

I miss playing with you so fucking much. I'm sorry I fucked shit up between us.

t.

xx

—

There's a new barista at the coffee shop near my apartment. She has no idea how to make a cortado. I switch my order to a latte whenever she's working, because her cortado technique is terrible. Even her lattes are below average. I kept wondering how she gets away with being so bad at what she does, until I realized that it's likely because she is achingly gorgeous.

I wonder if I would have done anything creative if I'd been a cis woman with a stunning face, the kind of face that makes everyone want to be you or fuck you or both. I honestly don't know. But I do remember the first time a stranger told me I was beautiful after I transitioned. I was standing at a crosswalk, waiting for the walk signal. I was on my way to see my electrologist, so I hadn't shaved for a few days and wasn't wearing makeup. A woman beside me said, This is strange to say to a stranger, but I find you really beautiful. I looked at her. She was in her early thirties with wavy blond hair and exuded a laid-back granola vibe. I didn't know what to say. I wasn't sure if she was flirting or sharing an elliptical "trans women are women" message. The traffic light changed, and we parted ways. I felt briefly elated. While waiting for my electrologist, it dawned on me that any time a cis person said I was pretty, my brain would automatically attach an asterisk to their compliment to qualify, "for a trans woman."

—

I finally received a text from Cookie: *I'm out of town with my hot gf, but I love your two songs! They might be the best ones you have ever written. I love what you did with my music, t! You made me cry.* She added a black heart emoji.

—

Albertine forwarded an email with the subject line *Film Soundtrack Query*, adding, *I thought you might want to see this. :)*

It was an invitation from Kit Gloves to write a song for the end credits of his next film. I'd become an overnight fan of his work after Marta took me to a midnight screening of his gay cult classic *Piss Night in Malmö*. The theatre was crackling with energy. As the lights dimmed, Marta stage-whispered, *I hope you're ready.* The film started, and the crowd roared. I still think the opening credits for *Piss Night in Malmö* might be the best I've ever seen. In a stylized blur, we watch a cavalcade of giddy queer misfits piss on each other in slow motion, perfectly choreographed to the fiery instrumental number "Rat Fink a Boo-Boo," by the Swedish garage punk band the Nomads. Piss play is not my cup of tea, but Kit Gloves somehow makes it strangely joyous and marvellously perverse. Marta never tires of quoting that film's final line: "At least we'll always have Piss Night in Malmö."

In his message, Kit Gloves explained that he's filming an adaptation of *All the Pretty Ghosts*, a novel by a trans woman named Cirrostratus. I was intrigued, so I went online. The extracts from her book seemed rad, but I kept wondering who the fuck she was. The image on her website was a drawing of a ghost, and her bio simply said, "Cirrostratus is just another pretty ghost who wants to stay in the shadows." I certainly understood why a trans girl would want to stay out of the limelight. The problem was that fuckers would crawl out of the woodwork and turn over every stone imaginable to try to find out who she was. And even if that didn't happen, there would likely be story after story speculating on her identity. She'd become the trans Elena Ferrante. I wished Cirrostratus luck in staying hidden.

Kit Gloves also wants *All the Pretty Ghosts* to feature a song I wrote in a fit of swoon called "All of the Above." I haven't played that one live for over a year, even though it's the sort of ninety-second bonbon crowds love. The last time I played it at a show, it felt like I was acting. Those emotions faded long ago. But I love the idea of reclaiming the song. And I love the idea of it appearing in a film by a trans filmmaker based on a novel by a trans writer.

I'm glad to see Kit Gloves is making films again. He vanished from the public eye after being besieged online for saying that Michael Cera playing Chelsea Manning is as fucked up as Tom Hanks playing Barack Obama.

—

Ping! I looked at the text message: *This is not a test. This is a booty call. I want your fist inside me* NOW. R U *in?* The message was followed by a string of emojis: glitter, a boxing glove, stars, and a dancing cat. Ah, Charlotte.

We'd had two more thrilling dates after Kiss and Bang, followed by weeks of radio silence. I'd just flossed, brushed my teeth, washed my face, and moisturized. It was already past my bedtime. I didn't want to see her.

Things are dropping off with Dex too. He's sweet and hot, but I'm tired of filling him with my fingers. Maybe I've had my fisting fix for the time being.

Fucking Charlotte. I debated leaving her hanging. She had some nerve. But she went after what she wanted, which was to bang oodles of randos. That was her call. Rather than turn into a pretty ghost, I shot her a quick reply to let her know she'd have to find another fist. Impulsively, I also sent her three identical emojis: ghost, ghost, ghost.

—

I got an email today from a girl I used to know from a support group. It was a group email with a link to a GoFundMe. I clicked on the link, and it was for a fundraiser called Goodbye to Goldie. It looked like Goldie, a girl we knew from group, had died a few weeks earlier, and now people were raising money to have a farewell picnic. Fuck fuck fuck. I'm not on social media, so news reaches me slowly.

Goldie was a boisterous peroxide-blond trans girl who worked in a trendy clothing store. I remember one time she showed up at group with a stuffed kangaroo. As ever, we went around the room, giving brief updates on our "gender journeys." When it was Goldie's turn, she introduced us to her kangaroo. This is Matilda, she said. I named her after a movie with a boxing kangaroo. I'm feeling low today, and she always lifts my mood. Then, Goldie said, almost offhandedly, that she'd noticed herself lactating a bit lately. A few girls snapped their fingers. I quipped that her body was probably trying to make food for Matilda. Everyone laughed, and Goldie flashed a sheepish smile. Liz reminded me of our "no talking during gender journeys" rule, and I apologized. But I still remember Goldie's face beaming that day. And now she's gone.

I spent some time searching for information and images online, but there wasn't much. Goldie's social media accounts were all private. Her profile pictures were all the same close-up of her flipping the bird, her fingernails painted in black shellac polish and her hands in black finger-less gloves adorned with white skulls.

I messaged my friend from group, and she confirmed that it was suicide. Fuck fuck fuck. I wasn't surprised, just stunned and sad. Like many people in my life, especially trans women, Goldie had felt like she was deeply fucked up and unlovable. "Broken" was a word Goldie had used a lot. Men had broken her. Meth had broken her. I try to do what I can to keep other trans girls alive, but I've never known how to help mend them. I can barely tend to myself. I felt awful that I'd rarely offered to hang with Goldie outside of group, aside from the one time we got our eyebrows threaded together. Afterward, we went for coffee, and her phone kept pinging. When I asked her about it, she said her "beau" was being a "dinkwad" (her words). She was one of those people with their own vocabulary. She silenced her phone and said we should connect on social media. I told her that I avoided social media, that when I'd joined briefly it felt like it was siphoning my brain. That's real, she said, laughing. Fuck, Goldie.

I messaged Clarice about Goldie. After texting for a while, I had to say goodbye because my vision was too blurry and my brain was spent.

I crawled into bed and hugged a pillow.

When my body felt somewhat still, I messaged Nisha to see if I could sleep over.

I spent the next few days in a haze. I spooned with Luna and pretzelled with Nisha. When stray song lyrics came to me, I jotted them down like a stoned stenographer. I let myself be held.

—

Goldie's death kept bringing me back to that awful night.

It all happened so suddenly. You were in my apartment. I'd forgotten you still had a key, Johnny. I'd always seen you as powerful and protective, like a mama bear. I loved your beautiful broad shoulders. Now you seemed distant and diminished. A mess of rage and sorrow in motorcycle boots, swaying in the doorway. You'd chipped one of your front teeth since the last time I saw you.

Your bloodshot eyes swung from me to Hayley and back to me. You looked wounded and woozy, like a grizzly hit by a tranquilizer dart.

You were trembling. You don't get to forget me, you said. I won't let you forget me.

Then.

A glint of silver. Your beloved butterfly knife.

I hurt too much, you said.

An awful smear of red.

I watched in disbelief and horror as you took a seam ripper to the fabric of your body.

My heart fell out of me.

My mind swam away from me.

You'd done the unthinkable. You punched a hole in the cosmos.

The next fifteen minutes felt like fifteen hours or fifteen seconds.

Time expanded and collapsed.

I plunged to the bottom of the ocean, where everything was muffled, murky, and unreal.

I watched myself screaming, sobbing, and pleading.

I watched myself try to staunch the red smear.

A cry of sirens shocked me back into myself. Emergency vehicles.

You once said I was a siren, luring queer sailors with my songs. One of your signature cocktails was called a Shattered Sailor on the Rocks.

Lights strobed through the windows. A swell of footsteps and voices. People in the room.

Everything was blurry. My nose was runny. I was holding Hayley, or she was holding me. Someone was asking questions, and I was trying to answer them. I was choking on my tears. I had no good answers. Nothing made sense. It felt like I had the flu or heat stroke.

The next week was like a time loop or a broken record. Your bloodshot eyes, your quivering voice, your chipped tooth, and your rage and sorrow were etched into the grooves of my mind.

After a few days, my brain understood that all three of us were okay, that the hole in the cosmos had been hastily patched with superglue. But my body didn't understand. It kept getting stuck in those endless, unfathomable fifteen minutes. I kept wanting to go back and ease your pain, to reassure you that I still loved you, that I'd never forget you. But I couldn't undo anything.

—

At first, Hayley said she was okay. Then, she stopped replying to my text messages. I tried calling, but it always went to voice mail. At some point, my texts stopped being delivered, so she must have blocked me. I asked several mutuals about it, but they said they didn't know anything. Finally, a friend of Hayley's messaged to assure me that she was doing okay— *There are rough patches*, they clarified, *but she's mostly okay*—and that she needed time and space to heal. I understood. That's when I realized that

I couldn't stay in the same city as you, Johnny. I needed to go to another city, any other city, to put space between us. I needed distance to feel safe.

—

LUNA TOLD ME THAT MAGRITTE, the person at the front door to the club we were waiting to enter, was legendary for looking at someone and simply saying, Not today. This was how she rejected people. I looked up the place on my phone. It was called Medicine Ball, so I assumed it used to be a pharmacy or a health clinic. Nearly every review mentioned Magritte. The place had only five-star reviews and one-star reviews, the latter mostly written by people who had been turned away at the door. The best five-star review I saw was by someone who had been rejected: "As soon as Magritte looked at me, I knew she could see into my soul. 'Not today,' she said. And I knew she was right. 'Thank you,' I said. She nodded."

We'll get in, Nisha said. No doubt at all.

I wasn't worried about being turned away, because Jay said we could come in through the side door to the club. But I was curious what Magritte would make of me. When I made my way to the front, she simply said, Welcome, and waved me in.

Nisha led Luna and me over to the bar. She leaned in and said something to the bartender. He pulled three glass bottles out of a cooler. The bartender grinned at us and yelled something that I didn't understand. Nish rolled her eyes and laughed. She said something back to him, shrugged, and dropped a few bills on the counter. She turned and handed Luna and me our rhubarb sodas. We clinked glasses and sipped.

What did you say to each other? I said in her ear.

He said, "I like transsexuals." He's always been a creepy person. I said to him, Not today.

I heard my own voice coming through the speakers. It was a cover of "Lola" we'd recorded with an adrenalized version of Robyn Hitchcock's "Sometimes I Wish I Was a Pretty Girl" on the B-side. I'd released that single a couple years before I transitioned.

I spotted Sam and Jay. They were both DJing in sparring headgear. And right then, I realized where I was. It was the same club where I'd seen Algy and Eloise play in a boxing ring. The punching bags had been removed, but it looked like the same chains were now being used to suspend a constellation of twirling mirror balls. I wished I could message Algy and Eloise and tell them where I was and let them know that Blood Moon had changed my life. I wondered what their lives were like now. I think Algy grew up in Chiang Mai, so maybe that was where they were.

Great jumpsuit! Sam yelled in my ear. I smiled, and we hugged. I was wearing a blue jumpsuit covered in white seahorses. She yelled something else, but I missed most of it as Against Me! kicked into their blistering cover of "The Crying Game." I furrowed my brow. Sam put her mouth against my ear and said, I used to play in a band called the Sea Whores! W-H-O-R-E-S! We were all trans and we all did sex work! You should have seen us! We were good!

When she pressed against me, I could feel her hardness against my thigh. I felt my cunt flutter. Sam's sparring headgear gave her a butch swagger. I imagined her cock rubbing against the opening of my cunt, up and down, brushing against my clit as I got wetter, making me wait before she eventually eased me open and filled me.

I put my mouth to her ear. I really wish I'd seen you! I said. Are you and Jay co-DJs? Do you have DJ names?

She pointed to a little flyer tacked on the side of the sound booth. I'm DJ Salinger! He's DJ Daugherty! I nodded. Feeling her cock against my thigh was driving me bananas.

A couple minutes later, Jay came bopping over, banging his head as Cheech and Chong's "Earache My Eye" came blaring out of the speakers. He leaned in and said something to Sam, who nodded vigorously. Jay grabbed me by the arm and pulled me away from Sam. I waved at Luna and Nisha as I walked past them. Be back soon! I yelled. They both gave me slow royal waves. I followed Jay through a blue door. As soon as the door closed behind us, things got quieter. My ears still felt muffled. I was glad I'd worn earplugs. Playing live had done a number on me, and I wanted to retain whatever hearing remained.

It's so good to see you, Jay said. He gave me a hug.

Same, I said. How are you?

I'm great. You're playing with us tonight, right? Like, you're still down to play a couple songs?

Yes, I said. It's gonna be fun! I haven't played for so long. Does your band know the songs?

He nodded. They're really excited. Would it be cool if we go back and I introduce you to them?

Lead the way, I said.

While Jay's band played, I stood with Luna and Nisha near Sam, who was the show's sound engineer. Emeralds for Eyes sounded like atmospheric garage rock. They were swampy, simple, and spacious. When I'd asked them before the show to describe their music, their bass player Fang had said, We're like the Cramps making out with the Yeah Yeah Yeahs. And he wasn't wrong. Their singer, Sandy, had charisma to burn. He reminded me of some rare footage I'd seen of Tomata du Plenty, the jittery, wide-eyed singer for the criminally underappreciated San Francisco electro punk band the Screamers.

We're going to do something a little risky tonight, Sandy said into the mic. I made my way to the side of the stage. This is Tracy, he said, making a game show "look what prize we have for you" gesture with his entire arm. I climbed onstage. She plays in a band called Static Saints. People made some noise. I waved and walked up to one of the mics.

Sandy knocked out the opening chords to Alice Cooper's proto-trans anthem "Is It My Body" on his Gibson SG. I'd never played with a band composed entirely of trans guys before. I was awash in a sea of testosterone, but I felt comfy. Everyone had their tops off, including Jay, and I'd have been tempted to join them if I hadn't been wearing a jumpsuit. I sang the opening lines to my two lovers near the soundboard. Nish had her arm around Luna, and they were swaying. At some point, I started singing to the band, especially Jay, who was killing it on the drums. I gave Sandy a look and tilted my head to let him know he should hop on a mic and sing with me. I was Karen O to his Lux Interior.

Toward the end of the song, he slung his Gibson SG behind his back and stuffed his microphone into his leather pants, which was hot and hilarious. And, of course, I took the bait and knelt down to sing into his crotch. I could only keep it up for a line or two before I burst out laughing. Sandy whipped out his microphone, and the band finished the song. There was a whoosh of applause, and I got up to give Sandy a hug. That was great, he said in my ear.

He tucked the mic back into its stand. Apparently, he said into the mic, looking over at me, it was my body after all.

I laughed and adjusted the guitar strap on the red Fender Mustang they'd lent me for the gig. I plugged in, turned up the volume, and strummed. It sounded right. I checked the tuning and the pedals. All good.

We're gonna play a song I've never played live before, I said. It's a protection spell against exes. It's called "Even Your Charms."

As Jay promised, the band knew the song like they'd written it. I didn't play guitar at all for the verses, letting the bass and drums carry me along in their undertow. Sandy picked up on what I wanted and stuck to playing root notes for the verses.

> Dark clouds are gathered at my door
> Seems like you wanna go to war
> But I don't love you anymore
> No, I don't love you anymore

Then, I unfurled those fat barre chords for the main refrain, hearing Sandy and Jay's voices merge with mine:

> Even your charms can't hold me now
> Even your charms can't hold me now
> Even your charms can't hold me now

I looked over at Jay, and emotions welled up inside me. He blinked and nodded. He knew. As we played the first tense instrumental bridge with its coiled major and seventh chords, I let some anger and grief spill out. Yes, it was an ex hex, but it was also an ode to autonomy.

> Do I have to spell it out?
> Just keep my name out of your mouth

Do I have to spell it out?
Just keep my name out of your mouth

Even your charms can't hold me now
Even your charms can't hold me now
Even your charms can't hold me now

Sandy, Jay, and Fang all joined me for the incantatory bridge:

This is an ex hex
This is an ex hex
A spell to protect us
And make you stay away

And now their voices dropped out and it was just mine, pushing you away, expelling you with my words, with all the life in my lungs.

Stay away
Stay away
Stay away

I hope you're okay. I want you to be healed and happy. I don't want to hurt you. You've been hurt enough. I want to steer clear, because you tore a hole in me that's proving hard to repair. I deserve to be safe.

I let the music take over for a few seconds and stepped back from the mic. I looked over at Jay. He was watching me. I gestured to lower the energy a little. He did.

We hadn't discussed how to end the song. I started singing, "Even your charms can't hold me now," and signalled for Jay, Sandy, and Fang to join in. We started out softly, and I ratcheted up the energy. We locked in. I made my guitar part sparse. Then, I stopped playing entirely. I looked over at Fang. He pared down his bass line and stopped playing. Throughout, we all sang the refrain "Even your charms can't hold me now." I could hear people in the crowd picking up the chant, too. I wondered if I should hire a children's choir for when Static Saints records the song. I visualized dozens of kids in the studio belting out, "Even your charms can't hold me now." Maybe their off-kilter wall-of-sound vocals would help conjure a queer and crooked spell of protection. *Village of the Damned* meets the Langley Schools Music Project.

Now, all four of us were singing that line, and Jay was keeping time with a bare-bones drum part. "Even your charms can't hold me now." Then, he took out the snare and hi-hat to reveal a simple kick drum beat. Then, there was no beat. It was just a roomful of voices chanting the same line. "Even your charms can't hold me now." Jay, Fang, Sandy, and I locked eyes, and the three of them stopped singing.

I sang the line one last time by myself. "Even your charms can't hold me now."

The room erupted.

As we were turning to leave the stage, I impulsively asked how they felt about playing one last song. They all nodded. Yes, yes, yes. I already knew what song I wanted to play. They said they knew it, which didn't surprise me. It was a simple song, and the band was tight. People were still clapping, though it was starting to taper.

I went to the mic and said, Hey, is it okay if we play one more song? There was a collective cheer.

I reached back and unzipped my jumpsuit, letting the top fall to my waist. I had a belt that kept the rest of it in place. Now all four of us were topless onstage. I waved at my friends standing around the sound booth. Luna punched her fist in the air and howled like a wolf. I howled back.

Standing there topless, I felt in control. Okay, I said into the mic, buckle up.

I turned to Sandy, and he kicked into the opening guitar riff to "All of the Above," which always felt like I'd pulled it from a forgotten Buzzcocks B-side. He circled through it a couple times and then I let loose with lyrics.

Is this longing
Is this falling
Is this love

Fang ebbed in with his bass. I sang to the three gorgeous trans girls at the soundboard.

Is this longing
Is this falling
Is this love

I turned my attention to the front row and sang to a trans girl with white, black, and orange hair. She reminded me of a calico cat. And she'd even given herself dramatic swooping cat eyes with eyeliner, a skill I'd never mastered.

Is this longing
Is this falling
Is this love

I was right in front of her. She smiled and leaned forward and gave me that "can I kiss you" look with her goth girl eyes. I smiled and leaned in, and our lips and tongues touched. I felt a jolt of wet electricity. She tasted like pink bubble gum. I heard Jay come in on the drums as the band dialled up the energy. I stepped back and opened my throat.

> Is this all
> Is this all
> Of the above

I went inside myself and came out again with more force, more wonder, more life.

> Is this all
> Is this all
> Of the above

As I moved into the final verse, I felt myself reclaiming this song of swoon. It was no longer tethered to a former lover. It was a song about swimming in a sea of possibilities, a song about the mysterious ways love enters our lives in various forms and moves through us.

> Is this longing
> Is this falling
> Is this love

With that, we crashed to a close and ambled off the stage with our arms around each other.

I fumbled with my jumpsuit in the bathroom. Why the fuck had I worn a jumpsuit to a gig? It's the worst when you need to pee. The absolute worst. And, yes, of course, I peed so hard that some of it splashed over the seat and onto the floor. Broken water park for the win. At least it was the backstage bathroom, rather than the public one. I spotted a poster for an upcoming show featuring two bands with magnificent names: Thin Lezzy and zz Bottom.

When I finally returned to the dance floor, my friends fawned over me. You are like a sparkler onstage, Luna said. I blushed. Sam asked me to pick a song for DJ Salinger to play. It took a sec, but an apt song sprang to mind. Sam's face lit up when I shared my selection with her.

A few minutes later, I was dancing madly with Nish and Luna to "Jesus Built My Hotrod." Luna had never heard the song before and kept cocking her head when Gibby Haynes did his "wang dang uh dong dang" bits. This song is wild! she yelled into my ear. I nodded and kept bouncing around, letting the song move my torso and limbs like I was its sweaty jumpsuit-clad marionette.

While watching Nisha flirt with Sam at the soundboard, I felt a tinge of sadness. It was strange, because I wasn't sad about Nish and Sam. Luna yelled in my ear, "Oh, love, you're a motherfucker!" I noticed DJ Salinger was blasting one-hit wonder Silas T. Comberbache's profane earworm "LAMF." "Oh, loooove, you're a motherfucker!" Luna yelled again, aiming finger guns at me. I broke out my finger guns, returning fire. Her face was ecstatic and shiny with sweat. Mirror balls reflected pink and blue rays of light everywhere. And I knew why I was sad. I needed to fly home soon. I needed to play these new songs with my band. I needed to stop avoiding my ex. But that meant I wouldn't see Luna and Nish for a long time. Luna beamed at me, and I beamed back. "Oh, looove, you're a motherfucker!" we yelled in each other's faces.

—

Nisha told me that a few of Sadie Tang's works were permanently on display at a gallery across town. We took transit over and met Luna in the gift shop. The last time I'd been to a gallery was my first date with Charlotte, the same night I met Nisha. That gallery had been housed in a former bank; this gallery was in a former railway station. The entrance featured a pristine refurbished caboose.

Before long, we caught the attention of the museum guards because Luna felt like prancing.

You are the gayest gay in the world, Nish told her.

Please don't get us kicked out, I added.

I am a very gay girl, Luna said. I feel extra gay today. So take me to the jail. I don't care. Gay is good. My god is a gay god.

After a while, Luna started to settle down. She didn't know anything about art, but she was fascinated by unsettling art. The more fucked up the art was, the more she liked it.

Why don't they tell us how much they pay for things? she asked. I bet this pile of stinky garbage bags was a million dollars. I respect the artist who gets a million for his junk.

Over here, guys! Luna called. She was a ways ahead of us. We made a beeline before a guard could hustle over and harass her. She was pointing at a sculpture of a human head.

This is the most genius artist ever, she said. This is worth a million dollars.

What is that? Nish asked. Is that made of shit? She recoiled.

Yes! Luna said. It's called *Shit Head*. Her expression was priceless.

I looked at the gallery label. Yep, it was a 1998 work called *Shit Head* by a British artist named Marc Quinn. The medium was listed as "Artist's feces." I had a vision of bringing this piece to art school and being skewered mercilessly during crit. Then, I imagined shoving open the doors of the art school like a Wild West gunslinger and immediately being offered a million dollars for my shitty sculpture. Luna was right: there was a demented genius at play.

Another genius, Luna said. She was standing in front of another work.

More shit? Nish asked. She looked queasy.

Of course, Luna said. She made a thumbs-up gesture.

I'm going to take a break, Nish said. See you in a bit. Text if you can't find me. She wandered away.

Luna had hit the artistic shit motherlode. This was an even earlier piece. It was a sealed tin can called *Artist's Shit* from 1961 by an Italian artist named Piero Manzoni. The label stated that it was "reputed to be full of the artist's feces." When I mentioned this, Luna laughed, because in this instance the gallery had purchased the tin can hoping that it was full of the artist's shit, but with no iron-clad guarantee.

This Italian guy, she said, is even more genius than the British shithead. I laughed. She had a point.

A nearby display case caught my eye, and I walked over to it, glancing at the label. I remembered reading about this work and seeing photos of it years ago. It was created by a Canadian trans artist named Chase Abernathy. He was one of the artists I was studying when I'd planned to write my dissertation on trans artists, before I dropped out of the PhD program. It was a work called *If You Can't Stay Out of My Ass*. The label said the work was made from "silicone and artist's feces." I remembered reading about how Abernathy had commissioned a company to create

one-of-a-kind dildos based on the faces of the Conservative Party pol-
iticians who had maligned and misgendered him in Parliament. They'd
demanded Abernathy return funding for an arts grant, calling him a ped-
dler of smut. I recalled that his work was unabashedly sexual, but it was
also brilliant.

Luna was standing next to me. Her eyes were electric. Dirty dildos, she
said. This is the most genius gallery.

Indeed, the curator seemed to have carved out a peculiar artistic niche
with this collection. I wondered if there was a scat-centric art book in the
gallery gift shop.

I felt two arms wrap around me. Nisha whispered in my ear, I found
Sadie Tang. Her work is really cool. She cupped my breasts for a few seconds, then slid her hands over my tummy, cupped my cunt for an instant,
and rested her hands on my hips. I turned around, saw the gallery guard
eyeing us from a distance. I gave her a quick kiss.

Hey, Luna, I said, come with us.

Luna looked like a kitten that had been rolling in catnip. Okay, she
said. But I must come here again. Maybe we missed some valuable poop.
It is giving me some really good ideas. She had a mischievous grin.

Sadie Tang's work was located on the other side of the same cavernous
room. I wondered which part of the terminus railway station this massive
space had been. Perhaps it was where they used to store the trains.

Looks like they keep art by brown and Black artists in the same room
as the shit, Nisha said, waving at the works we were passing en route to
Sadie's pieces. We'd just passed the famous filmed performance of Yoko
Ono's *Cut Piece*. We were nearing a car encased in orange Plexiglas by
Rirkrit Tiravanija. Up ahead I could see some silhouettes by Kara Walker.

Nish added, I'll bet you anything the curator is white. Anything. Do you want to make a bet?

I shook my head. I hadn't noticed until she'd pointed it out, but there was no way I'd take that wager. I flashed on *White on White*, an early abstract painting by Kandinsky or Malevich. I always conflated those two. That painting had an odd subtitle, something about supremacy. Why would "white" and "supremacy" both be in its title? Or was I misremembering? I spotted paintings by Kerry James Marshall and Basquiat just past the silhouettes by Kara Walker. Oh Lord. I wondered what this wing was called on the museum map.

The gallery had four works by Sadie, three of which I recognized: *Three Imaginary Girls*, *When We Were a Girl*, and *Decrying Shame*. The first two had knocked me out when I'd seen them as a teenager. The latter I'd seen at a gallery opening shortly after *The Crying Game* was released. I'd been intimidated to discuss the piece with Sadie because it felt so visceral and confrontational. Plus, it included her wearing a strap-on, and at the time she was informally mentoring me over coffee dates. It was a weird combo.

I knew I couldn't go into the sound booth and revisit *Decrying Shame*, because Sadie's presence was so palpable in that piece. It would be too intense. And I didn't want to blubber in front of two lovers, particularly in a quiet, white-walled gallery.

There were four lavender plastic chairs in front of the glowing light box portraits of *Three Imaginary Girls*. Each chair had a small accompanying side table, replete with headphones and the familiar yellow photo albums with the phrase "When We Were a Girl" scrawled on them in pink cursive. My heart bloomed seeing Algy up there with two other Asian trans women. I wondered how long it had taken Sadie to capture that defiant expression on Algy's face.

I know her, I said to Luna and Nisha. They looked up at Algy's glowing portrait.

So cool, Luna said. She looks like she could destroy me. It's a good look.

I sat in a plastic chair and put on the headphones; Luna and Nish followed my lead. We started flipping through the photo albums. This time around, I could pick out Algy's voice as the women recounted their imagined girlhoods. I looked over at Nish and Luna and saw that the dissonance between the Asian trans women on the walls and the white girls in the photo albums was dawning on them. Sadness and anger started to swirl inside me. I remembered an episode of *The Golden Girls* where Blanche explained that when she felt a whole bunch of different emotions bleeding into one another, like colours mixed on a painter's palette, she called that feeling "magenta." I found her colour theory lacking, but I appreciated the concept of magenta. I often tilt toward a muddle of emotions. Looking over again at Luna and Nish, I sensed they were also feeling magenta.

The work of Sadie's that was new to me was called *On Donuts*. I pulled a flimsy pamphlet from a clear plastic holder on the wall beside the description of the piece.

On Donuts by Sadie Tang.
Narrated by Björk.

Oh right, Björk. I'd read about this piece. "On Donuts" had originally appeared as one of the thirty-three short films in Sadie's only feature film, *Miscellaneous Kisses*. Like *Detachable Penis*, *Miscellaneous Kisses* weaves together fragments from existing films to fashion something fresh, surreal, and hypnotic. The three-minute short film "On Donuts" is a collage of close-ups from several black-and-white movies, each clip featuring a blindfolded woman with an enigmatic expression. A dreamy montage of sapphic, sepia-tinted Mona Lisa smiles. Viewers of *Miscellaneous Kisses* needed to conjure a donut for Sadie Tang's voice-over instructions in "On Donuts." For the installation piece *On Donuts*, Sadie transmuted celluloid into dough, inviting visitors to follow Björk's instructions by eating a donut in the gallery.

Get ready, Luna said. It's donut time!

Nisha and Luna were standing at a square white table. On it, several donuts were encased in small clear-plastic domes, and boxes of black latex gloves sat at each of its corners. Ah, latex gloves, a staple of Sadie's work. Nisha and Luna were already wearing lavender headphones.

C'mon, Nish said. Hurry up. Luna wants her donut, girl. Luna licked her lips and laughed.

Oh jeez. I joined them at the table and put on my headphones.

Nisha pressed a lavender button in front of her to start the installation.

I heard Björk's lilting voice in my ear. She said, "Instructions for eating a donut!" I exchanged looks with Nish and Luna. I gently squeezed my tongue between my teeth to keep myself from laughing. Björk sounded so giddy. It was infectious.

Then, Björk said, "One! Put on a pair of gloves." I reached for a pair of gloves, keeping my eyes averted from Nish and Luna because I knew that if we made eye contact I might start giggling. "Put gloves on both of your hands," Björk told us. "Enjoy the snap of the gloves on your wrists!" I followed her instructions and fumbled my fingers into the gloves. I snapped them against my wrists. At this point, the clear plastic domes opened to reveal the donuts. Luna's eyes lit up. She really did have a thing for donuts.

As Björk's narration continued, I became more immersed in the piece.

2. Select a donut. Don't think too much. Just find a donut. A donut is a donut.

3. Pick up the donut.

4. Look at the hole in the middle of your donut.

5. While staring at the hole, think about the last time you had an orgasm. Keep thinking about your orgasm. Don't talk about it. Try not to be embarrassed.

There was something very sensuous about how Björk said the word "orgasm." I sounded like "ooh-er-geh-zum." She imbued the word with a sense of wonder. I found myself thinking about the guttural, burbling, and gleeful noises I'd heard her make on recordings and wondering what sounds she made when she came. I glanced at Luna and Nish. They had their eyes closed. Oh fuck. I looked down at the instructions printed on the pamphlet to see what I'd missed while daydreaming about giving Björk an orgasm.

6. Take a bite of the donut. Just one bite. Chew it slowly.

7. Close your eyes.

8. Think about the person you love most in the world. Picture their face.

I bit into the donut, closed my eyes and pictured my grandma's kind face. There was a pause. I'd caught up with the narration. Then, Björk whispered her next instruction to me.

9. Open your eyes.

10. Look at the donut in your hand. Imagine the donut is full of magic and pleasure.

11. Take another bite of the donut.

12. Look at the half-eaten donut you are holding. Imagine the remaining half of the donut is filled with love and kindness.

Out of the corner of my eye, I glimpsed Luna gazing at her donut, a beatific smile on her face. I felt my own face relaxing.

13. Eat the rest of the donut.

14. Imagine the donut inside your body is nourishing you with magic and pleasure, love and kindness.

15. Remove the gloves from your hands and put them in a trash bin.

16. Enjoy your life.

That was amazing, Nish said. Eating that donut felt almost spiritual. And sort of sexual because of the gloves. Luna sidled up beside Nish, putting an arm around her.

And Björk's voice was kind of hot, right? I heard myself say.

Yes! Nish said. So hot! It was like ASMR that's actually sexy.

Yes, very sexy, Luna said. But now I am very hungry. You can't just give me one donut. I need all the donuts!

—

I thought of Sadie Tang frequently after we'd parted ways. I bought myself a copy of the thick lavender art book with Sadie's name embossed on the cover in bold white letters. I considered sending her a letter care of her university, but I still felt embarrassed by our last encounter. I wondered if she'd thought I was a creep when I drunkenly called her a pretty transsexual. Looking back, I'm almost positive she knew I had my own gender shit. When the internet arrived, I followed her work as closely as I could. I googled the snot out of her. Sadie kept making art, mostly installations featuring Asian trans women. Her work remained defiant, but it became increasingly joyous.

I lost track of Sadie in the tumult of my thirties. When I finally looked her up again, I learned that she had died in 2008 while being treated for thrombotic thrombocytopenic purpura (TTP), a rare autoimmune disorder that causes microscopic clots to form throughout the body's blood vessels. She was forty-nine.

Her later works were often rooted in Buddhism, particularly the *Heart Sutra*. Indeed, her final work, *Art Sutures*, was a way of writing over several of her previous pieces, treating them as palimpsests, uprooting them from their original contexts and making them about love, death, emptiness, and pleasure.

I was particularly fond of how she recut her classic video piece *Detachable Penis* for *Art Sutures*. It still used split-screen footage of waggling fluorescent dildos and Hollywood film stars saying things like "I love having a detachable penis," but she'd spliced in new footage that had the actors expressing more unguarded, expansive ideas, including "It's a wonder we don't love every person we meet," "It's a wonder we don't make love to every person we meet," and "Everything is foreplay until we can finally love without fear." In the artist's statement for *Art Sutures*, Sadie wrote, "We're all just detachable egos, but we're also connected to everything else, endlessly conjoined for life." She had slyly retained the erotic playfulness of the original piece while widening its scope to include loving kindness and interconnectedness.

In her film *Miscellaneous Kisses*, Sadie talks about compiling an index of places she's visited and building a time travel shrine furnished with artifacts from those places. She says that she picks a place, closes her eyes, stills her mind, and travels there for a spell. I don't have an index or a shrine devoted to time travel, but I've often jumped back in my mind to 1993, which was when I first glimpsed my future. I've always said that I knew I needed to transition when I awoke in a hotel room in San Francisco and saw the dress I'd been wearing the night before draped across a chair. It's a tale that's become fossilized in its retelling. A fuller version of that tale involves Sadie and the shadow that her death cast on my life. I read every obituary I could find on her and contemplated how my own obit would read. I wondered if I'd get the *New York Times* treatment. Maybe. *Esperanto A-Go-Go* had briefly made us critical darlings.

He dropped out of a PhD in art history to devote himself to helming the indie rock band Static Saints.

His band's *Esperanto A-Go-Go*, a concept album about universal languages, was selected by several critics as one of the best albums of 2013.

He was (in)famously photographed kissing Adam Horovitz (a.k.a. King Ad-Rock) of the Beastie Boys on a bench in Prospect Park.

According to one critic, he sounded like "Michael Stipe on designer downers."

I noticed that even in my imagined obit, my gender rankled me. I swapped pronouns to see how that felt.

She dropped out of a PhD in art history to devote herself to helming the indie rock band Static Saints.

Her band's *Esperanto A-Go-Go*, a concept album about universal languages, was selected by several critics as one of the best albums of 2013.

She was (in)famously photographed kissing Adam Horovitz (a.k.a. King Ad-Rock) of the Beastie Boys on a bench in Prospect Park.

According to one critic, she sounded like "Michael Stipe on designer downers."

I felt calmer. With Sadie's death, I realized that the masculine lane I was driving in felt unbearable. Plus, I sensed that this lane was going to end before long. I needed to swerve through traffic to get in the femme lane ASAP. I'd already wasted so much time merging and going with the flow. Sadie prompted me to alter the destination on my internal GPS. A body is a vulnerable vehicle.

When considering the trajectory of my career, I often turn to Sadie Tang. She did what she wanted to do—and in the end, she playfully unravelled all the stitches she'd spent her career carefully putting in place. Make your work as useful and beautiful as you can, she seemed to be saying, but don't cling too tightly to it.

—

I adore cafés and bistros in art museums. One of my favourite memories from a European tour a couple years ago was visiting the Louisiana Museum of Modern Art in Denmark. I stopped making visual art several years ago, but it's hard for me to pass up the opportunity to visit a stellar gallery. The Louisiana Museum has a buffet with an oversized, lopsided black-and-white sculpture by Jean Dubuffet visible through the café's huge windows. I tried to convince my band of the brilliance of the buffet/ Dubuffet visual pun, but they were unimpressed.

I remember puttering at the Louisiana Museum buffet, putting food on my cafeteria tray, trailing behind two older Danish women. They were decked out in black with the occasional piece of elegant, angular silver jewellery. While on tour in Scandinavia, people often spoke to me in the native language of whatever country we were in. At first, it threw me. Then, I realized that I was surrounded by tall, pale women with a minimalist aesthetic. I was no longer the sore thumb. I was just a thumb among thumbs.

While spooning almond rice pudding and cherry sauce into a small white bowl, I flashed on moving here, becoming an older Danish lady dressed in black, rocking a stylish grey bob, going to the gallery now and then with my cute wrinkly Danish girlfriend, gazing out the wide windows at the outdoor sculptures and the choppy blue sea behind them. I longed to be unexceptional, to no longer feel the unwelcome, unending weight of strangers' stares.

Try my Shirley Temple, Luna said.

What? I asked. I was in the gallery café with Luna and Nisha.

I said try my Shirley Temple. She pointed at her drink, blood-orange red in a tall glass. Both Nisha and I had gotten rhubarb sodas. Luna had sprung for a fancy girl drink, replete with blue-green seahorse swizzle stick and maraschino cherry.

I leaned in and sipped through her striped paper straw. It was sweet, but also quite delicious. I'd once written a song that included the phrase "grenadine and hand grenades." The sticky sweet grenadine was nicely balanced in this Shirley Temple.

So? Luna looked at me with wide and expectant eyes.

It's good, I said. It's great. Luna smiled and nodded. It's like an elixir, I added.

It's sooo sweet! Nish said.

Elixir! Luna said. I don't even know her! She laughed.

Nish and I laughed too. Luna had already used the same punchline earlier, near a vibrant, swirling painting by Hundertwasser, but the "lix" in "elixir" made it funnier this time.

Nish leaned in and said softly, Don't look right away, but that old guy keeps staring at us.

Luna spun her head immediately. I waited a few seconds and discretely snuck a look. An old man was gazing at us openly. He wasn't glowering or scowling. It was like he was vacantly watching a TV show. He didn't seem embarrassed when all three of us looked back. And he didn't look away, which surprised me.

I leaned in. When an old man stares at me like that, I said, I think it's one of three things. 1) He's a creep. He's into trans girls or he's a weird misogynist. I was gonna say he's a pervert, but I know a lot of super cool perverts. 2) He's curious. Like, he's an older guy and he's just thinking, Wow, it's amazing that there are trans women. Maybe he even thinks it's cool. Or, he's jealous and sees us as self-actualized and wishes he'd done all the things he kept hidden about himself... which brings me to the last possibility. 3) He's an invisible trans girl. He's had all this gender stuff churning in him for years but could never understand it or talk about it. And now he feels like it's too late, so he's stuck playing the role of an old man.   .

Nisha and Luna both looked from me back to the old man. There was a cane leaning against his chair. I wondered if it was the sort of sword cane that John Steed carried in *The Avengers*. Perhaps the old man had watched that show growing up and yearned to be as hot and cute as Emma Peel in her leather catsuit, like I did.

It's hard to be sure 'cause he's so far away, I said, but I'm not getting a creepy vibe from him. I think he's curious or he's a trans girl.

My brain has exploded, Luna said. You just made me feel sorry for him. Before, I was angry, but now I want to go over and hug him and tell him it's okay. It's not too late to join the club.

Yeah, wow, Nish said. You might be right. I never thought of that. My mind is also blown. An invisible trans girl. You're right. There are so many invisible trans girls.

I started humming a song.

I know that song, Nish said. She cocked her head. What song is that? It's driving me crazy. Is it Pulp?

I shook my head and kept humming.

You are driving us crazy, Luna said. She reached out, pretending to wring my neck, like a cartoon character.

It's the song "Secret Girls," I said. By the band Costumes by Edith Head.

Right! Nish said. She quietly sang the chorus.

And you will lose yourself in the city
(You will unravel your riddle)
And you will find yourself in the city
(You will secrete all your secrets)

That's a catchy song, she said.

I know, right? I said. And the singer later came out as a trans girl.

Right! she said. I forgot about that. Heidi something.

Heidi Thade, I said. Yeah.

"Oh, I'm a secret girl," Nish sang quietly.

"Such a secret girl!" I sang in response.

"We're the secret girls," she sang.

"Yeah, we're the secret girls!" I sang back.

We sang the last part together: "And we're coming! We're coming! We're coming for you!"

I leaned over and kissed her.

You two are amazing, Luna said. You should do music together. I want to learn that song so I can join your band.

Luna, you're so fucking adorable, I said. You can totally sing with us anytime. It's a song by a trans girl who had a band in the nineties. But she didn't come out as trans until years and years after the band broke up. To me, that song is just such an ode to invisible trans girls, y'know. That thing where you keep yourself hidden to stay safe, but it's so, so, so hard and it hurts like hell. I glanced over at the old man. He was shuffling out of the café with his cane. Nish and Luna looked over at him too.

Yes, Luna said. I remember being a secret girl.

For some reason, I noticed that I was incredibly thirsty. I gulped down the dregs of my rhubarb soda, but I was still parched.

Can I have another sip of your elixir, Luna?

She nodded and slid her Shirley Temple over to me. Elixir, she said. I don't even know her.

Nisha shook her head. You're prettier when you don't talk, she said. She squeezed Luna's cheeks and kissed her.

After taking a couple sips of Luna's elixir, I saw the old trans woman with a cane pause outside the café window to look at us one last time before leaving for good.

—

After performing with Jay's band, I realized just how much I'd missed playing with Cookie, Marta, and Poe. We have a fiery chemistry. We're more than the four of us. We blur into each other, like those robot lions that form Voltron. *Fuck it*, I thought. *I'll just tell Cookie.*

I spent a few minutes crafting a text message. I read it a few times, trying to imagine how it would land for her.

I'm going to preface this by saying that I know you'll probably say no and that you should probably say no, but I can't help

asking: Would you ever be interested in joining the band again?
You are a guitar genius. I miss playing music with you so much.
And I really miss having you in my life.

It felt too open hearted. But I didn't want to keep traipsing around this topic. I wanted her to rehearse with me, to be in the studio with me, to be on the stage with me. I missed her gift for unfurling riffs that would make everything sound better. Whenever I played without her, I was aware of her absence.

When I was a fledgling visual artist, I tried to perfect a technique called chiaroscuro, where you use light and darkness to make a painting pop. Rembrandt and Caravaggio were great at it. I can make good music, but it seldom sings the same way without Cookie adding a couple of light and dark sonic brush strokes. Her playing refines and redefines my songs. And after hearing her instrumental EP, I realized that we could also write songs together, which was really exciting.

I read my message one last time and hit "Send."

—

So many songs have been tumbling out of me lately that I probably have almost enough material for a new album. "Even Your Charms," "Broken Open," "St. Bernard," "O Yes, I'm Your Lioness," "My Body Is a Time Machine," "Rings of Saturn," "Maybe (I'm an Ocean)," and a new one tentatively titled "Halliwell-Orton" that I just started writing a day or two ago, after watching the eighties film *Prick Up Your Ears*. For that song, I found myself fixated on the word "frequency," with the idea of tuning in to your lover's frequency and the way that sex often becomes less fre-quent over time. I thought about how you can miss being your partner's person, being the body they reached for, being the ubiquitous "you" in their head. So far, the song revolves around repeating a few lines about frequencies: "We lost that frequency / Can't find that frequency / I'll miss your frequency."

I opened a new note in my phone and started jotting down song titles. Then, I wondered what to call my next album. I wondered if it should have the word "city" in the title. *Invisible City? Inoculated City? Serpentine City?*

I heard Nisha's voice. I guess she'd woken from her nap. I put my phone down on the bedside table and turned to face her.

What's that? I asked. I missed what you said.

I said do you think lovers are like jawbreakers? I must have made a face because she added, Like in the song. She yawned and pointed at her Bluetooth speaker on the dresser. I listened. When we returned from the art gallery, Nisha put on a Costumes by Edith Head playlist; it had been playing on repeat in the background for an hour or two now. I recognized the song, but I hadn't heard it in a while. It was called "Essex."

Maybe, I said. I haven't thought too much about it. Why? Are you gonna break my jaw?

No, Nish said. I like your jaw. I have, like, jaw envy. I hate my jaw. But, I mean, the song has those lines. Hold on. She grabbed her phone and jumped "Essex" back to the start. We both listened. I wondered if Heidi Thade was still making music, wherever she was now.

Suddenly, Nish started singing along with the chorus.

All I know is Essex sucks
And your lipstick tastes like wine gums
All I know is Essex sucks
And my heart's in your divine hands

And then she pointed at the speaker as she sang along with the "jaw-breaker" bridge.

> You're a jawbreaker, jawbreaker, jawbreaker
> Sucked through the crust,
> Through the mantle to the inner core
> I've got a blood-orange tongue
> Girl, you've got a hard core, hard core, hard core

Nish dialled down the volume and said, I think it's true that the more time you spend with people, the more you see their true colours. Like a jawbreaker. I think I've sucked through your crust and your mantle, Tracy. But I don't think I've gotten to your inner core yet. Do you have a hard core?

I don't think so. I'm pretty gooey and soft inside. How about you?

I think I'm soft too, she said. How did we get so soft?

I don't know, I said. It's kind of amazing because, I've gotten softer as I've gotten older.

She leaned over and kissed me.

—

I was watching a Korean revenge film when my phone pinged with a message from Cookie. It was 7 p.m. for me, so it must have been noon the next day for her.

Her text was one word: *Yes.*

I texted back, *Fuck yes! That makes me sooooo happy.*

She replied, *Same.*

Ah, stoic Cookie. I put my phone down and noticed my heart was thumping like crazy. Cookie was back in the fold! I put on David Bowie's "Diamond Dogs" and started dancing around the room. I imagined Dex's

St. Bernard, Anders, was bouncing beside me, gnawing on his rag doll. I'd fallen in love with *Diamond Dogs* as a kid. It's an album slathered in post-apocalyptic sleaze, but it also fucks with gender in a fun way. While I was bopping around in my apartment, my phone pinged a few more times. I paused Bowie to scan my messages. They were from Cookie.

Do you want to come to Tokyo?

I ran into Jim O'Rourke at a film festival.

He's a fan.

I think he'd be down to work with us.

In an instant, Cookie was back in the band and maybe we could all fly to Tokyo and have our next album produced by Jim O'Rourke. It seemed like a dream.

I'd been bracing myself to return home, wondering how I could avoid Johnny. And now I'd been offered a detour. We could go to Tokyo and work with a genius producer. I should have been overjoyed.

I sent Cookie a string of messages:

That sounds amazing. I'm so tempted!

But I think I need to go home. (Sorry!)

I'm tired of being afraid.

I want to work on the new songs.

And I want to write songs with you.

Would you be willing to fly back and practise with us?

Later, I'd love to record in Tokyo with O'Rourke!

Sorry!

Cookie messaged that she understood. She'd chat with her partner and figure out how to make this work.

I sent back a couple emojis: a glittering heart and a crying face. I added, *I love you, Cookie.*

—

Albertine messaged me: *Hi, Tracy. My friend who's housesitting while you're away says a handwritten letter has arrived. The return address says it's from Johnny Baxter. On the back of the envelope, it says "Please read me" and has a cartoon heart. What do you want me to do?*

I felt my inner core turn magenta. I wanted to read it. I wanted to incinerate it. I wanted to yell in Johnny's face. I wanted her to hold me. I knew that I needed to resist the gravitational pull of letting her back into my life. She'd eviscerated me. She'd wanted to make me suffer. Now that more time had passed, she probably wanted to smooth things over. But my body told me things couldn't be made smooth. I could never trust her again. I needed to have boundaries. We shouldn't be in each other's lives anymore. I had to shed that old layer of skin to continue growing, like a queen cobra.

I texted back, *I can't read it. I'm sorry. Can you ask them to shred it? Thanks.*

Albertine: *Yes, of course. I get it. I'm sorry I brought it up. I just didn't know where things sat with you and Johnny. Consider it shredded. I love you.*

When death is dragged into a relationship, maybe it never leaves.

When someone you love tries or threatens to kill you or to kill themselves

in order to control you or to punish you,

maybe that death threat

can never be retracted.

You're stunned, caught in the undertow.

After the event passes,

        death becomes an unspeakable thing,

                but it remains in the relationship.

You're always aware that the person you love could summon death again.

Perhaps they become like a bomb that can never be defused.

A bomb wired to your four-chambered heart.

A bomb that rides shotgun in your car.

A bomb that knows your address.

A bomb in a black leather dress.

A bomb you're afraid of.

A bomb you still love.

I've had one parent and two lovers drag death into our relationships.

Maybe I'm wrong.

          Maybe death can leave.

I hope I'm wrong.

          I hope death can leave.

A bomb that held the string to my kite

A bomb that held me in the night

Johnny dragged death into our relationship.

We're both still alive,

                fortunately.

But I had to leave

              for good.

I really hope you're okay, Johnny.

You are a handsome firecracker,

              a gorgeous Molotov cocktail

                            with an undercut.

I'm going to stop saying your name and stop talking to you in my head.

I want to disconnect the wires running to a phantom version of you.

Maybe one day you'll escape your past. I hope you do.

Either way, I need to be free.

I loved you deeply.

Goodbye.

NISHA HAD A SMALL GOING-AWAY PARTY for me at her place. Just her, Luna, Sam, and Jay. I debated inviting Dex, but we'd definitely drifted apart. We exchanged *goodbye and good luck* texts adorned with heart emojis in neutral hues. (Purple from him. Blue from me.)

For the first hour or two, I felt strangely distant from my friends. It was as though I was swaddled in bandages, like a mummy. My time in this city felt unreal, as though it were a dream. Only Nisha seemed to notice. I told her I didn't know why I felt out of sorts. We ended up in her bedroom. We made out a bit, mostly tribbing with our skirts pulled up and our panties still on. We barely said anything. And then, somehow, I was back in my body. I ran my hand over my scalp, feeling the bristles under my fingers. I'd stopped shaving my head a couple weeks ago, and it was in that slow, awkward growing-back-in phase. Maybe I should get a hat.

We spooned for a while. And then Luna was with us too. I wasn't sure if Nish had texted her or if Luna had knocked and come in. Either way, I found myself the middle spoon. We all lay there quietly. I could hear muffled music outside.

After a few songs, we got up and went back to the living room. Jai Paul's "All Night" was playing. Sam was resting her head in Jay's lap on the couch. He grinned when we came back into the room. Nish cracked a window, and we shared a joint. For sober girls, Nish and Luna were pretty into weed.

And now it was Jai Paul's "BTSTU." I've always loved the song's beat and its sputtering electronics, but the entitlement of the narrator drives me batty. Nobody wants a lover to say they're back and they want what's theirs. As the song swelled and hiccupped, I looked at Jay and Sam tilting into each other, and at Nish and Luna, who were sharing a conspiratorial laugh. *This is what I want*, I thought. *To be around people who adore me but don't want to possess me.* And I'll admit that I thought, *like you wanted to possess me.* And I noticed my ex slowly creeping back into my thoughts. It's easy to slide back into worn patterns, even unhealthy ones. As a friend reminded me recently, a dopamine hit from something bad can feel the same as a dopamine hit from something good.

And it struck me that maybe I want relationships that are like dresses. I need room to twirl. Better yet, I want them to be like dresses with pockets. You don't always need pockets, but you sure miss them when they aren't there. I never want another relationship that feels like a corset. Sure, a corset can make your tits look fantastic, but you're going to struggle to breathe.

At the end of the night, I said goodbye to everyone. I knew I wouldn't be seeing them again for at least a few months. I didn't cry. Okay, I cried a little. I did a weird *Wizard of Oz*-style goodbye. I think I called Nisha the Cowardly Lioness. Jay was Tin Man. I remember that. Maybe I told Sam she was like Toto? I'm not sure. We were all pretty fucked up. I think we just had weed, but my head feels fuzzy. At some point, Jay made mushroom tea, but I don't think I drank any. Maybe a sip or two. Jay kept saying the word "steep" until it lost all meaning. And then every time he said "steep," Luna added "boo beep" and swivelled like she was doing the robot.

During my woozy *Wizard of Oz*-style farewell, I sort of remember saying to Luna, I think I'll miss you most of all, Scarecrow. And she said something like, I want to be your Falcon, not your Snowman. And every-one started laughing. And I kept trying to explain, but I wasn't sure if she was confused or fucked up or if she was fucking with me. I think it was the latter, because she started adding little "boo beeps" as though she were a malfunctioning robot.

We all hugged, and my taxi arrived and whisked me back to my apartment. That was when I really cried. The soft heap of tissues on my bedside table kept expanding. I wondered if tears are traces of memories. Eventually, I drifted off to sleep.

—

After years of touring, I've gotten good at packing. While getting my things together for my flight home, I kept catching myself counting. It's one of those things I've always done. If you were to ask me about anything countable in this apartment, I could probably dash off a number. Dresser drawers: five. Books: lucky thirteen. Guitar picks: seven. Spoons: four. Rolls of toilet paper: five. Cubes in the ice cube tray: thirty-two. I often unconsciously count things, but it becomes especially prominent when I'm feeling anxious. I checked yet again how much time I had left before my flight: six hours. I still had nearly two hours before I had to taxi to the airport.

I popped across to the coffee shop for a final cortado and croissant. Then, I took my guitar out of its case and started working on a song I've been trying to finish. It's called "This Woman Is Not Me." The seed for the song was probably sown when an ex said to me, "I never thought I'd be the psycho ex-girlfriend, but here we are." And, it was true, that was what she'd somehow become. I thought about those times when we do and say unfathomable things. It's like those experiments where someone puts on a uniform and becomes the role associated with it.

I recently watched footage of Stephen Trask talking about writing songs for *Hedwig and the Angry Inch*. Now, I loathe *Hedwig*, but I have some love for its queer creators. Anyway, Stephen Trask was talking about how the chords for one song in *Hedwig* went from E to A to D—with a low F# note played with the D chord. I picked up my guitar and strummed E A F#/D. It sounded dreamy and slightly ominous. That last chord really made the progression. And, like that, I found myself singing two lines that felt buried in those chords.

> I'm coming apart at the seams
> Everything dies in my dreams

That opening gave me a vague sense of what the song wanted to be. I kept strumming the chords until I found the rest of the first verse.

> You love this woman it seems
> You love this woman it seems
> But this woman, this woman is not me
> My mascara is running, but not me
> This woman, this woman is not me

I could already imagine my band in our rehearsal space, finding the right rhythm for the start of the song. It would sound pretty, sad, and sparse, with Marta's bass and Poe's drums carrying us along. I'd be strumming the chords, quite low in the mix. There would be room to breathe. The first time I sang the phrase "not me," Cookie's guitar would come in, slashing chords that were trebly, distorted, and warm. Her part would elevate everything. Maybe a little feedback would start to swell during the last line. (With *Hedwig* in mind, I'm wondering if I should have written my memoir like a musical, breaking into song when emotions became overwhelming. On second thought, maybe that's what I am doing.)

For some reason, I knew the next section needed to be shimmery. Through a little trial and error, I'd found some chords that seemed to follow the *Hedwig* ones perfectly: F# D#m C# Bsus2. It was a progression that felt open—with the final chord adding a dash of suspense. The words for this section were like a bright-blue sky briefly troubled by a dark cloud.

> But everything, everything, everything is all right
> But everything, everything, everything is all right
> Everything dies, and that is a fact
> Everything dies, and there's beauty in that

For the final section, I only had four good lines so far.

> Everything is all right
> All the pretty things hide at night
> I was smote, and you were smitten
> Everything good gets rewritten

The guitars here needed to sound deeply distressed, almost as though the speakers were blown. I strummed the chords for this part—F# G# A#m—and sang what I'd already written. Sometimes when I did this, a line would unexpectedly tumble out of me, like the whirring wheels of a car suddenly finding traction and lurching out of a snowdrift and onto the road.

I saw an image of a woman astride a sleek black horse. I remembered something a lover had said once: Never date horse girls or hockey boys. They'll break your heart every damn time. She'd grinned, adding, I used to be a hockey boy, and now I'm a horse girl. I sensed the next couple of lines had to do with a horse, its rider, and a heartbreaker.

I played the chord progression and tried variations on those words. Finally, I found it.

> I was the horse, and you were the rider
> I was the heart, and you were the dagger

When the dagger appeared, I saw the narrator being cut down. I tried a few different ways of phrasing that idea until I found one that worked with the mood and the chords.

> You brought this woman down
> You brought this woman down
> This woman is not me
> Oh no, oh no

I played the chord progression on a loop, trying to find the next line, until the alarm on my phone pinged. It was almost time to leave for the airport. I plugged my guitar into my little amp, set up a mic, and recorded a rough demo of what I had so far. I didn't want to risk losing anything. I listened back. The recording was lo-fi as hell, but this unfinished song had some life to it.

I snapped my guitar case shut and summoned a car to take me to the airport.

—

I'm through security, waiting to board the plane. I remember being at the same airport when I was twenty, flying back to the same city after my first girlfriend, Astrid, broke up with me. I'd wondered if she'd be waiting for me when I landed. She wasn't. I'd hoped we'd get back together. We didn't.

I want to say that that was a lifetime ago, but it feels like several lifetimes ago. I feel as though I've repeatedly shunted from one life into another, like a caterpillar ambling from one leaf to the next. In some ways, it feels like I'm always moving ahead; in other ways, it feels like I'm moving through a labyrinth that circles back on itself, with recurring patterns I only glimpse now and then. I spot them and forget them. They're like epiphanies in short stories that reveal new ways of being and seeing, but you know they'll disappear before long, and the protagonist will return to her old habits.

Now I'm waiting in line to get on the plane. Visions of being here decades ago. A muzzle flash of déjà vu.

I used to cover "Too Cool to Live, Too Smart to Die" by the garage rock band Deja Voodoo with my friend Aaron in our band, Lubricated Sagan. I never felt too cool or too smart, but I always knew I was going to die.

In elementary school, I remember wondering why I needed to memorize meaningless historical dates for a test if I was just going to die anyway. In grade five, we were asked to write about what we would be doing in the year 2000. I couldn't imagine myself living that long. I'd never make it to twenty-seven.

But then, somehow, I did.

Now I'm showing my ticket and passport to a flight attendant, half smiling, trying to look like myself.

I watch the flight attendants mime what to do in an emergency. First, they do it in French; then, they do it in English. As they vacantly smile in the face of imaginary tragedy, I find myself wondering about the equation "tragedy plus time equals comedy." What horseshit. I have a sense of how the overhead baggage may shift during this flight, but I have no bloody clue how my emotional baggage will shift across time. Tragedy can become comedy, but then it can jump back to being tragic again. Plus, real life often defies genre. It's more like those strange plays Shakespeare wrote at the end of his career. I think they were called late romances. Kathleen loved those plays, but I didn't get them. In one of them, a character's wife dies and comes back to life ten or twenty years later. What the what?! I couldn't give myself over to the mystery. It was too unsettling. But sometimes that's how life can feel. Your friend's mom unexpectedly dies. Another friend finds out her partner is pregnant with twins. Your favourite musician in the universe rejoins your band. From time to time, there is magic.

Now we're in the air, and the lights in the cabin are being dimmed.

After my plane landed and the taxi delivered me to my door, I let everyone know that I'd arrived back home safely. I added that I'd need to lie low on my own for a few days to acclimate.

I don't feel entirely safe being back. I still hold some fear. It will take time to settle back into this watery, cloudy city and into my body. I crawl under the covers and let myself sink into sleep.

When I eventually awaken, I somehow have the final lines for "This Woman Is Not Me." I grab a pen and jot them down in my little red notebook.

> No, you were the horse, and I was the rider
> You were the deer, and I was the tiger
> There's a wildness in me
> Oh no, oh no

Everything comes apart at the seams
And every good thing dies in my dreams

As I write this, I realize the song will probably be released before this memoir is published, so you already know I finished the song. You are living in the future, dear reader, while I'm here in the present.

But I can tell you that I got chills when I saw myself morph from the horse into the rider and then, just like that, become the tiger.

At times, I feel a wildness thrumming in me. It's bewildering and bewitching.

—

When I'm creating something good—something that's beyond me—it can feel like the art is in control. I try to put my puny ego aside, to get out of the way and let the work tumble out. I surrender to it, letting it move through me. (Maybe I'm just a conduit for a parallel version of me in a parallel universe. She's the writer; I'm her imperfect amanuensis.)

During those rare moments, it sometimes feels like I'm the horse and the art is the rider. I try to find the chords it wants and the words it wants, to detect a gentle tug on the reins so I know where to go. (Ideally, the rider loves the horse, and the horse loves the rider.)

When I find the right chords and words, I often feel calm and warm, as though some soft hand is stroking my muzzle to let me know I'm a good girl. At times, writing this book has felt like that. (Horses have a deep need for safety.)

I wonder about all the ways I could have shaped my life for you. It's difficult to tell a story when it's still unfolding. (A single sheet of origami paper can be folded into a horse, a deer, or a tiger.)

—

Albertine just booked a ticket for Cookie. She'll be here next week! Having her rejoin Static Saints is surreal. I wonder if I should let Cookie take the reins sometimes. She sent me an ethereal instrumental track that I've been playing non-stop. She should be in control when we record it. (So much of life is knowing when to be the horse and when to be the rider.)

I'm chomping at the bit to be inside these new songs with Cookie, Marta, and Poe. I miss being in a band—the chemistry, the alchemy.

—

One of the saddest moments in my life was realizing as a child that I'd never actually know what it's like to be another person. I'd only ever know what others decided to tell me about their inner lives. I remember walking back from the grocery store near my elementary school, knowing that I'd always be stuck inside myself.

I wonder if you have a sense of what it's like to be me. I transitioned because being an invisible girl became intolerable. I needed to make my femininity legible. Now I'm trying to make other sides of myself visible.

I'm tender, and I'm wild. I'm a good girl and a heartbreaker. I'm a horse and a rider. I'm a deer and a tiger. I'm a capacious creature.

I'm a girl, and I'm plural.

—

Since returning home, my mind often swims back to that awful night, but I've gotten better at easing myself out of that locked groove. Whenever I notice a thorny memory surfacing, I'll pause, take a breath, and remind myself, *That was in the past. It's over. Please come back to the present.* When Nurse Lulu taught me to dilate, she advised me to be a "gentle little helper" if the dilator didn't want to leave my body on its own. Lately, I've become a gentle little helper to ease shards of trauma out of my body. My gentle little helper often softens her instructions by calling me "sweetheart" or "darling." I become a gentle rider soothing her fearful horse, with care as a carrot: *Sweetheart, that was in the past. It's over. Please come back to the present.* And the horse often grows calm.

—

I went to Marta's last night for dinner and drinks. Her weird energy was exactly what I needed.

After dinner, she refilled my wineglass and said, I know you don't want to talk about your ex. But. The thing is. I have a friend who's a witch—a legit witch, not some fake-ass witch—and I could totally ask her to put a protection spell on your place. I could do that for you, T. This witch likes me, so I think she'd say yes. Like, she really, really likes me. She raised her eyebrows and tittered. I thought, *Oh, I've missed you, Marta.*

I told her I'd think about it. Truth be told, I'm tempted. I've been having bad dreams lately. I'm also tempted to get a cat. It wasn't on my mind until Marta suggested it. Her tuxedo cat Pandan spent most of the night curled in my lap. The second or third time Marta topped up my glass of wine, she mentioned that a friend of hers was fostering a tortoiseshell that needed a good home. She pulled up a few snaps on her phone. The cat was unbelievably adorable.

Pip is a rescue, she said. She was found with two kittens at a construction site. Her kittens were adopted right away, but Pip doesn't have a home yet. She's a trauma baby. Super skittish, but super sweet.

Maybe I could meet Pip, I said. I hadn't had a cat for years, because I used to live with someone who was terribly allergic. I wasn't sure about the name Pip, though. Maybe I'd call her Lola or Félicette.

For real? Like really for real? Marta asked. I nodded. Fuck yeah! she said. She leaned over and clinked her wineglass against mine. Cheers, queers! We smiled and sipped. Pandan rolled onto her side and draped a paw over her eyes.

—

Now I'm sitting at the kitchen table, the afternoon sunlight filling the wide windows of my third-floor apartment, trying to divine how to end my two-story memoir in a way that feels open and expansive,

> an ending that's useful and beautiful,
>> an ending like a dress with pockets,
>>> an ending as luminous as a pearl,
>>>> an ending with room to twirl

Acknowledgments

THIS NOVEL WAS DEVISED AND REVISED while living as an uninvited settler on the unceded, ancestral, and current territories of the xʷməθkʷəy̓əm (Musqueam), Sḵwx̱wú7mesh (Squamish), and səl̓ilwətaʔɬ (Tsleil-Waututh) Nations.

—

I want to extend gratitude and love to an array of radiant critters who helped bring this book into being:

Readers of different drafts for generous and generative feedback: Onjana Yawnghwe, Bishakh Som, Gwen Haworth, Melissa Adler, Niko Stratis, and Zena Sharman.

Editors who graciously published early extracts: Jessica Johns (*Room*), Corinne Manning (*Intimate Isolations*), and Cameron Awkward-Rich, Hil Malatino, and Francisco J. Galarte (*TSQ*Now*).

Stephanie Sinclair for help finding the perfect literary home for this work.

The dream team at Arsenal Pulp Press (my long-time publishing house crush) for breathing life into this novel with such warmth and wisdom: Brian Lam, Robert Ballantyne, Cynara Geissler, Catharine Chen (for smart, soft notes and nudges during the editing process), and Jazmin Welch (for creating the swoony skin these words live in).

A quartet of writers I admire who took time from their own work to endorse mine: jiaqing wilson-yang, Bishakh Som, Megan Milks, and Andrea Warner.

An improbable quintet who opened my aperture in my twenties—and changed my vision permanently: Margot K. Louis, Rob Wright, Kobayashi Issa, Shunryu Suzuki, and Thich Nhat Hanh.

A dozen artists whose work was foundational to this book at various phases: Agnès Varda, Alexis Pauline Gumbs, Audre Lorde, Italo Calvino, J Dilla, Jorge Luis Borges, Leanne Betasamosake Simpson, Pamphila, Rowland S. Howard, Sue Tompkins, Wong Kar-Wai, and Yoko Ono.

A constellation of kith and kin, including Shannon Plante, Edith Irene Plante, Doreen Hamlyn, Wayne Hamlyn, Nunu Yawnghwe, Aggie Yawnghwe, Kay Higgins, Jessica J. Hanna Reimer, Travis V. Mason, Rojina Farrokhnejad, Ania Dymarz, Baharak Yousefi, Chantal Gibson, Raven Salander, John Elizabeth Stintzi, and DCB.

An energy field of queer and trans friends and writers too magical and mercurial to pin to the page. My work exists because of you—and maybe I do too.

All the folks I've made music with through the years, particularly my beloved bandmates while working on this novel, Gwen Haworth, Jay Pottle, and Carolynn Dimmer.

Every glorious and holy creature who has stirred, soothed, and mended my wobbly heart in the imperfect past, present, and future.

Melissa for an expansive, fizzy correspondence and for a distant sparky connection.

My jumpy, fuzzy feline, Gus, for teaching me about acceptance, boundaries, and bravery. Every day she reminds that although trauma burrows into our bodies, we still yearn to be held and beheld.

Onjana, my former partner, my first reader, and my favourite collaborator, who has been my dearest friend across at least a few lifetimes. This book about art, friendship, healing, and love is for you.

Photo: Agatha K

HAZEL JANE PLANTE is a librarian, musician, cat photographer, coastal creature, and writer. Her debut novel, *Little Blue Encyclopedia (for Vivian)* (Metonymy Press, 2019), received a Lambda Literary Award and was a finalist for both a Publishing Triangle Award and a BC and Yukon Book Prize. She lives with her gorgeous cat, Gus, on the unceded ancestral territories of the xʷməθkʷəy̓əm (Musqueam), Sḵwx̱wú7mesh (Squamish), and səl̓ilwətaʔɬ (Tsleil-Waututh) Nations.

hazeljaneplante.com